SMALL TOWN SPIN

A NICHELLE CLARKE CRIME THRILLER

LYNDEE WALKER

SEVERN RIVER
PUBLISHING

Severn River Publishing
www.SevernRiverBooks.com

This is a work of fiction. Names, characters, businesses, places, events and incidents are either the products of the author's imagination or used in a fictitious manner. Any resemblance to actual persons, living or dead, or actual events is purely coincidental.

ISBN: 978-1-64875-513-2 (Paperback)

ALSO BY LYNDEE WALKER

To find out more about LynDee Walker and her books, visit

severnriverbooks.com/authors/lyndee-walker

For Julie, whose heart and soul will always be in Mathews County. Thank you for sharing it with me, and for being the sister I always wanted.

In memory of Austin J. Hemmer, with special hugs to Sloane, Joe, and Cameron, who love him forever.

1

The news doesn't take sick days.

Generally, the number of blocks on a calendar that I don't work are rarer than comfortable shoes at a runway show. But four hours into a double shot of Claritin and DayQuil on a sunny April afternoon, I still felt like I'd been hit by a truck, and had only managed to finish one story.

"I think pollen season has won the afternoon, kiddo," my editor said, eyeballing me from the doorway of my cubicle. I tried to lift my head to reply, but dropped it back to my desk with a dull *thunk*.

"I'm fine," I said into the blotter.

"Go home, Nichelle." Bob patted my shoulder.

Happy to oblige.

* * *

Settled on my overstuffed navy sofa with my toy Pomeranian snuggled in my lap and the TV remote in hand, I managed three sips of my honey-lemon tea before my cell phone erupted into *Second Star to the Right*.

The dog sat up and growled. I patted her and dropped the remote, reaching for the phone. Parker.

"I really am sick," I said by way of hello when I picked up. Just in case he couldn't tell—a shoebox full of clothespins clamped on my nose wouldn't have lent my voice any more of a ridiculous twang.

"You'll thank me in a minute," he said. "I have a story for you. An exclusive, if you can drag yourself back out of bed."

"Drugs or gambling?" I asked, tilting my head to hold the phone against my shoulder while I reached for a notebook and pen. Parker was the star sports columnist at the *Richmond Telegraph*, and I figured if he was tipping the crime reporter (that'd be me) to a story, it meant an athlete had been busted for one of those things.

"Suicide," he said.

"Aw, hell." I blew out a short breath and dissolved into a coughing fit. "Sorry. Stupid pollen. I hate writing about suicides. Of all the depressing stories I do, those are the ones that get to me the most."

"I need you to do this," he said. "Personal favor. It—" His voice broke, and he paused. "It won't stay quiet forever."

His pleading note left no room for excuses—or allergies. Parker was a good friend. I could suck it up to help him out. Plus, sad subject aside, I couldn't hang up without getting the scoop. Story of my life.

I sighed, pen poised. "Spill it."

"Tony Okerson," he said.

"The football player?" Holy Manolos. "How do you figure that's going to stay quiet for three seconds? That guy is a living legend."

"Tony Okerson, Junior," Parker said, and I pinched my eyes shut. A kid. Shit, shit, shit. I noted the name and listened as he went on.

"So far, they've kept a lid on it, but it's only been a few hours," he continued. "The local paper will run a spread tomorrow and it'll be open season. Tony is one of my best friends, Clarke. They're devastated."

"I can't imagine," I said, my heart dropping into my stomach at the depth of pain in his voice. "I'm sorry, Parker. But what is it you want me to do with this?"

"Tony's convinced he can control the media spin. I told him he has a better shot if he talks to you and lets us break the story. You know cops and crime better than anyone. Can you be in Tidewater by four o'clock?"

"Tidewater? Not D. C.?"

"When Tony retired last year, they moved into their beach house. It's on a little island out there. Tony wanted his kids to have normal childhoods. Thought moving to a real-life Mayberry was the best way to keep them grounded and safe." Anger bubbled just under the sorrow in Parker's voice. "He said he'd talk to you tonight. I told him he could trust you. But this whole thing is making me antsy. I'm just waiting for someone to tweet him a well-meaning 'My condolences.' It'll be all over the Internet in an hour as soon as that happens."

"Jesus. What a mess."

"Yeah. I just...I'm not asking you to print anything that's not true, but I figure if you soften it, maybe the TV folks won't smell blood in the water, you know?"

I shook my head, staying quiet. The suicide of a three-time Super Bowl champion quarterback's son wouldn't go unnoticed for long. The size of the town where it happened was likely the only reason it wasn't already all over ESPN. And the sleepy little burg was in for a rude awakening when the cameras descended.

"What happened?" I asked finally.

"I don't know," he said. "They found him out by the shore early this morning."

"Cause of death?"

"I didn't ask. Tony sounded—" He paused. "Broken."

I knew the tone. Too well. But I didn't want to think about that, so I shoved the memory to the back of my mind and locked it away. Parker. His friend. Big story, handle with care. Focus, Nichelle.

"No note?" I asked.

"No."

"History of problems?"

"Not that I know of." The words choked off and I heard a couple of deep breaths before he cleared his throat. "I'm not really clear on the details. But they'll fill you in. Take care of this for me, huh, Clarke? I taught that kid to throw a baseball. Bounced him on my knee. Cheered at his games. He was a good boy. Smart. Talented. If we can keep it from turning into a media circus, let's do it."

"I'm on it," I said, ignoring Darcy's yip of protest when I moved her into the floor and sat up. "I'll be there as soon as I can. Text me the address?"

"I'll send it right after I hang up. And thanks."

"Parker?"

"Yeah?"

"I really am sorry." The words felt lame, but I knew from too much experience they were the only ones that fit.

"Me, too, Clarke." He sighed. "Me, too."

* * *

Antihistamines and vitamin D on board, I changed back into a soft cotton pencil skirt and a powder blue cashmere sweater, sliding my feet into copper Jimmy Choo slingbacks I'd picked up at a thrift store the week before. Spring always puts me in the mood for new shoes. To be fair, so do summer, fall, and Wednesday.

I poured the rest of my tea into a travel mug and scratched Darcy's ears before I climbed back into my little red SUV.

Parker had sent me the address, and my maps app told me it would take ninety minutes to get there, which meant I needed to hurry if I wanted to make it by four. I pointed the car toward I-64 and cranked up the Elvis radio station, thinking about teenage angst and what might have caused this nightmare I was about to walk into.

Once outside the city, I set the cruise and sang along with Elvis, admiring the bits of green peeping from the tips of the tree branches. In a week, those baby leaves would shade the entire freeway. There aren't many trees in the part of Texas where I grew up, and the ones there are don't get as mammoth as Virginia trees. Though I'm not a fan of Mid-Atlantic winters, I loved that it wasn't already a hundred degrees outside in early April. Save for the pollen, I'd have driven to Mathews County with my windows down. But I was miserable enough already.

I pulled off the interstate at West Point and scrunched my nose at the stench from the paper mill while crossing the bridge. I bet that's horrible when a person can actually breathe.

The wide road narrowed to two lanes through rolling acres of farmland, corn and hay just sprouting in the fields lining the street. Houses, farms, and churches—in almost equal numbers—were the only things I passed for miles. I turned again by a 7-Eleven and slowed through a green stoplight before I crossed a short drawbridge and pulled onto the island where Tony Okerson had moved to protect his children.

Parker was right: Gwynn's Island was tiny, with a small handful of stop signs and only a few more streets. I passed a long-closed gas station and a vacant building that might have once been a supermarket. If it hadn't been for the manicured lawns and the children darting across roads that looked more like gravel driveways, I'd have wondered if Parker'd sent me to a ghost town.

My map led me to a small iron gate at the head of what appeared to be a private drive. There was no name, only the house number on small blocks the colors of the sand and sky, set into the stone of one post. Perfect for a celebrity looking for a hideaway.

I buzzed and gave my name to the man who answered. His deep voice sounded spent: exhausted and raw. I steeled myself for what was sure to be a tearjerker of an appointment. I try to hold myself together in front of the families, but it's not always easy. My gut said this one would be harder than most.

The gate swung inward, and I idled up the drive. Waves crashed nearby, though I couldn't see the bay yet. Scanning the property line, I caught a glimpse of the water just as a surprisingly modest stone and clapboard beach cottage loomed around the last curve.

I climbed the steps of the wide front porch. It wrapped down both sides of the house, bedecked with Adirondack chairs, palm-blade fans, and three different swings. A red plastic bucket in the corner brimmed with toys. Damn. It hadn't occurred to me to ask Parker how old the kid was. What was I getting into, here?

The front door stood open behind a wood-framed screen, and soft chimes rang through the house when I pushed the doorbell.

A petite woman whose honey-gold skin and sun-streaked hair said she spent a good deal of time outside appeared in the entry. She tried to smile, but it didn't come off.

"Nichelle Clarke, from the *Richmond Telegraph*?" My words sounded more like a question than an introduction because her face portrayed a level of pain I wasn't sure I wanted to tackle, no matter how big the story was. I didn't want to let Parker down, though. "Grant Parker sent me."

She nodded, snagging a friendly-faced Golden Retriever by his thick red collar as she pushed the door open. "I'm Ashton Okerson. Please, come in."

I stepped into a perfect oasis, my heels clicking on travertine just the right shade of blue-gray to match the panoramic views of the Bay I could see through each of three doorways.

"I'm so sorry for your loss," I said, shaking her hand. She didn't look much older than me.

"Thank you for coming to help us. Tony says Grant swears this interview will make it easier. I don't see how anything could." She closed her eyes for a long blink. They shone bright with tears when she opened them. "But thank you. Make yourself at home in the living room." She pointed to the doorway straight ahead. "I'll get my husband."

The wall to the right of the dining room held an artful collage that showed off a gorgeous family. I studied the center photo. Tony Okerson's blond, all-American good looks were framed by a flawless sky, his arm slung around Ashton, the surf in the background. An equally-handsome teenager knelt in the sand in front of them, a football tucked under one flowy-white-beach-shirted arm. Twin little girls with pigtails the color of sunshine leaned from behind Ashton and Tony, grinning.

I stared at the boy. He was the reason I was there, because he was the only male child in the picture. What could bring such tragedy to this peaceful place?

Looking around, I didn't see or hear any sign of Ashton or Tony. Maybe he'd gone for a walk. I would. If I lived in that house, I wouldn't even need shoes, and I could eat as much white chocolate and southern fried everything as I wanted, because I'd walk a million miles up and down that beach every day.

I strode to the open glass wall that ran the length of the living room, searching the shoreline before a soft sob pulled my attention from the water.

One of the little girls from the picture. Hugging a football and crying. I froze. I didn't want to scare her, and I was a stranger. My throat closed and tears burned my eyes. Before I could get my mouth open—though I wasn't sure if it was to speak to the child or call for her mother—I felt a hand on my shoulder.

I turned to find myself face-to-face with one of the most famous athletes in the western hemisphere. The anguish in his green eyes screamed that he'd give back every trophy and Super Bowl ring to have his son safe upstairs.

Oh, boy.

I closed my eyes and hauled in a deep breath, pasting on a smile and putting my hand out.

"I'm so sorry to have to meet you under these circumstances, Mr. Okerson," I said, clearing my throat between the words and brushing at my eyes. "My allergies are giving me the hardest time today."

He nodded, offering a small half-smile. "I understand," he said, and his gentle handshake told me he did. "Please, call me Tony. Come, have a seat."

"Um." I gestured to the little girl.

He peeked around the corner, his broad shoulders slumping. "She won't talk to anyone."

I followed him to a sprawling azure sectional. Ashton came in from the hallway and bustled around the kitchen, disappearing out onto the deck with a plate of cookies.

I shot Tony a look and started to get back to my feet. "Can I help her with something? I feel like she should be, um, not doing housework."

He shook his head. "She's been like this since the sheriff left. Keeping herself busy with mundane things. Almost like she can fix it." He watched his wife fill a pitcher with iced tea and put glasses on a tray, sighing and lowering his voice so only I could hear him. "Like part of her thinks if she goes about a normal Thursday, TJ will come home and this will be a bad dream. God, I wish she was right."

I nodded, trying to smile when Ashton brought the tray in and set it on the coffee table. She filled the glasses and handed me one, then offered one to Tony, who waved it away. Ashton sank into the couch next to her husband, laying her left hand on his knee.

"I'm not sure ...?" She let the question trail off, her turquoise eyes begging me for guidance.

"What to tell me? I understand that." I leaned forward and put the glass on the table, studying them.

Sorrow seeped from every pore. Clearly, I shouldn't vault into asking them about TJ's death. "I want to write a story more about who your son was than how he died, though I'm afraid I need to know that, too," I said. "What kind of music did he like? What was his favorite color, food, time of the year?"

Ashton opened her mouth and her face crumpled. One hand flew to her lips and a muffled sob escaped. "I can't. I can't talk about my beautiful boy in the past tense. My God, he's really gone, isn't he?" She buried her face in Tony's orange polo. "How did this happen to us?"

"I'm so sorry," I said, her muffled sobs tugging at my heart.

Tony nodded over the top of his wife's head. "Thank you. I know you didn't mean any harm. We asked you to come here. Grant said he dragged you out of a rare day off. This is just...surreal. We're still trying to process it."

"I'm sure that's a difficult thing to do," I said, my thoughts running back to the little girl on the deck. It would be especially hard for her to understand. I knew.

They sat for a moment, him staring at nothing, smoothing her hair as she cried. I tried to blend into the sofa. Some days my job felt more voyeuristic than I'd like. When Ashton sat up, I turned my attention back to them.

"TJ's a good kid," Tony said. "Good grades, lots of friends. No trouble. He's an old soul in a young man's body. Didn't ever seem like he wanted to be anything but grown up and responsible. He loves his little sisters, is really active in the church."

I scribbled as he talked, my Benadryl-fogged brain trying to pick through that to a place where this boy had killed himself. Nothing about that said "suicide."

"Girlfriend?" I asked.

"All the girls chased TJ," Ashton said, sniffling. "But Sydney was the only one he ever wanted."

Maybe unrequited teenage love?

"Did she want him, too?" I asked.

"Oh, yes. They've been dating seriously for over a year. Talking about growing up and getting married, like we did. They're in love." She glanced at her husband and he squeezed her hand. "We're not stupid. We told them they had to wait until they were through with school. Do it in the right order. We had TJ when we were still in college. We managed, but it was hard."

I nodded, jotting that down.

"Had the two of them had a fight?"

"No. She's studying in Paris this semester. She wants to be an artist. They Facetimed and talked on the phone every day. She's coming home next week, and he's so excited to see her," Ashton closed her eyes and tightened her grip on Tony's hand. "I guess she's coming home tonight, isn't she?"

Maybe he missed the girl? I put a star by that.

"Forgive me, but I have to ask: is there any history of depression in your family? Had TJ ever shown signs of it?" I bit my lip. Past stories had taught me that teen suicides almost always fall into one of two camps: kids who are outcasts or bullied, or kids who are struggling with the onset of mental illness.

"No," Ashton said, her face serious. "I've been over every minute of the last three weeks in my head today, wondering if I missed something. I have a psych degree gathering dust in the attic. I know the signs. For TJ to spiral that far, that fast, we'd have noticed. I'm a full-time mom and Tony's retired. We have nothing to do but helicopter our kids."

Hmmm.

"How many sports does TJ play?" I asked. They were obviously more comfortable with the present tense.

"Football and baseball." Tony tried to smile. "Quarterback and pitcher. Grant says he's better at baseball. I disagree."

I nodded, another lump forming in my throat at the reminder of the hurt I'd heard in my friend's voice on the phone. Parker had been a breath from being a major league pitcher when a blown rotator cuff ended his baseball career.

"He said y'all were old friends?" I knew Tony Okerson was a UVA alum, like Parker. "From college?"

Tony nodded. "The summer before my senior year, they assigned me a freshman buddy from the athletic program. I had fun showing Grant around the campus. He was serious. Laser-focused. I knew he had the stuff to make it in professional sports five minutes after I met him. He's a good friend."

"That he is," I said. Or, he had been since he'd forgiven me for suspecting him of murder. I'd played matchmaker as a peace offering, setting him up with our city hall reporter at the end of summer. They were getting serious.

I looked out the window at the surf, then back at Tony and Ashton. They didn't want to be there. Didn't want me there. Didn't want to deal with any of this. Their son's death was a circus trainload of elephants in the room, but I couldn't flat-out ask them to describe it. So I chose the round-about road.

"Tell me about TJ," I said, raising my pen.

And they did. They told stories and laughed and cried for an hour. I wrote down everything from Ashton going into labor at a UVA football game (Tony made it through the third quarter before the offensive line coach whisked him off to the hospital just in time to see his son come into the world) to TJ's first day of kindergarten, to his belief that wearing the same socks and underwear for all of January helped his dad win the Super Bowl (ick, but an endearing sort of gross). When the story came around to that morning, Ashton dissolved into sobs again.

"He wasn't in his room," Tony said, clearing his throat. "I went to get him up because we always run in the mornings, and he wasn't there. I thought maybe he was already outside. It's spring break, but he's been up early every day. He went to a party last night, though, and we told him he could stay out late."

Party? My ears keened on the word. I stayed quiet and let Tony talk.

He stared past me at the dark flatscreen TV on the wall over the fireplace.

"I ran, probably a mile and a half down the beach. The shore gets rockier the further you go around the island. I saw the remnants of a camp-fire, and I know the kids build them this time of year when they're out on the water late. Then I saw TJ's jacket. I picked my way down to the water. He was slumped on a rock. It looked like he was sleeping."

I frowned. What about that screamed "suicide?" I hadn't heard anything to make me think this kid had killed himself, yet his parents told Parker he had. How was I going to ask them that without making Ashton cry harder?

I tilted my head and caught Tony's eye.

"I'm afraid I don't follow…" I said.

He nodded, his eyes gleaming with unshed tears. "There was a bottle of Vicodin in his pocket. It was empty."

Ah.

"He'd just picked it up yesterday," Tony continued. "His knee has been bothering him since he took that bad fall in the state championship game in December, and he twisted it in baseball practice last week." He bent his head and buried his face in Ashton's hair, tightening his arms around her. I ducked my head, jotting notes and trying to sort through their story.

A whole bottle of narcotics would do it. But why?

I looked around. The mirror image of the little girl I'd seen outside, but wearing a Mathews High football jersey that swallowed her tiny frame, waved at me from the kitchen doorway. There was a ring of chocolate around her mouth and a light missing from her blue-green eyes. The combination broke my heart.

I wiggled my fingers at her. She stepped into the living room.

"Mommy?" She paused at the end of the couch, and Ashton and Tony broke apart, wiping their eyes.

"What is it, angel?" Ashton flashed a half-smile and opened her arms. The little girl ran to her and climbed into her lap.

"I want TJ to come home," the child said, her whisper muffled by Ashton's shirt.

Dear God.

Tony Okerson looked at me over his daughter's head, pain and pleading twisting his famously-handsome face. "Please, Miss Clarke. Don't let the press turn my family's loss into a sales pitch."

I wasn't sure what I could do to stop it, but I offered a shaky smile as I stood, promising him I would, anyway. There was nothing else to say.

"Thank you for coming," he said, tears falling faster than he could brush them away.

"Of course. Thank you for sharing your memories with me."

I scratched the dog behind his soft, floppy ears as I let myself out the front door, tugging it to make sure he couldn't escape. I climbed back into my car, the effects of the medicine washing away with the adrenaline and emotion of the afternoon.

The image of the Okersons clinging to their wounded little girl burned the backs of my eyelids as I dropped my head and let the tears fall for a few minutes. By the time I rubbed my hands over my face and started the car, it was after six, the sun low in the sky. I wondered where the drugstore was. Another dose of Benadryl was definitely in my future. And since I was poking around town, I might as well meet the local law enforcement.

I glanced at the Okerson house one more time in the rearview as I started up the driveway. Something wasn't right. The details didn't add up. And I was already too invested in these people and their story to walk away without trying to find out why.

2

A dazzling pink sun sank into the Chesapeake Bay, rings of orange, violet, and gold flowing across the horizon and into the water. I slowed the car and watched from the rock-lined road that ran along the north side of the island, letting the beauty erase some of the turmoil I'd lugged from the Okerson house.

A dull honking behind me broke my reverie, reminding me I'd stopped in the middle of the street. I checked the rearview to find a John Deere occupied by an older man in starched jeans and a white straw hat. I waved an apology and gunned the engine.

I hadn't passed anything but churches and a couple of seafood places on the island itself, so I drove back across the little bridge, wondering as I breezed through the only stoplight in town if it ever turned red.

I stopped at the 7-Eleven on the corner that led back to the real world and shuffled inside, hoping they had cold medicine of some variety to get me through a couple more hours and then get me home. Leave it to me to take a sick day and wind up working 'til ten o'clock. The news doesn't wait for pollen. Or anything else, in the age of Twitter.

I found a packet of Sudafed and a small vat of diet Coke. Sipping the soda, I moved to the register.

"You're not from around here," the words were flat—a statement, not a question—from the wiry redhead behind the counter.

"Just passing through," I replied, trying to smile through my sinus pain.

"There ain't nothing out here but fields and water and the people who work them," she said, pulling my change from the till with a raised eyebrow that said she wanted to know why I was there. "You come here, you leave, but you don't pass through."

"Seems like a nice place." I turned for the door.

I hauled myself back into the car, shivering in the breeze and thinking I probably needed a couple of Advil, too. I laid a hand across my forehead. Fever. Hooray. After swallowing the Sudafed, I dug a vial of Advil out of my bag and took two, leaning my head back to rest for a second.

I tried to search for the sheriff's office address on my cell phone. No signal. Great. There weren't but so many places for the sheriff to be in a map dot this tiny. I turned the opposite of the way I'd come into town. I could find the office.

* * *

Or not find it. I tried following the arrows through the halls of the big red courthouse with the sign out front that said "sheriff's office." It was locked, paint buckets outside and drop cloths covering everything I could see through the window.

Twenty minutes later, I'd circled town three times and wondered if the police had closed up on account of remodeling. I stopped in the parking lot of an ancient service station that had been reborn as an antique store. The old-fashioned gravity-fed gas pumps out front were topped with blue and white globes emblazoned with "Esso extra" and flanked by vintage Standard Oil signs. The front walk displayed a charming array of merchandise.

If I wasn't crunched for time and feeling like absolute hell, I'd have browsed for an hour. As it was, I dragged myself to the door and asked the gray-haired gentleman behind the counter where I could find the sheriff.

"At the courthouse," he said, bustling around the end of the high, polished wood counter. His brow wrinkled deeper with concern when he stopped in front of me. "Why don't you come in and have a seat, sugar? You don't look so good."

"Allergies," I said. And decongestants for dinner.

"What business d'you got with Zeke?"

Zeke? Sheriff Zeke. All right. "Just a few questions."

"You look like death on toast." He settled on a stool behind the counter. "Sit down."

"I appreciate the hospitality, but I need to go talk to the sheriff," I said with an effort at smiling. From the look I got in response, I probably managed a wince. "I tried the courthouse, and the office looks like it's being painted."

He nodded. "They moved out of the new office for the painters and back to the old office. At the courthouse. Go to the stop sign up yonder and turn right, then go behind the shops on Main."

"I'm afraid my cold medicine is fogging my brain. The courthouse is a block down on the right," I said.

"But the place where the courthouse used to be in the middle of town is where you want to go," he explained with a patient smile.

"I see." I didn't, really, but I'd go wherever he said if it meant I was closer to getting home.

The little Okerson girl's haunted turquoise eyes flashed through my thoughts and I stood up straighter, thanking him and trying to stride back to the car. Mind over matter, my mom always said.

I found the sheriff's office right where he said it would be and parked next to a pickup from the same era as the gas station/antique store. After blowing my nose, I climbed out of my car and started down the sidewalk. The hastily-stenciled "Sheriff" sign hung over a door next to what had to be the coolest vintage fire station in Virginia, a soaring two-story red brick building with twin open garage bays and an honest-to-goodness fireman's pole. The sheriff's temporary front door stood open to the April breeze, voices carrying to the sidewalk.

"Dammit, Zeke, you got to do something about this," a deep baritone boomed. "Those old bats are gonna skyrocket the divorce rate 'round here, and we don't have the manpower at the courthouse to handle the uptick in paperwork."

"It's not my jurisdiction, Amos." A tired sigh followed the words. "And they're not doing anything that's against the law."

"Neither are we," the baritone protested.

"Didn't say you were," the sheriff replied. "All I'm saying is I can't help you."

A tall, barrel-chested man in a sport coat, slacks, and polished black boots stormed through the door, nodding at me as he passed. The pickup's door groaned a protest when he jerked it open.

I peeked around the doorframe. The cavernous room held a handful of mismatched office furniture. A twenty-something woman with spiky hair the color of the fire engine next door sat behind a dispatch unit in one corner, flipping through a magazine. A man in a chocolate-and-tan uniform slumped in a wooden swivel chair in the center of the desk tangle.

"Excuse me," I said, wincing at my nasal twang. The Sudafed hadn't even made a dent.

They looked up—his sun-bronzed face softened into an interested smile, while she raised a brow. I smiled, focusing on the sheriff. He didn't look old enough to have a name like Zeke. I'd put him mid-forties, with dark hair, curious eyes, and a medium build that spoke more to leanness than muscle, but was fit all the same.

"What can we do for you, miss?" he asked.

"I'm Nichelle Clarke, from the *Richmond Telegraph*," I said. "I came out to talk to Tony and Ashton Okerson, and I want to ask you a few questions about TJ."

The dispatcher returned to her magazine when the sheriff nodded.

"Not much I can tell you that his folks couldn't, but come on in." He waved to a chair across his desk. "I'm Zeke Waters."

"Nice to meet you, sheriff," I said, falling into the chair he offered. It took effort to lean forward and scrounge a pad and pen out of my bag. "I don't suppose you have a tox report back on TJ yet, do you?"

I knew the answer to that was almost surely "no," since it hadn't even been a day, but it was a small town. Maybe there wasn't that much for the coroner to do.

"We probably won't have it for several weeks," he said. "We don't have a crime lab or a coroner, so everything goes to Richmond for autopsy and testing. From the looks of the scene, they'll find a combination of narcotics and alcohol. Most kids who try to kill themselves don't actually pull it off, either because they don't really want to die or because they do it wrong. I can't tell you how much I wish TJ was in that group. The whole damned town is already in an uproar, and it's only going to get worse when word gets outside our little corner of the world."

"And y'all assume it was a suicide because?" I raised one eyebrow. I couldn't figure why it was the first place everyone went.

"Because smart kids don't chase a whole bottle of narcotic pain meds with booze if they don't want to die?" Sheriff Zeke leaned back in his chair and folded his arms across his chest. "TJ Okerson was a smart kid."

"But his parents say he wasn't troubled. Good grades, steady girlfriend, popular ... I've written about teen suicides before. This doesn't fit. Are you opening an investigation into his death?"

"Of course we are," he said. "I examined the scene and talked to the other kids who were out there with him last night. A couple of the boys said he was talking about missing his girl, and worried about his baseball season because of his knee."

I scribbled. "So he was a little upset. There's a difference between bummed and suicidal."

"You trying to tell me how to do my job, Miss Clarke?" Sheriff Zeke's tone flipped from conversational to stiff. "Because this is not my first rodeo. I know everything you're saying."

"Then why are his parents convinced he killed himself?" I asked.

Losing a loved one to suicide is hard, because the guilt that stays with the survivors can eat a person alive. I'd only been at the Okerson's house for a couple of hours, but I liked them. I didn't want them living with the "what if." And my gut said something was off. Even if the sheriff was looking at me like I was a moron.

"Because right now it's the most plausible answer. He was upset. Alcohol is a depressant. And I don't see a scenario where anyone made a kid as strong and fast as TJ Okerson swallow a fistful of narcotics."

"But you don't even know that's what killed him," I protested. "You don't have the tox screen back."

"It's the most likely possibility." He sighed. "Look, it's not like I assumed this all by myself. His parents said he got the pills yesterday. They're gone, he's dead, no evidence of trauma. How does two and two add up in Richmond? Because out here, it's usually four. This is a small town. I hate like hell the idea that a kid with everything in the world to live for decided he didn't want to anymore. But it happens."

I studied him. His whole posture was one of resignation and exhaustion. He didn't want this case any more than I did.

"I'm sorry. I didn't mean to sound like I was questioning your investigative skills. They just seem like such nice people," I said. Maybe he was right, maybe he wasn't. But arguing with him wasn't going to get me anywhere but frozen out of the loop. "Was there anything else unusual about the crime scene?"

His face and voice softened again. "Beach party. Bonfire. Beer bottles. Just kids blowing off steam on vacation," he said. "I was out there for over three hours this morning combing the shoreline. It's a sad situation. Got everyone on edge. But I've been at this for more years than I want to admit. The simplest answer is usually the right one."

I nodded, adding that to my notes.

"Thank you for taking the time to talk to me," I said, fishing a business card from my bag and handing it to him. "It was nice to meet you. When you hear about the tox screen, will you give me a call?"

"I'm about to get buried by the media, huh?" he asked, tucking the card into the top drawer of his desk.

"Very likely. But if it helps, national folks don't ever hang around long."

"Our local paper and some of the TV stations and the paper in Newport News are about the only reporters we ever get in here," he said. "This will be different."

I smiled. "I'm sure it's nothing you can't handle."

"I'd rather not have to."

I smiled understanding and turned for the door.

Back in my car, I contemplated napping for a full two minutes before I started the engine and turned out of the square, aiming the headlights toward home.

For most of the drive I tried to convince myself that Sheriff Zeke was right, but my gut said he wasn't looking hard enough. Honestly, I wanted him to be wrong. Murder was a sexier story all the way around, both because it would be easier on the people who loved TJ in many ways, and because murder sells papers. Plus, something about the sheriff's words nagged the back of my brain. I just couldn't grasp what through the germs and exhaustion.

After arriving home, I filled Darcy's food and water on my way to bed, thankful for her doggie door. Perching on the edge of my cherry four-poster, I kicked off my heels, too beat to even put them back on their shelf. I figured out what bugged me about the sheriff's story as I snuggled into my pillows.

Why would TJ Okerson be worried about his upcoming baseball season if he planned to swallow a fistful of Vicodin?

3

My head was no less stuffy the next morning, but I had work to do. I trudged into the newsroom at seven-thirty to write my story on TJ before the morning news budget meeting, texting Parker on my way. I wanted him to check the article before I turned it in. I was paranoid that my allergy meds had made my head so foggy I'd get something wrong.

TJ Okerson's favorite color was green. He loved football, the beach, and his twin little sisters. As a junior, he led the Mathews Eagles to a state championship last season, appearing set to follow in the footsteps of his famous father, retired Super Bowl champion quarterback Tony Okerson.

"He had the best smile," his mother, Ashton Okerson, said. "I know the saying is that someone's smile lights up a room, but TJ's smile lit up the world. My world, anyway. He made it a better place."

Ashton and Tony talked to the Telegraph *exclusively about their son Thursday evening, after Tony found TJ's body on the beach near their home on Gwynn's Island that morning. Local law enforcement officials said the death appeared to be a*

. . .

I paused, staring at the blinking cursor. I didn't want to type the word "suicide," because my gut said there was something else there. On the other hand, the Okersons believed sheriff Zeke. I didn't want to upset grieving parents and friends, either.

I blew out a short breath and sipped my coffee, scrunching my nose when my beloved white mocha syrup tasted more like tomato sauce thanks to my stuffy head.

"How's it coming?" Parker asked from behind my left shoulder. I smiled and turned to face him, waving a hello to his girlfriend as she dropped her bag to the floor in the cube next to mine.

"Slowly," I said, studying his face. The dark craters under his emerald eyes were unusual, and told me I should probably keep my mouth shut about why it was coming slowly. Parker loved this kid, and I didn't want to make my friend sadder. "These stories are always hard. And his parents were so nice," I finished simply.

He shook his head. "Of all the kids I've ever met, TJ was the least likely to do something like this."

I laid a hand on his arm and caught Mel's eye. She looked tired, too. She just shook her head, a pained look on her face.

"I'm so sorry," I told Parker.

"What did the cops say?" he asked.

"That they're looking into it, but they think it was a suicide."

"Why?" He stepped back and shook his head.

"Why what?"

"TJ loves his baby sisters. He loves his family. I just saw him two weeks ago. He was happy. Why would he do this?" Parker sat heavily on the edge of my desk and dropped his tousled blond head into his hands. Mel massaged his shoulder and offered me a helpless shrug.

I tried to pull in a deep breath, but the stuffy nose netted me a small gasp.

"His parents don't know. The cops don't know," I said. "It doesn't sound to me like a typical suicide, if there even is such a thing."

Parker raised his head and leveled his green eyes at me.

"Are you saying what I think you're saying?" he asked.

"I'm not sure what I'm saying," I replied hurriedly. "I just ... my gut says there's something off, Parker." So much for keeping my mouth shut.

"Are the cops out there really looking into it, or are they placating Tony and Ashton?"

"I can't tell. The sheriff seemed like a nice guy, but I don't know him or anyone else in the department. I'm flying a little blind, here. He said he's waiting for tox results, but they don't have their own lab, so that could take a while."

"How long a while?"

"A couple of weeks. Maybe three," I said. "It's not as complicated as a DNA analysis. Just testing his blood for hydrocodone levels and alcohol. It depends on what's in the queue."

"Painkillers?" Parker raised an eyebrow.

"There was an empty bottle in his pocket. His folks said he just got the prescription refilled."

"And alcohol? TJ wasn't stupid," Parker said. "He knows better than to drink and take painkillers."

"I think that's their evidence that he did it on purpose," I said gently. "It's the why that doesn't fit for me."

"Yeah." He shook his head again as he stood. "I should let you finish your story."

"Bob wants it early. Thanks for the scoop. I hope I do it justice."

"You will," he said, turning for the hallway that led to his office. "Keep me in the loop, huh?"

"Absolutely. I'm not sure how far I can get a foot in the door down there. It is a small town. Like, one stoplight, the-7-Eleven-clerk-gave-me-the-stink-eye-because-I-don't-belong small. But I'll keep after it."

"Thanks."

* * *

I finished typing my story, alternately giggling at funny anecdotes the Okersons had shared and swallowing tears at the memory of the little girls who missed their brother. Reading through it, I hoped it was good enough to make Ashton Okerson's day a teensy bit easier.

I copied Parker when I emailed the article to Bob, just in time to sprint to the staff meeting. Well, it felt like sprinting, but was probably more like dragging ass thanks to what I suspected was a full-blown sinus infection.

I stopped short when I rounded the corner into my editor's office and found Shelby Taylor parked in my usual seat.

Standing just inside the door, I shot Bob a clear WTF look and got an apologetic shrug in reply.

"Good morning, Nichelle," Shelby purred, folding her arms over her ample chest and grinning up at me. "You look as fresh as ever."

I didn't even have the energy to glare. Shelby was our copy chief, but made no bones about the fact that she wanted to be our crime reporter. And she'd tried everything from sleeping with the managing editor to ratting me out to the criminal underworld to get it, too.

I leaned toward her and coughed. She wrinkled her nose and shrank back into the orange velour of Bob's Virginia Tech chic armchair.

"You should consider things like the freedom to take a sick day when you're trying to steal someone's beat," I said.

"I don't get sick," she snapped. "Seems like you should take more vitamins."

I turned to Bob. "What the hell is she doing in here, and can you make her leave?"

"Now, ladies," he said. "Nichelle, Shelby's filling in for Les for the next week."

"She's what? A whole week?" I tried to groan, but it sounded more like a snort. "Why? What happened to Les?"

Our managing editor had never been one of my favorite people, seeing as how he was a brown-nosing weasel who wanted Bob's job as badly as Shelby wanted mine but, given the choice between my rival and her boyfriend, I'd take Les twice over.

"He's recovering from surgery," Shelby chirped. "Andrews asked me himself if I'd step in."

Right. Rick Andrews was the *Telegraph's* publisher, and didn't care about much of anything but the paper's bottom line and image. Les was generally so far up Andrews's backside the big boss didn't have time to notice any of the rest of us. I had a hard time believing he knew Shelby existed.

"How is it that we work in a newsroom and I hadn't heard Les was having surgery?" I asked. "Is he going to be okay?"

"It's a minor procedure," Shelby said, fiddling with the file folder in her lap.

"A minor procedure he needs a week to recover from?" I perched on a plastic office chair. "I'm practically dying, and here I sit."

"Are y'all talking about Les's hair plugs again?" Eunice Blakely, our features editor, asked as she ambled into the room and lowered herself slowly into the orange velour armchair opposite Shelby's. Eunice's war correspondent days had ended when a helicopter crash in Iraq earned her a half-dozen screws in her right hip. In the years since, she'd made our features section a consistent award-winner, and made herself our resident mistress of southern cooking and wry observation.

I sucked in my cheeks to keep from smiling.

"I think it will look good when it's healed," Shelby argued.

"But isn't the point for people to notice he looks different? Why hide? Also—why are you here?" I asked Shelby. "Les doesn't usually come to the news meetings."

"I want to know what I need to be on top of today," Shelby said with a grin. "Just trying to learn as much as I can from this opportunity."

Bob rolled his eyes, but she didn't notice, and I coughed again to cover a laugh. He knew as well as I did Shelby was there because she wouldn't miss an excuse to crash the meeting.

The rest of the section editors filed in and Bob flash-fired through the rundown, not turning to me until the end.

"We have an exclusive on a sad story today," he said, his gaze flicking to Spencer Jacobs, our sports editor. "We're going live with it on the web as I speak, because the police report will be in the local paper in Mathews County this morning."

He paused and sat back in the chair, eyes on me. Whispers flitted through the rest of the room.

"What's Nichelle got?" Eunice finally asked Spence. "And what's it got to do with you?"

"Tony Okerson's teenage son is dead," I said quietly when Bob nodded an okay.

"What?" Spence sat up straight, fumbling for a pen. "How? And why don't I have this at the sports desk?"

"Parker asked me to handle it," I said. "The Okersons are his friends. And your guys don't have much experience working with cops."

"It's her story, Spence, and you get her whatever she needs to do a good job of it," Bob said. "Listen up, folks. We have the only interview the Okersons are giving. When this breaks nationwide, it's going to be huge, and this poor little town isn't going to know what hit it. Everyone and their Poodle will want into this story, and no one here is sharing anything. Not a word. Are we clear? If you get a call from a member of another media organization, you forward it to Nichelle or to me. Nothing goes out without approval."

I nodded. Parker and Bob were close, and I could tell from the forceful note in Bob's voice that Parker had given him the same speech I'd gotten on the phone the day before.

"What's the *Telegraph*'s official statement?" Shelby asked.

I snuck a glance between her and Bob. He looked irritated, and she was too busy staring daggers at me to notice.

"Just send all inquiries to me," Bob said, impressive control in his tone. "I don't see a reason for you to get any questions. But if you do, I'll field them."

"What if you're not here?" Shelby asked. "If I'm putting in long hours and find myself needing to answer someone?"

"Take. A. Message," Bob said through clenched teeth, and I snorted. I didn't mean to. It just slipped out.

Shelby shot me another glare as she strode from the office.

I smiled, keeping my seat as the section editors ran for their computers, looking for my story. Curiosity is part of the gig when you work in a newsroom.

"Don't be so quick to gloat," Bob cautioned, leaning his elbows on his desk. "She's going to be as far into everything as she can get until Les comes back to work, and you are going to be up to your neck in this Okerson thing. I'll do what I can, but she has Andrews's ear, and his memory is about as long as Les's hair."

"That's so wrong." I didn't even try to suppress a giggle.

Bob grinned. "I think you sympathize with my ill will toward Les."

"I do at that," I said. "And I am going to nail this Okerson story. Something's not right, chief. I have a bad feeling about this whole thing. That interview was one of the hardest things I've ever done in the name of a story. And that's counting getting shot. It just rips your heart right out to talk to these people. They're so nice."

"I got the feeling from the story that you were hedging the cause of death." He sat back and laced his fingers behind his head. "What gives?"

"It doesn't fit. He was cute. Popular. Family has money. He had a girl. A looming career playing ball, for chrissakes. Why?"

Bob chewed on that for a five slow taps of my foot before he answered with a question of his own.

"What'd you make of the sheriff?"

"Eh. He seems nice. He's not stupid. He's also not excited about the media shitstorm. I think I can get on his good side. I just don't know how far he's going to dig."

"Well, kiddo, your gut has a good track record. Poke around if you must. But I know I don't have to remind you that you need to stay on top of your regular beat. And we cannot screw this thing with Okerson up."

I nodded, fishing a Kleenex out of the pocket on my soft lavender cardigan and swiping at my nose.

"March yourself to Care First and get an antibiotic." Bob drew his brows together in a parental glare, and I smiled.

"Yes, sir."

"And then get some juice and get to work. Find out when the funeral is and if you can go."

"To the funeral?" Aw, man. I didn't think I could handle that.

"There will be cameras on every inch of lawn at that church," Bob said. "I want you inside."

"You got it, chief." I grabbed my bag and turned for the door. The elevators seemed a Himalayan trek away, and the room seesawed a half dozen times when I stood up.

"Feel better," Bob said, turning to his computer. I saw my story flash on the screen, a photo of TJ Okerson from the state championship football game under the header.

I did not have time to be sick.

4

A sinusitis diagnosis and two Amoxicillin capsules later, I was back at my desk with a steaming mug of honey-lemon tea, a sweating bottle of orange-pineapple juice, and a big question mark hanging over TJ Okerson's death. I dialed Richmond police headquarters and asked for Aaron White, the public information officer and generally one of my favorite sources.

I trusted Aaron's opinion more than Sheriff Zeke's.

"I'd ask if you have twenty minutes for me to come by, but I think I have the plague, and I don't want to stand up unless it's absolutely necessary," I said when he picked up. "So, I need to ask you a couple of questions. Got a minute?"

"For you? Usually. What's up? We don't have much for you this morning, unless kids ripping off car stereos is news."

"This isn't about a case. At least, not your case. But we'll come back to the kids later." Lots of car stereos could be worth a few inches of space. We could run a warning to residents in the area.

"Why are you asking me about a case that's not mine? How sick are you?"

"Sick. But the news doesn't write itself. Did you see my story this morning about the Okerson kid?"

"Ah." He fell quiet. I twisted the phone cord around my index finger. Aaron had two daughters, neither of them much older than TJ.

"Aaron?"

"I saw it. Those poor people."

"Indeed. So, the thing is, I'm not entirely sure it was a suicide."

"What? Why not? What does local law enforcement say?"

"The sheriff thinks he killed himself," I said, tapping a pen on the calendar blotter that covered the top of my paper-strewn desk. "But it doesn't track. I get the empty pill bottle and the booze at the party. That's damning evidence. But this kid, according to his parents, anyway, had none of the markers of being suicidal. Not one."

"How well do most teenagers' parents know them?" Aaron asked.

"I have no frame of reference. Only child of a single mom. We've always been tight. But I suspect you're looking for 'not well?'"

"As much as I hate to say it, that's usually the case."

I pictured Ashton Okerson's crumpling face, heard her "helicopter our kids" comment ring in my thoughts.

"These folks didn't seem to think so," I said.

"Not that they told you," Aaron said. "I mean no disrespect. Tony Okerson is a damned fine ballplayer and I hear he's a good man. But he's spent a lifetime working the media. If they didn't know what was up with their kid, they're not admitting it to you. Not now."

I sighed. Tony said they went for runs every day. Ashton knew all about his plans to marry his girlfriend. That more mirrored my life than your typical primetime teen angst my-parents-are-morons drama, but he had a point.

"So I should dig more." I said. "Thanks, Aaron."

"Anytime. Holler if you find something else you want to bounce off me. Such a sad story."

"Your girls home for break yet?"

"They came in Friday, bearing a small mountain of laundry." His tone told me he didn't mind a bit. It was the first year both of his daughters were away at college, and he was over the moon to have them home.

"Hope you have enough detergent," I said.

"Me, too. Though if I were the sort to do it, I could borrow some from the evidence locker. That might be an interesting one for you: narcotics seized three hundred gallons of Tide in a bust yesterday," he said.

"How did I miss that?" I asked. "And what the hell are drug dealers doing with detergent? Do I want to know? I can't imagine shooting up Tide is going to end well for anyone."

Aaron laughed. "No, I don't suppose so. But this isn't for shooting up. It's currency," he said. "They've been having this issue in New York for over a year. Looks like it's trickled down here. Tide is expensive, right? And it's something that's not usually stolen, so no one locks it up. People make a run for it with a shopping cart full, then they trade it to the dealers for drugs. The dealers take it back to another store and get a full refund, plus the sales tax. Nifty little scheme, huh?"

I flipped my notebook to a clean page and scribbled that down. "I swear to God, if these criminals directed their creative energies to good things, we'd have a cure for cancer. How the hell do people come up with this stuff?"

"It's job security," he said. "As long as there are creative crooks in the world, we've got jobs."

"I can always count on you for the bright side," I said. "Thanks for your help."

I asked him to email me what he had on the car stereo thefts and the detergent bust before I hung up.

Maybe it was mind over matter, but I felt a bit more human, and the room only rocked once when I stood. I grabbed my bag, tea, and juice, hoping I'd continue to improve on the drive to Gwynn's Island. The answer to the nagging feeling in my gut wouldn't come looking for me in Richmond.

* * *

I dropped my cell phone in the cup holder for easy access when I climbed into my car, dialing my friend Emily's office in Dallas when I got to the freeway. A perky-voiced receptionist answered and I asked to speak with Emily.

"Doctor Sansom is very busy this morning," she said, her tone sweet but guarded. "May I tell her who's calling?"

Once I had given her my name, Em was on the phone in four seconds.

"It's been ages, girl," she said, her earring clicking against the receiver. "What is going on with you? I thought you wanted to be Lois Lane, not Nancy Drew. Then I see you on Anderson Cooper talking about all kinds of crazy stuff. And, I hear Kyle moved to Richmond. Do tell."

"You're not charging by the hour, right, Dr. Sansom? Just so we're clear?" I tried to sniffle quietly, hoping I sounded a little farther from death's door than I felt.

Emily had the best laugh. Her head-thrown-back, full-blown chortle had been one of my favorite things about her since she loaned me her Strawberry Shortcake eraser in third grade and became one of my best friends.

It rang in my ear for a good ten seconds. "Shut up, Nicey," she said. "I've been meaning to call and bug you about Kyle since Christmas. My days keep getting away from me. What's going on? Do I need to clear my June weekends?"

"There are no wedding bells in my future," I said. "Kyle is...complicated. We're getting to know each other again. It's been ten years, and we're such different people than we were then."

"Last time I saw Kyle he was way hotter people than he was then, that's for damned sure."

"There is that." I grinned. "And he's very sweet. But I don't know."

"I'm guessing there's another guy," she said.

"Did they teach you to be psychic at shrink school?"

"Something like that. What's he like? Must be something else to keep you away from Kyle."

"He's something else, all right. Sexy, mysterious. But I didn't call to talk about my love life." I also didn't want to spill details on Joey. Talk about complicated.

"What did you call to talk about?" She stopped. "Shit. Have you been crying? Is your mom okay?"

"Mom is great, thank God. Five years remission this summer. I just have a sinus infection. None of that's why I called, either. Tony Okerson's son died Wednesday night."

"Tony Okerson, the football player?"

"The very same."

"Um. Not that I don't love hearing from you, but I'm confused."

"The local sheriff says the kid killed himself. I'm not convinced."

"I see." She paused, her voice softening. "You sure you're not projecting? It wouldn't be abnormal, with everything you and your mom went through."

"That, friend, is the million-dollar question." I sighed. "But I've covered other suicides, and this is different, Em. That's part of why I called you. I want your take on this kid."

"You know I can't analyze someone I've never met based on third-hand information. Certainly not in the space of a phone call."

"I know you can't give me expert opinion I can quote," I said. "I'm not asking you for an interview. I just want to know what you think."

No answer. I waited.

"Because I love you, tell me about him," Em said finally.

"Back at you."

I gave her the rundown. The only noise as she listened was the sound of her earring hitting the receiver when she nodded. "It just doesn't add up," I finished. "No matter how I try to force it, the puzzle doesn't fit. Or am I crazy?"

"You are not crazy," Em said. "Whether you're right or not, I don't know, but I hereby pronounce you as sane as anyone else. I'll go with your theory, though. There are statistical anomalies in everything, but if what you're telling me is true, this would be so far outside the curve we'd need binoculars to make it out."

"Why?"

"Well first, teenage boys who are suicidal are more successful at their first attempt, because they tend to do more permanent things. Taking pills is an iffy option. Maybe it works, maybe someone finds you and you get your stomach pumped. Or you change your mind and stop after two and have a bad hangover. Intentional overdose is more common among women. We tend to be more unsure of what we want."

Her voice dropped and I knew she wasn't just talking about pills.

"Yeah, yeah, I have commitment issues. We can discuss that later. Keep talking. What do guys do instead of taking pills?"

"Shooting, hanging, jumping off bridges," she said. "Things that have more permanent results."

I filed that away. "Okay. What else? You said 'first.'"

"I did. The rest is pure conjecture, because I haven't met anyone involved. But unless there's something you didn't tell me, or something they're not telling you, I can't find a reason. If the kid didn't have a psychotic break in the space of a few hours, you didn't give me anything that indicated he would consider suicide. There are warning signs."

I nodded. "That's what I thought."

"I'm not saying run a story crying conspiracy," Em said. "But if you think something's off, check it out. This will be hard on his family. The closure would help them. I don't suppose I have to tell you that."

Nope. "Thanks, Em," I said.

"Anytime. Now, about this mystery man," she said.

My phone beeped. I pulled it away from my head and checked the caller ID.

"Speak of the devil," I told Emily. "Let me call you later?"

"Sure, honey. Good luck."

I thanked her again and clicked over.

"Hello?"

"Nichelle?" Joey's deep tenor, with his slight Italian-by-way-of-Jersey accent, always made my stomach flip.

"Hey there. What's going on with you?" I put one foot on the brake as I took the West Point exit.

"What's going on with you? Have you been crying?"

"I wish. Tears are easier to get rid of than germs."

"You're sick? Are you at home?"

"That'd be fabulous," I said. "But no. I'm chasing a story to Tidewater."

"You should rest."

"Nice theory. I'll try it out later. I hope. What's up?"

"Just calling to say 'hi,'" he said.

"That's a new one."

"I was thinking about you."

My stomach flipped again. "That's nice to hear."

"I'm glad. Get done out there and get home. Feel better."

"Thanks."

I clicked off the call, a smile tugging at my lips. He was thinking about me. Kyle's face flashed quick on the heels of that and I sighed, considering Em's words. But I had time to figure Joey and Kyle out.

The clock was ticking on TJ Okerson's story.

* * *

The light was green again when I crossed the bridge to the island. I drove every street, which took all of twenty minutes at Sunday-stroll speed. It was quiet, the children I'd seen the day before tucked safely behind locked doors in the wake of the tragedy. I wasn't looking for an interview—just to get a feel for the place TJ had called home. It was Mayberry-like, in the most charming sense of the label. And it was an island. But for the ninety-minute drive from my office and my favorite coffeehouse, I'd consider moving.

I slowed as I approached the Okerson house, then slammed the brake and turned around when I saw Charlie Lewis's satellite truck from Channel Four parked along the side of the road. She was likely camped outside Tony and Ashton's gate, and I didn't want to lead her to my actual destination if she hadn't thought of it yet.

I crossed the bridge again and turned toward Mathews, parking in a visitor space at the high school. The building was TV-show-high-school-set perfect, red brick with bright white columns.

I walked into the front office and a plump blonde woman with a turquoise sweater set and shimmery pink lip gloss smiled and asked if she could help me.

The question was, *would* she help me? I introduced myself, and her smile faded. I didn't like my odds.

"We saw your article this morning." She gestured to the computer monitor on her desktop. "Lyle Foxhead at our local newspaper is my sister's boyfriend. He was tore up over the Okersons talking to you and not him. He rang their phone off the wall all yesterday and half the day today. How come they talked to you? You ain't from here. Of course, they're come-heres, too."

"Come heres?"

"People who aren't from the county. They come here to live. But they're not part of us. Not part of the area like the rest of us."

"I see." I wasn't sure I did. She made it sound like a club there was no way to pledge. "Well, as a journalist, I can certainly understand Lyle's frustration." I smiled. "The Okersons and I have a mutual friend who recommended they talk to me. So this is not a case of 'they just didn't trust him.' And I'm sure y'all know it's been a very trying couple of days for them."

She gave me a critical once-over. "A mutual friend?" She appeared to soften a bit.

"Grant Parker and I work together."

"Is that a fact?" She grinned the way women do when Parker walks into a room, and I knew I'd found my in.

"We're close." I smiled. "He went on and on about how hospitable the folks around here are."

"Did he, now?"

I nodded.

"I do pride myself on my manners," she said, fluffing her already-pouffy hair. "I'm Norma. Welcome to Mathews."

"Thanks. I'm wondering if some of TJ's teachers might talk to me."

"I don't know," she still looked guarded, but she reached for the phone on her scarred wooden desk and dialed a number.

She dialed three different people, the layers of pity in the smiles she flashed me between calls getting thicker each time. "This is just such an emotional subject for our faculty." She shook her head as she cradled the phone.

"I understand," I said, sure it didn't help that I was an outsider. I offered a last smile and moved toward the door, sniffling. She cracked.

"Wait!" She brandished a tissue box, picking up her phone again. "I know who you can talk to."

I took a tissue and wiped my nose as she murmured into the handset. She turned back to me, grinning.

"If you'll just go down this hallway to the back doors, follow that stairwell outside then down, and take a left at the foot of the stairs, you'll find the gym. Coach Morris will talk to you. He's used to reporters. And he and Lyle don't get along."

"Disagreement over a story?" I asked, wondering if the coach distrusted the press.

"No. Coach Morris used to be my sister's husband." She shook her head. "I don't know what's wrong with her sometimes."

No drama there. "Thanks for your help."

The school was eerily quiet for the middle of the day. It took me minute to remember what the Okersons had said about it being spring break.

I found the gym easily, but Coach Morris proved more difficult. After lapping the basketball court and checking the equipment room twice, I flagged down a couple of lanky boys with bat bags slung over their shoulders.

"I'm looking for Coach Morris?" I leaned on the wall as a sudden wave of dizziness hit, making me wish I was closer to the bleachers.

"He's probably in his office." One boy gestured to a side hallway. "It's in the locker room. We can get him, if you like." He poked the second boy, who trotted off that way.

I smiled a thank you before I ambled to the bleachers and sat. The boy tugged at the bottom of the basketball net, watching me with a curious expression. Looking toward the hallway where the other boy had gone and finding it empty, I studied the kid in front of me. Straight teeth, clear skin, good hair. And a baseball player.

"Did you know TJ Okerson?" I asked, knowing the answer from looking at him.

"Everyone knew TJ." He plucked at the white strings.

"So I hear. How well did you know him? He was a pitcher, right?"

The boy nodded. "A great pitcher. I pitch, too, but no one could touch TJ. His dad's arm is legend. Some days, I wished he'd stayed in D.C."

"I bet it's hard to compete with a guy like that."

He met my eyes for the first time since I'd mentioned TJ's name, his tone flat. "There's no way to compete with a guy like that. Can't be done. There's only standing in his shadow and waiting for him to get hurt."

Holy shit. I held the boy's gaze until my eyes went blurry. He didn't blink.

"I'm sorry to keep you waiting," a deep voice from the far end of the bleachers broke the tension and I turned. "I'm Terry Morris."

"Nichelle Clarke," I said, smiling and putting out a hand.

"You can go on home, Luke," the coach nodded a dismissal at the kid and he shrugged and wandered toward the outside door, glancing back at me once.

I focused on the man who probably knew TJ as well as anyone, wishing I felt better and trying to put Luke's steely gaze out of my thoughts for the moment.

"Thanks for talking to me," I said. "I don't think I'm the most popular girl in town today."

"Norma tells me you're the gal who wrote the story about TJ in the Richmond paper. Any enemy of Lyle's is a friend of mine." Morris smiled. He was good-looking, probably in his early forties with light brown hair, a warm tan, strong jaw, and nice smile. His physique suggested he took advantage of his job as a gym teacher to keep in shape.

I didn't mention that I didn't want to be the enemy of the local press. If Lyle was any good at his job, he knew the people I needed to talk to and could be a great source for me.

"I'm going to jump right in here," I said, reaching for a notebook and clicking out my pen. "Was TJ troubled? Did anything seem to be bothering him lately?"

"Besides his knee? Nope." Morris shook his head hard enough to muss his hair. "TJ was a happy kid. Smart. Gifted on the field. Nice. I don't think anything much ever bothered him. He led a charmed life."

I considered the scenarios on my list of reasons for a kid like TJ to commit suicide. Aaron's comment about the Okersons floated to the top.

"What about his parents?" I asked. "His dad is a big deal. Did they put a lot of pressure on him?"

"Not that I ever saw, really." Morris held my gaze. "I mean, TJ was a perfectionist, and sure, he worried about what his dad thought. But Tony wasn't one of those dads who came to every practice and bitched at the kid all the way through. He offered pointers. You'd almost think he was a bad parent if he didn't, wouldn't you? But full-on pressure? No. Luke there, the boy who was here a minute ago—he gets more of that. His daddy won a state baseball trophy for us twenty years ago, and it was the greatest thing he ever did. He rides the kid pretty hard."

I scribbled every word. Damn. I hate cases involving kids on either side, but on both? My head developed a dull ache at the thought. I put a star in the margin by that comment.

"Tell me about TJ's knee," I said, remembering the night Parker had told me about his career-ending shoulder injury. It had messed him up. Maybe TJ was just young enough that a serious injury had pushed him a tiny bit too far?

"He pulled the ligaments in the last football game of the season."

"Ligaments, plural?" I asked.

"Yeah. I joked with him that he didn't know how to do anything halfway. He wanted to play the rest of the game. I coach the offensive line. I didn't know how bad he was hurt. That kid had a tolerance for pain like nothing I've ever seen. The docs said it was a miracle he could walk by the time the game was over."

"No kidding?" I kept writing.

Morris nodded. "They had a physical therapist at their house three days a week for the whole winter, and he was ready to start when baseball got going this spring, but then he came off the mound funny last Thursday and twisted it. He was limping and babying it pretty good all day Friday. They've been on vacation this week. I told him to rest it. Hadn't heard anything from them about what the doctors said."

And TJ's dad hadn't given me those details. Could Parker find out more for me?

"What about his girlfriend? Any trouble in paradise?"

Morris shook his head. "Not that I could tell, no. She's been out of pocket for a while, but he still had a picture in his locker. Talked about her all the time."

Locker.

"Has anyone been by to clean out TJ's locker?" I asked.

Morris shook his head.

"May I see it?" I asked.

"Sure, I guess. As long as you don't take anything." He shrugged. "Let me make sure the boys are gone."

He disappeared and I cradled my head in my hands and took a few deep breaths. I dug in my purse for the Advil and choked two down dry before Morris returned.

"All clear." He grinned.

The locker room stank of sweat, mildew, and spray deodorant in heavy enough doses that even I could smell it with my stuffed up nose.

"Right down here," Morris said, pointing to the third row of lockers. "Number nineteen."

I perched on the bench in the center of the aisle, smiling at the small-town feel of the lack of locks in the locker room. Closing my eyes for a moment, I pulled TJ's open.

When I opened my eyes, a beautiful girl with long brown hair and a Mona Lisa smile stared at me from the inside of the door, her photo outlined by a magnetic frame decorated with hearts. Girlfriend. Check.

I picked through the rest of the contents, not finding much of anything but normal teenage athlete stuff. Deodorant, three baseball gloves, socks, jockstrap (I didn't pick that up). A bag hung from the hook in the back and I started to open it before something in my peripheral vision pulled my eyes up. Toward the back of the shelf in the top of the locker lay a piece of lime green paper. I pulled it down. It was curved, crumpled on one edge, with huge block letters printed on one side.

Wednesday night, Cherry Point beach, get your party on before the season starts. Go Eagles!

A flyer for the party TJ had gone to. Who invited him? I turned the paper over looking for a name. There wasn't one.

"It doesn't look like there's much here to see." I put the flyer back where I'd found it, peeking into the bag. Dirty socks, a pair of cleats, and a set of knee pads. Strike three.

"He was a good kid," Morris said. "I sure am going to miss him. He won games, yeah. But he was just nice to have around. Why in God's name would he do something like this? Could it have been an accident?"

I shook my head. "The police don't think so, I think because of the number of pills that were missing. No one takes a whole bottle of Vicodin unless they're trying to hurt themselves." Quoting Sheriff Zeke felt put on, but I could see the pain on Morris's face, and I didn't want to add my suspicions to it without more reason.

"I just don't understand." He slumped against the bank of lockers. "It's so sad."

"It is," I said. "Everyone keeps telling me he was such a wonderful kid. I'm so sorry for your loss, coach. Thanks for talking to me."

"Anytime," he said. "I'm always available for a reporter who's not sleeping with my wife."

So not touching that.

I made my way back through the silent building to the parking lot and drove the two minutes to the police station, finding the old pickup in the parking lot again. Letting myself in, I sat perched on the edge of a bench in the front entry. The spiky-haired dispatcher was probably at lunch, the office quiet except for an animated discussion between the sheriff and the same agitated man I'd seen there the day before.

"How is it possible that you can't put a stop to this foolishness?" he asked, tugging at his red suspenders.

"Amos, they are not breaking the law." Zeke spaced his words out for effect.

"Trespassing."

"It's a parking lot."

"Invasion of privacy."

"In plain sight?"

I cleared my throat and they both turned to me. The sheriff actually looked happy to see me.

"I have other business to attend to with Miss Clarke here, if you'll excuse me," Sheriff Zeke said. "She's from the newspaper. In Richmond."

Amos blanched, but recovered so quickly I wondered if I'd imagined it, offering a hand before hustling out the door.

"You have excellent timing," Zeke said.

"I try. He seems upset."

The sheriff rolled his eyes, but didn't offer a comment. Since Amos wasn't what I was there to talk about, I left it.

"I went by the high school and had a chat with the baseball coach," I said. "I just thought I'd stop by since I was out here and see if you'd had any new developments in your investigation."

"I'm still waiting to hear from the lab," he said. "But my statement for today is that according to the story I can piece together from witnesses, we have no suspicion of foul play. No matter how much you might want me to."

"I don't want this child to have been murdered. I'm just looking at every angle of the story."

"Or maybe trying to spin the story into something more sensational than it already is?"

Zeke sighed when my eyebrows went up.

"That's probably unfair," he said hastily. "But I've had twenty-seven phone calls from media outlets today. Every TV personality in the east is on their way here, and I expect they'll be arriving in time for dinner. I'm sorry for the Okersons. But right now, I have to find a way to keep this from becoming an epidemic. A kid like TJ Okerson committing suicide gets blasted all over the TV and the Internet, and there's liable to be a whole wave of kids who hurt themselves trying to be cool."

"I had the same thought this morning," I said. "Which is part of the reason it makes sense to look for other causes of death, right?"

"I can't waste taxpayer money running an investigation into an open and shut case," he said. "I'll pay for that next election season."

"You're that sure after two days with no lab results?" It sounded sharper than I intended, and the sheriff bristled. I raised one hand. "I mean no disrespect. I just think—there was a boy at the school today. Luke something. A baseball player. He seemed very jealous of TJ. Was he at this party?"

The sheriff shook his head. "You don't give up, do you?"

"Not easily."

"I don't believe there's an official list of who was at the party. I haven't heard the Bosley kid's name."

I stared, waiting for him to say something else. Like, "I'll look into that."

He returned my somber gaze without so much as a twitch of his lips.

Looked like I'd be the one checking out young Luke. A mustachioed deputy in a uniform that matched Zeke's and a wide-brimmed hat came through a side door, pausing and giving me an interested once-over. I tucked my pad and pen back into my bag.

"Thanks for your time, sheriff," I said as I stood, not wanting to leave on a sour note. "Again. Good luck tonight."

"You're not staying for the show?" Zeke asked.

"I've seen it."

The farther I was from Mathews when the satellite trucks invaded, the happier Bob would be. I was sure I had messages stacking up at the office, and my cell phone had been binging email arrivals all afternoon. Professional courtesy forbade me from outright ignoring them, but being sick and trekking around Mathews all afternoon were excellent excuses for putting them off.

5

After a five-minute chat with the elderly receptionist at the local newspaper office (Lyle wasn't there), I left a message and took a copy of that day's final edition home. I wanted to know what else was news in Mathews County.

I got Aaron's email about the car stereo thefts and the detergent and sent Bob a four-inch blurb about each for Metro from my cell phone before I aimed the car toward Richmond.

Dead tired, I turned into my driveway an hour and a half after I left the *Mathews Leader*'s office. I examined the flowerbed next to the mailbox, noticing that my hyacinths were pinking up, before I saw the black Lincoln parked under the low-hanging tree in the neighbor's front yard. I smiled.

"Joey?" I coughed over the last half of the word as I let myself in through the kitchen door. The first time I'd ever laid eyes on Joey, I'd come home from a long day to find him in my living room, waiting with a story tip. Apparently, the Mafia doesn't consider an invitation necessary. After that first scared-shitless encounter, he'd saved my life once and shown up to talk increasingly often. We'd developed a slow-growing relationship of sorts. He wasn't exactly a "good guy," but I'd been unable to find evidence that he was a bonafide bad guy, either. The only thing I'd nailed down was that he was good to me. Years of up-close-and-personal with the worst of society had blessed me with a good creep radar, and Joey didn't set it off.

Since he liked to stop in without calling (and clearly, I had shoddy locks), I'd given him a key shortly after Christmas.

"Straight to bed." I heard the low, warm voice from the hallway before I saw him, and my stomach flopped. Since we'd never been to bed together, I figured he was worried about my illness. I hoped, anyway. It's impossible to feel sexy with a nose full of yuck.

"Is that an order?" I asked.

"Absolutely." He stepped into the kitchen, his olive skin dark with scruff along his jaw, his full lips parting over a smile. I really was sick, because my pulse didn't even flutter. "You sounded horrible on the phone. And no offense, but you don't look two steps out of a funeral home."

Great. I smoothed my hair back and then gave up, too sapped to be self-conscious. Darcy yipped and pawed my ankle and I scratched behind her ears, dizziness washing over me when I bent down.

"Whoa." I grabbed the back of one of my little bistro chairs and hauled myself into it. "Hang on, Darce."

"Bed. You need rest. I can't believe you drove your car." Joey shook his head, a line creasing his brow. "I already took Darcy outside, and I fed her, too."

I smiled a thank you, staring after he turned away.

Damn, he looked good. His suit jacket was slung over the back of the other kitchen chair. He stepped to the stove in a perfectly-tailored charcoal vest and pants, his cornflower blue shirt making his skin glow warmer in the soft light. I marveled at the fact that this man was in my house. Cooking.

"This story is the kind you don't skip out on," I said.

"I saw it. Sad stuff." He lifted the lid off a pot and stirred and I caught a whiff of something delicious through the sinus fog.

"What is that?"

"My mother's minestrone will cure anything," he said, settling the lid back in place and turning to me. "It's full of vitamins, and it tastes good, too. It'll be ready in about half an hour."

"I have less than no appetite." I folded my arms on the table and dropped my head onto them, muffling the words. "I just feel...gross. Stupid germs."

"Which is why you need to eat. And rest." He looped one arm around my waist and fit the other under my knees, scooping me out of the chair and walking toward the bedroom.

"In all the times I've imagined you carrying me to bed, this is not what I had in mind," I said, laying my head on his shoulder.

"You imagined what?" His voice dropped. "Let's hear that story."

"I probably shouldn't have said that," I said. "My brain isn't firing on all cylinders. Disregard."

"Not on your life." He settled me on the edge of the wide cherry four-poster that dominated the floor space in my tiny bedroom. "But we'll table it for when you feel better." His dark eyes sparkled and my stomach cartwheeled.

"You really are an interesting guy, you know that? I never would've expected you to play nursemaid."

He chuckled. "Thank you. I think."

"Shutting up now," I said. "All the cold medicine I've taken this week is affecting my filter."

I kicked my eggplant Jimmy Choo slingbacks onto the floor and splayed my toes. "Everything hurts."

"Pajamas, medicine, and under the covers," he ordered.

I saluted. "Yes, sir."

He crossed his arms over his chest and leaned on the doorframe. "Well?"

"If I had the energy, I'd throw a pillow at you. Get out."

He raised both hands. "You said something about your filter being off. Can't blame a guy for trying." He stepped into the hall and shut the door.

I dug for cute pajamas and finally came up with a matching set. Wriggling them on, I climbed under the covers and called an all clear.

"So, what's the deal with this kid? Looks like he had it all and he just killed himself? Why?" Joey perched on the edge of the bed.

"That's what I said." I forced myself to focus on the story, so I wouldn't go all giggly at the sight of Joey on my bed. "I'm trying to figure it out, but honestly? The more I poke around, the more I think he didn't kill himself."

"Oh yeah?" He raised his eyebrows. "How come?"

"Well, because of what you said. It just doesn't add up. None of the suicide markers I've written about before are here. I mean, there were four kids who jumped off the Lee bridge three summers ago. I talked to more suicide prevention specialists and counselors and shrinks that summer than I did cops. This doesn't fit what any of them told me. Plus, my friend Emily is a big shot psychologist in Dallas. She can't talk to me on the record, but she says it doesn't fit, either, unless there's some big secret. And I can't see anybody in that town breaking wind without everyone knowing. Yet for some reason, the sheriff out there seems determined to mark it a suicide and close the file."

"Maybe you should think about why he's so eager to be done with it," Joey said, adjusting the covers so he could massage my foot. "Is he covering for someone?"

"Oh, Jesus, I hope not," I sighed. "That feels really good."

He smiled.

"I guess that's something to check out, though," I mused. "There was this kid I met at the school today. Luke ... I can't remember, but the sheriff said his last name, so he knows him. Or his family. Kid was pretty blunt about being jealous of TJ. And I didn't care for the vibe I got from him. I've been around more murderers than anyone ever should, and there's something about that kid. He might not have killed TJ, but it's not because he's not capable of it."

He switched to the other foot and I leaned my head back and let my thoughts roam.

"There's something else going on out there, too," I said, eyes still shut. "I've been to the sheriff's office twice in two days, and both times, there was a guy hanging out there badgering him about something that the sheriff swears isn't illegal. I sort of asked today, but he didn't take the bait. Could be an interesting aside if I can catch up to the other guy, though."

I sat up, thinking about the paper I'd brought home. Maybe there was a clue in there.

"I don't suppose you feel like bringing me the newspaper that's in the front seat of my car?" I smiled at Joey. "Not that I'm not loving the pampering, but I grabbed a paper in Mathews today. I'd like to get a better feel for the town and the people."

"I need to check the soup, anyway." He patted my foot and replaced the covers as he stood. "I'll be right back."

"Thanks." I grinned at the warmth in his eyes, pushing aside the where-could-this-possibly-go thoughts that came often when I was with Joey. He was sexy and exciting (and sweet, too, which was a cool bonus). We were having fun.

I grabbed the remote off the night table and clicked the TV on, CNN flashing up by default. Anderson Cooper was in California covering an earthquake. I wondered who they'd sent to Mathews. I flipped to ESPN, and found a young reporter in a polo shirt and blazer standing on the football field at Mathews High, talking about TJ.

"Okerson seemed on the verge of following in his father's footsteps, leading the Mathews Eagles to the state title last year. But he took a hard fall in the fourth quarter of the championship game, resulting in a knee injury that might have ended someone else's playing days. Tony Okerson talked to ESPN about his son's recovery last month."

They cut to a clip of that interview, and I watched Tony's relaxed smile, his eyes not the haunted ones I'd seen in his living room the day before.

"I'm very fortunate to have access to some of the best sports medicine folks in the country," he said. "Because of that, we were able to get TJ the treatment he needed soon enough after the injury to save his playing career, if that's what he chooses to make a career of."

The screen flashed a diagram of the ligaments in the knee, and a doctor from Johns Hopkins came on, talking about the type of injury TJ had, and why it was so unusual for him to recover. I fumbled a notebook and pen out of the nightstand drawer and jotted down the name of the injury, pondering that.

"He had a better tolerance for pain than any kid I'd ever seen," Coach Morris had said.

What if he hadn't recovered as fully as everyone thought?

I flipped back to CNN, where a young female reporter I didn't recognize was "Live from Mathews County, Virginia," standing on the front steps of the high school. She didn't have anything I didn't know, and everyone had been gone by the time she got there. Maybe no one else had talked to the coach. I'd have to watch Charlie's broadcast at 11 and check the Newport News media websites to be sure of that, though.

I flopped back into the pillows and sighed. I probably ought to get my story written, but I didn't want to do anything except sleep. Maybe I'd feel more like working after I ate something.

Joey strolled back in with the paper and my bag and handed both to me, glancing at the TV. "Media circus, huh?"

"I knew it would be. It'll be a miracle if they get through the funeral without someone getting nasty. I'm waiting for the commentary about his famous father pushing him too hard."

"Was he?"

"Not that I've been able to find. Grant Parker at my office is an old friend of the family, and he would have told me if that was the case. I think. Maybe I'll ask. But I did ask the baseball coach today, and he said he never saw any evidence of that."

Joey nodded.

I glanced back at the TV, which showed a shot of the Okersons' front gate with a voice over about the idyllic little town being rocked by the popular athlete's suicide.

"Dammit, I can't afford to be sick right now," I grumbled. "Going up against Charlie is bad enough, but I'm trying to beat out everyone in the country, here." I shook an antibiotic from the bottle I dug out of my bag and swallowed it. "Pharmaceutical industry, do your thing."

"You need to get well so you can do your thing. The soup should be ready." Joey walked out of the room.

I spread the *Mathews Leader* open over my lap. The front led with a short write up on TJ, most of the page dominated by a photo of him hoisting the trophy after the championship football game. Lyle had quoted the sheriff and the football coach, who was reached by phone in the Outer Banks. That was the kind of connection I didn't have out there, and I was glad to see it. I knew how it felt when the networks descended on one of my bigger trials.

The second story on the front was also Lyle's, and made me giggle because it was such a one-eighty from the Okerson story. A giant snapping turtle had wandered up from the water and chased a preschool class down

Main Street. The photos of the ensuing melee, showing Sheriff Zeke and a deputy facing off with the turtle—which was roughly the size of a child's picnic table and looked mean, with its hooked upper lip—were fantastic. It was the perfect portrayal of why I loved my job, wrapped up in one printed page. I never knew what each day would bring. And that was often truer for reporters in little towns, who covered a bit of everything instead of one dedicated beat.

Since I was pretty sure the turtle population wasn't what had Amos's suspenders in a twist, I kept flipping. I made it through all sixteen pages without finding anything suspect, but I did learn the names of the mayor (Jeff Ellington), plus the high school principal (Bill McManus) and PTA President (Lily Bosley). I found TJ's obit, too—it took up all but a business-card-size ad slot on page five.

Joey came in carrying a tray just as I set the paper aside.

"That really does smell good," I said. "And I can't smell much of anything. Thank you."

"Anytime." The way his lips edged up made me drop my eyes back to the newspaper.

He set the tray next to me and chuckled. "Find anything in the paper?"

"Not really. Some names I might need, but not what I was looking for."

"Maybe some rest will help you figure something out."

"I have a story to write. And then we'll see about that." I set the paper aside and laid the tray across my lap, lifting the spoon. "I didn't know you could cook."

"You didn't ask." He took a seat in the small chair in the corner.

"And me with the whole 'questions are my livelihood' thing, too." I took a bite. The soup was blistering hot, but amazing.

"This is fantastic. Thank you."

"I'm glad you like it."

I continued to mull over the story aloud between bites. By the time I put the empty bowl on the night table, I could've sworn I felt a little better. "Is there magic in that stuff? Or liquor?" I asked.

Joey shook his head. "Just vegetables."

"It was nice of you." I said, reaching for my laptop. "Truly."

"Someone has to make sure you take care of yourself. But I get the feeling you want me to go."

I frowned. "I don't want you to go. And I'm certainly not trying to be rude. But I have work to do, and sleep to get, so I'm afraid I'm not going to be great company. I'm shocked my cell phone isn't already buzzing with Bob wanting a story. I really should have done it when I got home."

"No offense taken." He stopped in the doorway. "Feel better. Maybe I'll see you next Friday?"

"Girls' night with Jenna," I said, scrunching my face apologetically.

"Saturday?"

"You're on. I better be back to a hundred percent by then."

"Keep eating the soup. I put the rest in your fridge. It works, I'm telling you."

"I'm a believer." I smiled.

"I'll call you tomorrow. Sleep well." He stared at me for a moment, then crossed to the bed and dropped a kiss on my head. "Be careful."

"You know something I should know?" I tried to keep focused on his words, when all I wanted was to melt into a puddle on the bed.

"Nope." He raised both hands in mock-surrender and backed toward the door when I arched one eyebrow at that. "I swear it. I'd never heard of Mathews, Virginia until I read your story this morning. Probably why Okerson moved out there in the first place, right?"

"You know anyone who might know something?" I asked.

"About this kid? I can't imagine why."

"Or his dad." I felt an idea looming. "Tony Okerson was a big deal football player. Who knows who he might have come into contact with? I've never heard or seen anything about him being into gambling or anything ..." I let that trail off, almost feeling traitorous for wondering such a thing.

Joey nodded thoughtfully. "But that doesn't mean he's not. You'd be surprised at some of the athletes and celebrities who are. Hurting the kid to get at dad is low, but not unheard of."

"Yeah?" I didn't care for this idea, except that it'd be an exclusive. I didn't know any other reporters with an in at the Mafia.

He sighed and shoved his hands into his pockets. "Why do I have a feeling I'll regret this conversation someday soon?"

I opened my mouth to object and he shook his head.

"Tell you what," he said. "I'll see if I can find out anything for you if you swear that you won't go poking into this alone and you promise to watch yourself and call someone for help if it looks like it might be more dangerous than playing fetch with Darcy."

The dog popped out of her bed and yipped when he said her name.

"Who am I going to call for help?" I asked. I didn't want to make him a promise I couldn't deliver on.

"Your friends at the Richmond PD?" He dropped his eyes to the floor. "Your friend at the ATF?"

I nodded slowly, catching the resentful note in his voice, but unsure what to do about it. My long-ago ex-boyfriend was a Bureau of Alcohol, Tobacco, Firearms, and Explosives supercop. He was also interested in no longer being my ex-boyfriend. Joey didn't like Kyle. Kyle didn't like Joey (what he knew about him, anyhow, which wasn't much). I liked them both. Em was right. It was a mess.

"I promise," I said.

"I'll see what I can find." He backed out the door with a wave. "Get well."

I heard the kitchen door click shut and sank into the pillows for a second, closing my eyes and breathing deep. Kyle. Joey. Equally gorgeous. Equally exciting. Almost equally problematic.

Pushing the covers back, I sighed. "Since I'm not deciphering my love life anytime soon, what say we figure out what happened to this kid, Darcy?" I asked the dog, slipping out of bed. She pricked up her ears and bit her favorite old stuffed squirrel.

After washing my face and making some tea, I climbed back in bed and opened my computer. My fingers hovered over the keys, but I didn't get a single word into the lead before my cell phone lit up.

I glanced at the screen and frowned at the unfamiliar number. Not Bob.

"Clarke," I said, pressing it to my ear.

"Zeke Waters in Mathews County," came the reply. "Remember that epidemic we talked about? It's been thirty-six hours. And I have another dead kid."

6

"You and the local paper are the only media being notified tonight, and I only called you because TJ's parents brought you into this," Waters said tightly, letting me through the yellow crime-scene tape blocking access to the area under the drawbridge. Deputies combed the rocks with flashlights, and I tried not to slip as I tagged after the sheriff.

I'd had the sense to leave my Jimmy Choos at home in favor of a pair of Tory Burch ballet flats when I'd dragged myself out of bed and back to the coast, but I wasn't expecting rocky shore terrain. The flats were slick, and my balance was already off from being sick. I hadn't come this far to wait by the road for an interview, though.

Sheriff Zeke swept the area with a wide orange beam, and I swallowed hard at the memory of the summer I'd had the four jumpers in Richmond, scanning the rocks for blood. I turned to the sheriff when I didn't see any.

"Is this bridge high enough—or the water shallow enough—for a jump to be lethal if they didn't hit the rocks?" I stared at the far bank, which I couldn't really see, but the deputies were all on this side.

"No," he furrowed his brow at the question, looking up at the underside of the bridge. "This wasn't a jump. The kids have parties here a lot."

"Another party?" I clicked out a pen, glancing at the stout man with the dark beard and glasses who appeared next to me, holding a tape recorder. Lyle, probably. "Same kids?"

"Some, yeah," Zeke said.

"Cause of death?" I asked.

"Not immediately apparent," he said. "I'm sure the tox screen will reveal it."

"Then why did you tell me on the phone you suspected it was a copycat suicide?"

"There's a note," he said. "Maybe another overdose, or intentional alcohol poisoning."

"Are you releasing the name of the victim?" Lyle asked.

"Sydney Cobb," Zeke said, one hand flying up to rake over his face. "It's Sydney Cobb."

Something rang familiar, but I was too beat to get it on the first try.

A look flashed between Sheriff Zeke and Lyle.

"What am I missing, guys?" I asked.

"She was TJ Okerson's girlfriend," Lyle muttered. "Those of us who work here all the time know that."

I sucked in a sharp breath. Of course. "Sydney was the only one he ever wanted," Ashton had said. The picture in TJ's locker floated to the front of my thoughts.

"She left a note?" I asked.

Zeke nodded. "'It hurts.' That's all it said."

I closed my eyes for a second, then scribbled that down.

"Listen, folks," Zeke said, "every hotel in Gloucester and Hampton is full of news crews, and what happens here has the potential to happen in other places because of that. This is new territory for me, this national stage thing. But I want to do everything I can to keep any more children from dying."

I nodded, catching every word. I was pretty sure I still had the suicide prevention stuff in my files from the other cases. "I have some public service announcement stuff on this topic I can use in my copy," I said. "But once we run it, it's going to go all over, just like TJ's story did. We can't control what the other media outlets do."

Sheriff Zeke sighed. "I know." He dropped his head. "Dammit! If TJ

Okerson was standing here right now, I'd take a swing at him, hand to God. The Cobbs ...I've never heard a human being make a sound like the one that came out of Tiffany Cobb when I showed up at her house tonight. Sydney stopped answering her phone a little after seven, she said."

"They were having a party that early?" I looked up from my notes.

"It was dark. They're upset."

Huh. I glanced between Zeke and Lyle again, but they didn't look like that was out of the ordinary. Damn. So now this girl had killed herself because of what had happened to her boyfriend, who may or may not have killed himself? It was a shitty story all the way around.

"How old was Sydney?" I asked.

The sheriff reeled off all the vital statistics and I took them down while Lyle stood by with his tape recorder. When Zeke excused himself to check something for a young deputy, I turned to Lyle. "I went by your office today," I said. "I wanted to introduce myself. I'm Nichelle."

"I know who you are." He shoved the tape recorder into his pocket and looked up at the underside of the bridge.

"Listen, the Okersons have a friend who works with me," I said. "It wasn't personal."

He nodded. "Hard to take it any other way when you've covered every jaywalking ticket in a town like this for ten years. Then something like this happens and I don't get the call."

"I can certainly understand that. Y'all had great photos of the snapping turtle rodeo, by the way. And your story on TJ was good. The football coach didn't talk to me."

"Coach B will talk to anything in a skirt, but not seriously. We had a female photographer on our staff for exactly half of one football game. He told her women weren't allowed on the sidelines, and she clocked him. She got fired."

"And arrested?" I asked.

"Nope. Zeke said he deserved it, and coach didn't want to admit it hurt bad enough for him to press charges."

"See? I didn't know to call him, and I might have punched him, too, so thanks for the heads up."

He grunted a reply, eyes roaming around the scene.

I followed suit, standing in silence and hoping to overhear something useful.

"What a week," Lyle finally said.

"Jesus, you can say that again," I said. "I've spent more time in your town than in mine."

"I've worked out here for a long time, ma'am." Lyle leveled a gaze at me. "I've never seen anything like this. This is a great town. Good people. God fearing. Hard working. Two dead kids in two days? And these kids? TJ and Sydney were the goddamn homecoming king and queen, for chrissakes. This is going to hit these people hard. And Zeke is right: it could spread like brush fire. I wish y'all would all go home and just let it die with Sydney."

I took a deep breath. "I can understand, and even sympathize. But you know as well as I do that that's not going to happen. So what can we do to help, Lyle?"

He stared at the ambulance on the other side of the bridge embankment, sucking on the inside of his cheeks and pursing his lips. "I don't know."

I dug a card out of my bag and jotted my cell number on the back. "If you think of something, call me."

He stuck it in his pocket, only half paying attention to me.

I pulled out my cell phone to text Bob an update and sighed when I saw that it was almost ten. "I'm never going to get well," I muttered, picking my way back toward my car.

Once out from under the shadows of the bridge, I spotted Zeke talking to his deputies up near the edge of the road. Passing a patrol car, I glanced into the open trunk and saw a box of bagged objects. Rocks, beer and Coke bottles, a crumpled piece of neon green paper, and assorted other teen party scene stuff. A mason jar crowned the pile. I paused, glancing toward the sheriff, who had his back turned. None of them were paying the least bit of attention to me.

Stepping closer to the trunk, I ran the beam of my little pink flashlight over the jar. The label looked like it had come off an inkjet printer, the three x's across it all faded in the middle.

In my years covering crime I'd seen dead people and drugs, interviewed murderers and prostitutes, and snuck into illegal gambling halls: but I'd never seen a jar of moonshine. Not the unregulated, not-sold-in-stores kind, anyway. Yet I was pretty sure I was looking at an empty one.

I fished my cell phone out and snapped a quick photo of it, then stuffed the phone back into my bag.

"Find something interesting?" Zeke asked, waiting behind me with crossed arms when I turned. My face must have betrayed me, because he put up one hand before I could get a word out. "Wait. Do I want to know?"

"Is that a moonshine jar, sheriff?"

"It is." He closed the trunk of the patrol car.

"You're pretty cavalier about that for a cop."

"Miss Clarke, moonshiners are Alcoholic Beverage Commission police business, not mine, first of all. Second of all, I have my hands full right now. I couldn't hunt for a still if I wanted to."

"Was there moonshine at the party the night TJ died?"

"There was. The kids drink it because it's easy for them to get. Teenagers are the perfect target market for moonshiners, because they're the ones who want booze and can't buy it, which has always sort of been the whole point of moonshine, right?"

I shook my head. "And you're really not doing anything about this?"

"I do when I catch them. The kids, that is. Underage drinking is against the law. But chasing moonshiners isn't my jurisdiction."

"Was Sydney drinking that tonight?"

"Very possibly," he said. "That jar was found near her. I'll run prints to be sure."

"Where do they get it? Is it a local operation? I mean, I cover a lot of shit in Richmond, and I've never run across bonafide illegal moonshine."

"I know of three stills on the island. When anyone drops by to check them out, they're family heirlooms gathering dust. But I'm sure that's not always the case."

I nodded, seeing a phone call to the ABC police in my future.

"Thanks again, sheriff." I pushed the button to unlock my car door and waved a good night. "I'm sure I'll see you soon."

* * *

Back home, I brewed a cup of coffee just after eleven, thanking my lucky stars I hadn't passed a bored state trooper as I lead-footed it home from Tidewater. Bob had called me twice and I had a story to write before I could sleep. Two, actually. And no promise of rest for my Saturday, either.

Settled on my couch with my laptop and a cup of Colombian Fair Trade, I stared at the screen.

"Two dead kids. Jealous baseball player guy. Moonshine. This is jacked up, Darcy."

I had no pointed reason to suspect that Sydney's death was anything other than exactly what it looked like.

But something nagged. I was too tired to get it, so I started typing.

For the second time in as many days, a well-known teenager in tiny Mathews County on the Virginia coast is dead.

Sydney Cobb was surrounded by friends Friday night, students toasting the short life of Mathews High quarterback TJ Okerson. Sydney was TJ's longtime girlfriend, his mother told the Telegraph *in an exclusive interview Thursday.*

"She left a note," Mathews County Sheriff Zeke Waters said as deputies around him scoured the rocky shoreline for evidence. Waters said Cobb's note read "It hurts."

I pulled from my story on TJ to finish the piece, and sent it to Bob with a promise that the day two on TJ was coming. After some thought, I'd left out the moonshine jar. I didn't want anyone else nosing around that until I had time to check it out.

Pondering it, I clicked over to my Google tab and typed "moonshine." The number of hits was staggering. I gathered from a scan of the pages that the Internet could teach me how to distill my own booze, and decided to look over that in the morning.

I dug out my notes from Coach Morris and wrote a day two on what a great kid TJ was, and how his parents didn't pressure him, which I was more sure about after seeing Tony on ESPN earlier. He'd even said something about TJ being healed enough to salvage his career if that's what he wanted to do. Which didn't sound like a psycho-pushy-dad thing to say. Maybe I could head off some hateful commentaries by highlighting that.

By the time I emailed Bob the second story, my coffee was cold and I was past ready to crawl into bed. I hustled Darcy outside, trying to focus on something more pleasant than dead teenagers and grieving parents in the last few minutes before my head touched the pillows. A few hours before, I'd been looking forward to the dreams I might have after Joey's surprise visit. By bedtime, I just hoped to keep them more Joshilyn Jackson than Stephen King.

7

Interesting quirk of Virginia law number three forty seven: all liquor stores are owned and operated by the state. Number three forty eight: the Alcoholic Beverage Commission has its own police department. With sworn peace officers and everything.

They're about as chatty as most other cops with reporters they don't know, too.

After the second guy in a row said "no comment" and hung up on me, I slammed my phone back into its cradle and jerked my tea cup off the desk with such force that it sloshed out all over a pile of press releases. Fabulous. I rooted through two drawers before I found a napkin, muttering every swearword I knew as I blotted my desktop.

"Tough day?" Parker's voice came from behind me, and I jumped and whacked my knee on the underside of my desk.

"What in God's name are you doing here on a Saturday?" I asked, spinning my chair to face him.

"I can't just sit around my house," he said. "Mel's at some kind of city council workshop, and I was going stir crazy, watching all the shit about TJ and his girl on every station. So I thought I'd come see if I could help you. I dragged you into this, and you've been sick and all. What can I do?"

His green eyes looked pained.

I sighed. "I wish I had an assignment for you. Have you talked to the Okersons? How are they?"

"How you'd think. Ashton wouldn't be functioning at all if she didn't have the service to plan and the twins to take care of. Tony is going over every minute of the last week in his head a hundred times a day, trying to find what he missed. And now they're upset about the girl, too. They adored her. Tony plays golf with her dad."

I nodded. "It's a suck situation, Parker. I'm sorry."

"What the hell, Nichelle? I mean, really. I read your piece this morning. You talked to the coach. Did he say anything else?"

"Not really."

He shook his head. "I just don't get it."

"That makes two of us. Hey—has Tony ever mentioned TJ having a drinking problem? Not normal teenage crap, but like an addiction? Hangovers? Excess? Moonshine?"

"Moonshine?" Parker laughed, but the smile faded when he caught the serious look on my face. "No. Why?"

"Look, I left this out of the story this morning because I want to look into it before it goes all over the TV, but there was an empty moonshine jar at the scene where the girl was found last night. I did some reading when I got here this morning, and it turns out alcohol isn't the only kind of poisoning you can get from drinking it. There's no way to know for sure what killed TJ or Sydney until the tox screen comes back, but I know good and well Sheriff Waters out there is assuming his case is closed while he waits for that report. I want to know where the kids are getting this stuff. I'm just not sure how to find out. I don't have a contact at the ABC police."

"Your guys at the PD must have one."

"It's Saturday. Aaron wasn't in yet when I tried, but I'll call him again in a bit and see if he's willing to share one with me. I have a drug bust and a car-on-pedestrian crash to talk to him about, anyway. Keeping up with my regular job and covering crime in Mathews on top of being sick is even too much fun for me. This kind of blows, to be honest."

"I imagine. How you feeling?"

"Better, I think. I'm on day two of antibiotics, and I had some magic soup for dinner last night. But I need some rest. Like, even just going home on time and getting in bed would be nice."

"You're dedicated. It's part of what makes you good."

"I might settle for mediocre and healthy this week." I grinned. "No, I wouldn't. I love it. And I want to help your friends."

"Good luck. I'll go hang out in my office and pretend to work, but if you come up with something I can do, holler. I'll be around. Even if you want me to go on a coffee run."

"Grant Parker is offering to run my errands? Cue the *Twilight Zone* theme." I widened my eyes and glanced around.

He flashed a ghost of the famous grin that made women in twelve counties call for smelling salts. "Just trying to make it easy for you to do your thing."

"I appreciate that, and I'm not one to look a gift coffee in the mouth, but listen: you did me a favor, too, Parker. This is a huge story with national exposure, and you insisted Bob give it to me."

"I wish I hadn't been in a position to do that."

"I do, too." I waved a stack of pink message slips. "I also wish I didn't have thirty reporters to talk around this with. I should probably get to it."

"Call me if you need me." He disappeared in the direction of his office.

I sipped my tea and surveyed my desk. I picked up the first message slip. CNN.

"Here we go," I said as I dialed the phone.

I made it through half the stack in an hour, politely saying as little as I could get away with, mostly describing the emotion in the Okerson house for them. After a particularly dogged woman from NBC sent me into a coughing fit (which was an excellent excuse to hang up), I took a break from giving interviews so I could conduct one.

"It's Saturday. And you said you were sick," Aaron barked when he picked up.

"I'm aware of that, and I am sick. Though more human today, I think. So far, anyhow." I clicked out a pen. "I'm behind. This Okerson thing put together with the sinus infection is killing me. But I have a regular job to do, too."

"Aw, nice of you to take a break from the glamour for me."

"You know I love you best."

He chuckled. "Which one do you want first?"

"The man versus car. What happened?"

"Guy was walking along the side of Patterson at close to eleven last night. Kid driving the car was sending a text. He mowed the pedestrian down and hit a tree. Knocked himself out. Phone was still in his hand when our guys got on the scene."

"Holy shit, Aaron." I blew out a breath. "Is everyone OK?"

"Driver was at St. Vincent's overnight, but they expect him to make a full recovery."

Thank God. "And the victim?"

"He wasn't so lucky. Doctors said he bled out about an hour into surgery."

I closed my eyes for a second before I scribbled that down. "Just walking down the street. And this kid did a stupid thing and gets to go the rest of his life knowing he killed someone. Jesus."

"Right? If I were smart enough, I'd make a device that disabled the text feature on any cellphone inside a moving car. These are the most senseless things we see."

"Amen to that." If there was one habit my job had made me positively phobic about, it was texting while driving. It caused several tragedies a month. I'd been known to snap at friends I was riding with when they reached for their phones.

"You want the drug bust, too?"

"You know me too well. That's the other one that caught my eye. Is Stevens around today, or are you giving up that info, too?"

"I saw him this morning," Aaron said. "He's got a lot of paperwork to go through. They've been working undercover in that club for eighteen months. I'll put you through to him."

I wished Aaron a happy weekend before he transferred me. The new narcotics sergeant relayed the details of a huge marijuana growing and trafficking ring operating out of a bar downtown. Almost a thousand plants, plus a literal truckload of ready-to-move product.

I thanked Stevens and hung up before I realized I'd forgotten to ask Aaron about the ABC police. I hit redial.

"He wasn't there?" He asked by way of a hello when he picked up.

"No, he was. But I forgot that I meant to ask you something else. I need some information from the ABC police, and so far this morning I've been stonewalled twice, just calling random officers. Do you have any friends over there who might talk to me?"

"A couple, but I doubt they're in today," he said and then reeled off names and phone numbers. "Anything interesting you need them for?"

"Maybe. There's something nagging the hell out of me about these dead kids in Mathews."

"It's because they're kids," he said. "I saw your piece this morning, and I've worked with you long enough to read between the lines. I know I don't have to tell you how common copycat suicides are."

"See, I thought so, too. And maybe you're right. But since no one else seems to be looking at anything other than the obvious answer, I'm going to make damned sure of it before I let this go. Those children have parents who deserve to know what happened."

"It's a small town and this will be a sore subject for a long time," he cautioned. "Just watch yourself. You can't go accusing people of murder willy-nilly."

"When have you ever known me to do anything willy-nilly?"

He was quiet.

"Yeah, don't answer that. But I'm not pointing fingers. I'm just poking around. If you're right and there's nothing to it, I'm totally safe, right?"

"Depends entirely on what you're poking around in. Why do you want the ABC police?"

"Out in the sticks? Why do you think?"

"That's what I was afraid of." He sighed. "I swear, you need a vest. And a gun. Folks who run illegal booze like their firearms, Nichelle."

"Noted."

I hung up and dialed the numbers he'd given me, but got voicemail both times. I didn't leave messages. I'd try again Monday when I could put them on the spot.

Turning to my computer, I wrote up the two stories I had for metro. I finished the second and opened my email program before I realized who I was sending my copy to for approval.

"Aw, hell." I attached the files to an email to Shelby. That was just what I needed. "I ought to add the *Twilight Zone* theme to my iTunes," I said as I hit send. "First Parker's offering to be my gofer, and now I miss Les."

"Your piece on the Okerson kid this morning wasn't your best work." It took me a second to realize that the voice came from behind me and was male, not Shelby prattling inside my head.

I turned the chair slowly.

Spence leaned against the wall behind my little ivory cubicle, arms folded over his chest and a studiously disdainful look on his face.

I'd never had reason to be crossways with our sports editor, who was generally full of witty commentary and whatever baked goods Eunice had brought in, though you couldn't tell it by looking at his lanky frame.

"Good morning to you, too, Spence," I said. "You have any constructive criticism to offer, or did you come in on Saturday just to be insulting?"

"TJ Okerson was left-handed, which made him a more formidable pitcher," he said. "That's worth mentioning in a story where you interviewed the baseball coach."

"No one told me that," I said.

"A sports reporter would know it."

"And the sports editor would, too." I leaned back in my chair. "I'm tired. I'm still sick. And it's been one hell of a long week, here, Spence. If you've got something to say, just say it. You want my story?"

"It's not your story. Or, it shouldn't be your story."

"Dead people are kind of my thing." I paused. "Uh. You know what I mean."

"Sports are my thing. It's my whole life outside my wife and kid. This is the biggest sports story to come out of Virginia in half a decade, and it gets assigned to the crime desk? What kind of bullshit is that?"

"The kind of bullshit you'll have to take up with Bob." I closed my laptop and put it in my bag. "I didn't ask for this assignment."

"I know. Your good friend Parker asked you to take it. As a favor. If he worked for me, I'd have canned him. But our big shot star columnist reports to Bob." He sneered.

I stared, dumbfounded. I had never heard Spencer Jacobs sound the least bit annoyed with...anything. And I'd worked with him for almost eight years.

"If it's that big a deal to you, seriously, talk to Bob."

"I was told pretty explicitly yesterday that I was to get you what you need to do a good job," Spence said, pushing off the wall. "So here's what you need: a background in sports journalism and some better interview skills."

"I'm sorry, have we left the newsroom and gone back to seventh grade? I'd feel sorry for you, except you're being an asshat. So go be one somewhere else. If you want to help, I'm happy to take suggestions and tips, and more than happy to share credit for the story. But if you're going to hurl insults and be petty because they picked me and not you? You can bite me. And you should go hang out with Shelby. Y'all have something in common."

I stepped around him and hauled my bag onto my shoulder, striding to the elevator. Technically, I should have waited for Shelby to okay my stories, but I was beat, and Spence had shaken me way more than I wanted him to see.

Parker poked his head into the elevator as I turned to the buttons.

"You have a lead?"

"Yes. A hot one. On a nap. Also, steer clear of Spence. Someone pissed in his Wheaties, and he seems to think it was us." I punched the button for the garage.

"Nice." He stepped back as the doors started to close. "Feel better. Call me if you need any help."

"You have yourself a side job, sir."

The doors whispered shut and I sagged against the wall. Some days, an eight-to-five desk job sounded better than others.

8

Joey's minestrone was even better the second day. I laid the bowl in the dishwasher after lunch, and settled myself on the couch for a nap. But sleep eluded me with all the nonsense running around my head.

I could sort of go with the sheriff on Sydney's death. I remembered being a teenager. Overly emotional the-world-has-ended came from way simpler stuff than your boyfriend dying.

But why would TJ do it? That was a puzzle with a billion jagged pieces, only half of which I had to work with. I kept going back to Parker's words from that morning, but I couldn't pin down why it was bugging me so much.

Was Aaron right? Was I making something out of nothing because the case involved young people?

Or was Emily right? Was I projecting personal memories into a mysterious suicide? I tried to be honest with myself about both, but kept returning to the summer of the jumpers. I hadn't prowled around Richmond thinking those kids had been pushed. There was something different about this story. I just needed to figure out what.

The moonshine was different. It had been at both scenes. Sheriff Zeke seemed pretty sure both of the dead kids had been drinking it. Was it a bad batch? Possibly. But no one else was sick, or dead.

Wait.

What if there was something in it? I mean, who could taste anything mixed with thousand-proof rotgut?

Possible. Especially if Luke "Waiting for TJ to Get Hurt" Pitcher had been at the party.

I kicked my blanket into the floor, sat up, and grabbed the phone.

"What's up?" Parker asked when he picked up.

"I can't rest, so we might as well work," I said. "This thing out in Tidewater is making me slightly nuts."

"You can say that again."

I'd been tiptoeing around this with Parker for days, but I needed an answer.

"Parker, you knew this kid. You know his family. Level with me. Does your gut say he overdosed on Vicodin?"

He didn't answer right away.

"It does not," he said finally. "But that sounds crazy, doesn't it? The bottle was empty. The cops say it's open and shut. Tony said they told him they're just waiting for the toxicology results so they can close the file."

"I don't think it's crazy," I said. "I've covered teen suicides before. This doesn't fit. The cops are telling me it's open and shut, too, but I can't let it go."

His voice perked up. "What else is there to do?"

"Play Nancy Drew."

"Want a Hardy Boy?"

I laughed. "I think I might."

"What can I do?"

"See if you can get anything else out of Tony and Ashton," I said. "I could go talk to them, but they'll speak freely to you. I want to know if TJ had any enemies. I know he was a popular kid. The guy from the local paper said he was the homecoming king. But someone always hates those kids, you know? I want to know who. If you can find out anything from them about a kid named Luke from the baseball team, that would be damned handy."

"I can do that."

Bob's orders from the staff meeting popped into my thoughts. "I also need an invite to the funeral. I like Tony and Ashton and I want to pay my respects, plus Bob is set on having an exclusive with the networks crawling all over the island."

"No problem. Come with me—Mel is doing something else Monday."

Something else besides going to his friend's kid's funeral with him? Really? I kept quiet about that. "Okay, sure. Thanks."

"Listen, Clarke, I know you have this whole sort of Lois Lane thing working with these big exclusives," he said. "If I'm being honest, that's why I called you with this in the first place. I knew it would get me on Spence's shit list. I'm not stupid. But, I also knew if there was anything amiss, you were the person who'd find it. I want Tony to know what happened to his son. Whatever that turns out to be."

"Me, too. Though I wish you would've warned me about Spence. He was well and truly pissed. Caught me totally blindside."

"Don't worry about Spence. I'll handle him."

"Hard to ignore him when he sneaks up behind me hurling insults. I have a feeling Shelby's got a new best friend."

"She won't look twice at him. He's got a wife and a kid and he can't get her promoted."

"I was hoping having to fill in for Les would get her off my ass. Why can't she decide she wants to be a feature reporter? Or, I don't know, cover the schools? She's not a bad writer. I'd just like for it to be someone else's turn in her crosshairs for a while. Especially if Spence is going to be all butthurt over this story assignment."

"I understand that." There was a commotion in the background and Parker muffled the handset for a minute.

My mind wandered back to moonshiners. Who could I talk to about that? If I could find out who was making the stuff, maybe I could find out who bought it and took it to the parties.

Lyle seemed to know the town he covered well, but I didn't want to tip my hand to another reporter, and I certainly didn't want the TV folks getting wind of what I was working on. The old man at the antique store with his adorable accent and fantastic treasures floated through my thoughts. I bet he knew everything that went on in Mathews. And he liked to talk.

"Sorry about that. FedEx," Parker said. "Anything else you want me to find out? I'm heading to Tidewater."

"I'm going to drive back out there myself. I just thought of someone who might be able to help me with an angle I'm working."

"Care to share?"

"Not yet. Let me see if it goes anywhere first."

"I'll let you know what I find out at Tony's."

"Thanks, Parker."

"Thank you. Go get 'em, Lois."

* * *

I dialed Joey's number on my cell phone after I got on the Interstate. I considered calling Kyle Miller, former love of my life and current Mr. Possibly as well as ATF supercop, but decided to wait until I had something more to tell him. Kyle had an irritating habit of blowing off my suspicions, and I wasn't in the mood for a fight.

"You feeling any better?"

Good Lord. Just Joey's voice on the phone made my toes tingle. Part of me was afraid of his questionable occupation. Another part was just downright chicken of falling so hard for a guy it could never work with. Yet I couldn't stay away from him. Oy.

"That soup is totally magical. Your mom should sell it at health food stores." It was kind of funny to think about Joey's mom. I hadn't ever considered Captain Mystery in a family setting. "I'm probably seventy-five percent today, and I'm on my way back to Mathews."

"Something new? Besides the other dead kid I saw in your story this morning? TV hasn't shut up about that all day."

I knew that, and I was hoping that going between broadcast times would keep me clear of most of the cameras. Though I was slightly worried they'd find the adorable little antique store and its owner as interesting as I did.

"Sort of. I left something out of the story and I'm wondering if you might be able to find me a lead on it."

"Me? What is it?"

"You know anything about moonshine?"

He chuckled. "Like, corn whiskey, moonshine? Only that it tastes God-awful."

I huffed out a short breath, noticing I could breathe through one nostril for the first time in days. "Seriously? The Internet says some of this is major interstate money. Especially around here where there are still so many places you can't buy booze on Sundays. You have to know something. Or someone who does."

"Why are you poking around moonshiners?" He switched gears without answering, which didn't escape my notice.

"Because the dead kids were drinking moonshine. Or, the girl was. TJ might have been. I'm working on that. Aside from the possibility that someone could have spiked their booze with poison, I read that if the stills aren't properly cleaned or any one of a billion things goes wrong with the process, moonshine can kill people. I found a crap ton of stories from the twenties and thirties about people going blind and dropping dead in speakeasies."

"I guess that's a hazard of drinking it. Why would a bunch of kids mess with that stuff? It has a nasty kick."

"My first guess is because they want to drink and they're underage. Which stores care about, but moonshiners don't. The ABC police have been cracking down on underage sales all over the state lately. There's only so much beer they can swipe from their folks before they get in trouble. So they get the moonshine because it's cheap and readily available. Especially if it's being made right there on the island."

"You could be onto something. Do me a favor?"

"If I can."

"Watch it. If the wrong person gets word that you're trying to prove their rotgut killed these kids, you could wind up in very real danger."

"I would blow you off, but that hasn't ended well for me, historically. So I'll be careful."

"Thanks. I'd tell you to drop it, but that doesn't ever work. So, you know, call me if you need me. Try not to get shot."

"Thanks. I'll do what I can. Call me if you find anything?"

His voice dropped. "I'll take any excuse."

My pulse fluttered as I hung up, pulling the car off the freeway at West Point. The drive seemed to go quicker every time.

* * *

By the time I turned into the antique store parking lot, I had a pretty good mental list of questions—hopefully enough roundabout ones to avoid suspicion.

I counted three other cars, but no news trucks. I stepped in the front door and smiled at the man with thick bifocals behind the ornate old cash register. It was the kind with big round buttons on individual levers and a pull handle that totaled sales and opened the drawer. And it worked—he rang up a glass perfume bottle as I walked into the shop.

He turned to another customer, explaining the history of a gorgeous footstool (it once graced the foot of the bed in the biggest suite at the island's only hotel, which had burned down years before) to a fifty-some-thing woman in designer jeans and a Louis Vuitton belt that matched the dark honey color of her gold-tipped Chanel flats. She forked over cash and left with the stool, and he turned to me.

"You don't look two breaths from the grave anymore, Missy," he said. "You found Zeke, I take it?"

"I did. Thank you for your help."

"You didn't tell me you were a reporter." He pursed his lips. I smiled. News about strangers probably zipped through Mathews faster than Speedy Gonzalez on uppers. "Been reporters crawling all over since."

I twisted my mouth to one side. "I'm sorry. I didn't see where my job was pertinent to our conversation."

"Oh, don't apologize to me." He chuckled. "There's lots of folks complaining about it, but me? I've done more business the last three days than I have all month. People go crazy over famous folks. Everyone in three states who ever watched a Skins game is looking for a genuine article from the town where Tony Okerson lives."

I smiled. "Well, I'm glad it was good for something." I put out a hand. "I'm Nichelle."

He nodded. "Elmer. Elmer Daughtry. I don't suppose you came looking for a chair or a chat about the weather." He turned to the secretary behind the register, deep mahogany with detail work that looked like it might have been carved by Thomas Jefferson himself, and poured two glasses of iced tea. He handed me one as he settled on a tall chair, gesturing to a backless barstool between the door and my side of the counter. "What do you want to know today?"

I perched on the stool and sipped my tea, sizing Elmer up. He was sweet, and he wasn't mad about the press being in town, which was helpful. But he was shrewd, too. Maybe my roundabout questions weren't the best approach.

"Honestly? I'm looking for information on moonshine, Elmer. And I figure you probably know everything there is to know about the county. So I thought this might be a good place to start." I pulled a pen and notebook out of my bag.

"How do you know I'm not a moonshiner?" His face was so serious my stomach wrung.

"You don't seem like the type?" I said, my voice going up at the end and turning it into a question.

He laughed. "You have a good gauge for that type, do you, city gal?"

I sighed. "No."

"Well, you're right that it's not me. I drank my share of it when I was a younger man, but this is about as hard as my drinking gets these days." He brandished the tea glass. "I might know where to get some, though."

"I'm not interested in buying any." Or, I wasn't until he said that. "I want to know who's making it. I hear there are a few stills on the island."

"You hear right. There's families around these parts been into moonshine since prohibition."

"That's fascinating. How do they keep from getting caught?"

"They hide. Some have so many generations of kids spread all over the county, if there's a whisper of the law coming by to check a still, it gets empty quick."

"Surely the police must be able to tell if it's been used recently?" I raised an eyebrow.

"I expect they can. Don't do them no good if they don't catch you in the act. Or catch you with a truckload of shine." He paused and gave me a once-over. "You work in Richmond. I seen some other stuff you wrote about in the paper. You got friends in law enforcement. They can't tell you this?"

"Not like you can," I said simply.

"Want the local color, huh?"

"Exactly." I grinned. "So how do people making this stuff not get caught with big batches of it?"

"Used to be they outran the law," he said. "You know that's where NASCAR came from, don't you?"

"Where ... I'm not sure I follow."

"That's always a good one for the tourists." He nodded sagely. "Years ago, moonshiners used to soup-up their cars so they outran the cop cars. Had to have good shocks to carry big loads of shine, too. Eventually, the boys started racing their cars. And there you have the birth of NASCAR."

I stopped writing as he talked, leaning one elbow on the counter, totally engrossed in his story.

"No shit?" It popped out before I could stop it.

"God's truth." He winked.

"So, where could a girl find a jar?"

"Why you want to know?"

I paused. I liked him, but I wasn't telling anyone why I was asking about this yet.

"I'm trying to get a feel for how things work out here. It's a little different than Richmond." Every word true.

"I imagine it is. The Sidells, the Parsons, and the Lemows are the three families you'd want to ask about."

I scribbled the names. "And they still make it?"

"Hard to say about this generation, but their daddies and granddaddies did. Only ones I can tell you for fact still do are the Parsons, because they run a still on the other side of these woods every once in a while, and I can smell it."

"What does it smell like?" I had a vision of driving around the island at night with my windows open, but Joey and Aaron's stern faces flashed right behind that. Maybe I'd bring backup if I was going to hunt moonshiners.

"Mash. Like spoiled corn," he said. "They use commercial hog feed, mostly. It's distinctive, that's for sure."

I wrinkled my nose at the thought, adding that to my notes.

"Thanks for your help, Elmer." I drained my tea glass and stood up, dropping the pad and pen back into my bag.

"Thanks for the bump in business," he said. "Holler if there's anything else I can do for you. Not much of anyone to listen to my stories anymore."

"They're missing out," I said. "It was nice to see you again."

He nodded a goodbye.

I opened the door and almost walked into Charlie Lewis. Damn. I felt my face fall, but recovered before she noticed. I hoped.

"I thought that was your car, Clarke," Charlie purred, looking around the shop, cameraman in tow. "What are you up to in here?"

"Shopping," I said with a grin. "Isn't it a cute little place?"

"Darling." She stared pointedly at my hands. "You don't have a bag. Nothing in here caught your fancy?"

"It's all out of my price range, honestly. I'd rather spend my money on shoes. But you might find something, with your big TV bucks."

"Uh-huh." She surveyed the store and seemed to buy my story, turning and following me back to the parking lot. Thank God.

"Listen, I'm stuck out here covering this mess with these dead kids because your boss gave you this story. My sports anchor is pissed at me, and I'd rather spend my days doing something besides chasing your tail around the sticks."

"Your sports guy, too, huh?"

"Too?" she arched one perfectly-waxed eyebrow.

"Spencer Jacobs could have grown another head before I'd have expected him to jump my shit about a story like he did this morning," I said.

Charlie stared for a minute, then dropped her head back and laughed.

"What's funny?" I asked.

"Who'd have ever thought we'd have a common enemy?" she asked. "For years, my motivation has been to kick your ass. And the past few days, all I've wanted was for the sports guy to have to admit he couldn't have done a better job on this."

"That sounds exceedingly familiar." I nodded, a reluctant grin spreading across my face.

"What say we show them a couple of girls can do every bit as well with this as they can?"

"Sounds good to me," I said. "I know a fair amount about sports."

"I don't know much about anything but soccer, because it's what I played in school."

"Maybe we could help each other out?" I asked. "With the sports stuff."

She grinned. "Of course. I still want to kick your ass."

"Not this week, Charlie."

"We'll see. But we'll show the sports section?"

"We will. I was told this morning that TJ Okerson being left handed was a big deal."

"Left-handed. Got it." She glanced at her cameraman and he nodded. She turned back toward her truck. "I have a live feed to set up for down at the bridge. Nice work this morning. How'd you catch that? My scanner won't pull from this far."

"Lucky break." I winked.

"Fair enough."

I waved as they drove off, glad she hadn't come in five seconds earlier and heard me talking to Elmer.

I pulled out of the parking lot, checking the clock on the dash: four-thirty. I wanted to explore a little after the story Elmer had told me, so I turned away from town on the main road, passing the fork that led to the freeway.

If I were going to make moonshine, I'd do it out here in the woods.

9

I was almost to Gloucester, according to the road signs, when a cluster of flailing arms and screeching loud enough for me to hear over the closed windows and radio drew me into the parking lot in front of a squatty building with a dancer silhouetted on the front door. I stopped the car and looked up at the sign in the parking lot. Girls, Dance, Girls. A strip club? Here?

"Why not? There are men out here, too, right?" I muttered, turning to the source of the commotion.

The man in front of me was large, and bellowing at a pair of ladies in floral-print dresses and wide straw hats.

I climbed out of my car, my jaw dropping when I recognized Temper Tantrum: it was Mr. Suspenders from the sheriff's office. Amos, wasn't that his name?

"This is a public place and we have every right to be here!" A gray-haired woman with cracked lipstick the exact shade of the coral flowers blooming across her flared skirt drew herself up, inches from pressing her nose against bellowing Amos's.

"You old bats are going to wreck half the marriages in Tidewater!" Amos stomped a booted foot in the gravel. "What in hell's that got to do with family values?"

"I'll thank you to keep your insults to yourself, Amos McGinn. Your momma would wash your mouth out with soap, God rest her soul. She's probably tunneled halfway to Richmond rolling in her grave at your sinning."

I leaned against the back of my car, taking in the scene. It didn't seem, after watching for a minute, that anyone was in danger. But this had to be what Amos was hassling the sheriff about. And it might make a fun story for Monday. They were so busy hollering at each other, no one had noticed me.

"You and I clearly have two different ideas of what constitutes a sin, Miss Dorothy."

They argued more, and I turned my attention to the woman standing next to Dorothy. She was quiet, outfitted from head to toe in lavender church gear. She was younger than Dorothy, but looked older than Amos. And she had a camera in her hand.

Holy pasties, Batman. I pursed my lips and smothered a laugh, the comments I'd overheard in the sheriff's office flitting through my head as I pieced this puzzle together.

The church ladies were taking pictures at the girly bar and notifying the wives of the married men hanging out there. That's one way to get rid of a business a gal doesn't like, I guess. And from what I could hear and see, Sheriff Zeke was right: not only was it not his jurisdiction, it wasn't against the law.

What it was was a great story. The kind that would bounce all over Facebook and Twitter if I got the tone right, which made the bottom-line folks at the *Telegraph* happy. I whirled for the car door, digging for a pad and pen.

"Don't you point that thing at me!" Amos glowered at Dorothy's companion, who ducked her head and took a step back. I settled in for the show.

Dorothy swatted his shoulder. "Don't you threaten us! We have as much right to be here as you do. More, even, because we are doing the Lord's work and you are sinning."

"Stop saying that! It's not like anybody in there's nekkid or there's anything but dancing going on. It's... art. Like the ballet."

"With boobies." Dorothy shook her head. "I can't believe you just compared this to legitimate culture."

"You wouldn't know culture if it popped out of your Sunday bulletin in a bright red G-string—" Amos's words cut off, and I looked up from jotting that down to find him staring at me.

He looked pissed.

Uh-oh.

"Now see what you did?" He stomped past Dorothy, his boots kicking up little clouds of dust. "That's a damned reporter from Richmond. We'll be the laughingstock of the state by morning."

"A reporter?" Dorothy turned and straightened her hat, putting a restraining hand on Amos' arm as she skirted him. "I've seen TV cameras all over town this week."

I smiled and put out a hand. "Nichelle Clarke, from the *Richmond Telegraph*. I think I have a good hold on what's going on here, but would you care to explain the details, ma'am?"

She shook my hand. "Happy to. I think you are Heaven sent, young lady."

"Dorothy, have you gone completely off your nut?" Amos shouted. "Being in the paper isn't gonna make you famous. It's going to let the world in on how backward and crazy y'all are. And those of us who aren't will be lumped in with you." He turned to me. "This is not news."

"I think it's my job to decide that."

Dorothy thumped Amos on the back of his head with her tidy lime green pocketbook. "There is nothing backward or crazy about wanting my home rid of this filth." She turned back to me. "I'm Dorothy Scott, head of the First Baptist Ladies' Auxiliary. We managed to keep this place out of Mathews proper, but then they came right across the line and opened up here. We don't want our men's minds poisoned."

"For the love of God, Miss Dorothy, shut up," Amos groaned.

"Don't you take the Lord's name in vain with me, Amos!"

"What exactly is your mission here, ma'am?" I asked.

"For the past week, Emmy Sue here and I have been making sure these men's wives know where their grocery money is going."

Amos threw his hands up. "I hear the laughter from Richmond already."

I suppressed a chuckle. No sense in making him madder.

"Why do you object to this business?" I asked Dorothy.

"It's a house of ill repute! Young girls in there gyrating while these heathens watch them." She fanned herself.

"I can't even get a lap dance in there!" Amos bellowed.

That was a state law. I knew, because a club in south Richmond had been busted for violation of it in their back room. More than a few of my cops had groused about the law being stupid as they helped the handcuffed strippers into patrol cars.

Dorothy sighed, her voice rising to the condescending tone people often use with children. "Lust is a sin, Amos."

"Appreciating an art form and the beauty of the human body is not."

I kept scribbling as they continued to bicker, while the lavender-swathed Emmy Sue snapped photos of a couple dozen license plates.

"Is this a church-sponsored activity?" I asked.

Dorothy sniffed. "Not strictly speaking, though the board of the auxiliary voted unanimously to support my efforts."

I took down the correct spelling of everyone's name, except Amos's, because he wouldn't give it to me and said he'd sue the paper if I quoted him.

"I think your wife is going to find out you were here, anyway," I said. "But have it your way. I don't mind unnamed sources."

Dorothy pumped my hand and thanked me, but stiffened when I stepped past her toward the door of the club.

"Where are you going?" she asked.

"Inside," I said. "Part of my job is to have every side of a story before I start to write."

Her jaw loosened, but she recovered quickly, pursing her lips. "I suppose if it's part of your job."

I waved at Amos. "Thank you both for your time." I walked to the door as he berated her for talking to me and she shooed him off, turning to her station wagon with Emmy Sue in tow.

It took my eyes a minute to adjust to the dim room when I opened the heavy wood front door. The interior looked like I expected, with matted red carpet, leather-paneled walls, and about fifty tables and booths scattered through the room. The stage was front and center, with a catwalk that ran halfway to the back door and sported a pole at the end. The bar ran the length of the left wall, a mirrored backdrop half-covered by liquor bottles behind it.

The smell was the thing I didn't anticipate. My stomach rumbled at the distinct scent of very good barbecue. I looked around and sure enough, about half the sixty or so guys in the place were watching the dancer (who, in Amos's defense, was not naked. She wore what would amount to a skimpy bikini on any nearby beach), the other half stuffing their faces with brisket and ribs.

"Excuse me." Amos's voice came from behind me and I scooted out from in front of the door. He shot me a go-directly-to-Hell-do-not-pass-go-do-not-collect-two-hundred-dollars look and joined two other men at a table near the pole. A hot-pants-and-crop-top-clad waitress put a beer in front of him before he even asked.

I scanned the room for Boss Hogg, but didn't see anyone who stood out as the establishment's proprietor.

"Can I help you, honey?" A voice drawled at my elbow. I turned to find a pretty waitress in the same uniform looking at me with a raised eyebrow. "You just sit anywhere, we don't have hostesses."

I smiled. "I'm not here for the show." I offered a hand and introduced myself. "I'm a reporter from the *Richmond Telegraph*. I was hoping the owner was around and would have time to chat for a minute."

"Let me see," she said as she turned toward the bar. Another waitress walked past and mine grabbed her elbow. "Hey, is Bobby around anywhere?"

"I think so. Want me to go look?"

"That's all right." She turned back to me. "Make yourself at home. I'll be right back."

She sashayed toward the swinging door at the far end of the bar and I pulled out a chair at the nearest table, looking around at the clientele.

Mostly blue collar guys, though there were a few suits in the mix. On the whole, it was pretty tame. In college, I did a story on a strip club near campus that boasted fully nude women and fall-down-drunk frat guys who hooted and hollered demeaning phrases by the truckload as they flung money onto the stage.

The music here was way louder than the men, and a pickle jar sat on the far end of the catwalk, customers dropping a few bills into it every couple of minutes. It was a much more civilized girly bar than I'd ever heard of. More like an old-school roadhouse.

"You looking for me, honey?"

I turned to find the waitress I'd talked to, smiling next to a petite woman in jeans, a pale yellow cashmere sweater, and gorgeous stilettos in the same color. Even in the shoes, she was probably a foot shorter than me.

I glanced at the waitress, who nodded before scooting off to a nearby table where a man in a checkered button-down was waving for a beer refill.

The other woman pulled out the chair opposite mine and offered a firm handshake. "I'm Bobbi Jo Ramsley, and this is my club. Sasha said you're a reporter. What can I do for you?"

I pulled my notebook from my bag and clicked out a pen. Introducing myself, I smiled at Bobbi Jo. "I hear you've caused some controversy with the local ladies' auxiliary."

She rolled her green eyes skyward, pushing a wayward lock of blonde hair behind her ear. "None of those old biddies would know pornography if it bit them in their spandex-girdled asses," she said.

I jotted that down, giving her a once-over. She was pretty, her pale face devoid of makeup. And either the light was extremely forgiving, or Bobbi Jo wasn't over thirty.

She grinned. "I know. I'm young. I'm female. Why do I run a bar like this?"

"To be perfectly fair, I don't know that I've ever been in a place quite like this," I said. "The food smells divine."

"Thanks. My grandmomma was one of the best cooks on the island. I use her barbecue sauce and side dish recipes, and Sam's got a way with a smoker. I think it's magic, or something."

I nodded, my stomach gurgling again. Three days of tea and soup wasn't enough, apparently. Bobbi Jo flagged a waitress down. "Bring us a C-cup and two setups, an iced tea and a..." She looked at me. "What would you like to drink?"

"Is it sweet iced tea?"

Bobbi nodded.

"Iced tea, please."

The waitress nodded and moved toward the kitchen.

"A c-cup?" I asked.

"Barbecued chicken breast. Good size. I can't eat a whole one by myself."

I swallowed a giggle and made a note.

"I do have to admit, I am dying of curiosity here, Bobbi Jo," I said. "How did you come to run a barbecue joint with a sexy floor show when you don't look like you're any older than me? And if you are, I won't leave 'til you tell me what kind of moisturizer you use."

She laughed. "I'm twenty-nine. For the first time, anyway. And the short answer to your question is, the economy sucks. It sucks everywhere, but out here, it sucks worse."

I nodded, keeping quiet and waiting for her to elaborate. She obliged.

"So many places in the county have gone out of business in the past few years." Bobbi Jo leaned her elbows on the table, fiddling with a sugar packet from the bowl in the middle. "The mill cut a lot of jobs. When my grandaddy died two years ago, he left me his farm and a nice chunk of cash. There was a drought the first summer and the crops withered in the fields. I decided that wasn't a reliable way to make a living. And my friends—I bet ten girls I graduated high school with moved away in the last year. When there's only a hundred people in the class, that's a lot, you know?

"I started reading about how economic systems can collapse, and we had some of the warning signs. I love Mathews. I love the people and the town and the island, and I didn't want to see that happen here, but you can drive over the bridge and see for yourself how close we came to being a ghost town. So I read up on recession-proof businesses. Guess what's number one on that list?"

I looked up from my scribbling. "That makes total sense."

"Doesn't it?" She thumped a fist on the table. "And there wasn't a club around here. I thought I'd found the key to saving the whole damned town, and Dorothy Scott and her old band of bats decided they wouldn't have it. Look around. I'm a woman. I'm not in this to demean women, and I'm not 'peddling smut,' either. The girls don't look any different on stage than most of them do when they go to the beach, and the waitresses are dressed in Hooters uniform knockoffs. Though, Dorothy'd probably pitch a fit if Hooters wanted to come to Mathews, too."

I looked at the stage, where a new dancer in a neon pink bikini and fabulous black patent Louboutins (I had that pair at home) strutted toward the pole. She jumped and grabbed it, flipping upside down and curling her legs around before she arched her back and reached her arms over her head.

"Damn. That looks like something out of Cirque D'Solieil." I said.

"Exactly!" Bobbi Jo nodded. "There are so many women around here with so much talent. Becca there studied dance at RAU for four years. But when nobody's going to the ballet, the ballet can't pay new dancers, right? She came home and moved in with her momma. She was working at the 7-Eleven, for Pete's sake. Now, she's doing what she loves and she makes enough to have bought her own house last month."

"And some killer shoes," I mumbled, scribbling. This story was fast becoming more about what Bobbi Jo was trying to do for the town and how her club was different than about the showdown in her parking lot.

"So, it looks like you're definitely helping the economy, but you're not in Mathews," I said.

She sat back in her chair, frustration plain on her face. "Unfortunately, thanks to Miss Dorothy and her friends, I am not. We must have had ten town hall meetings last summer, and no matter how much I tried to explain or what I argued, she convinced damn near every woman in the county that their husbands were going to run off with my dancers if they allowed the club. First off, more than half the dancers are married. Second, I have a way stricter contact policy than the state. They can't even grab the girls' hands or give them money. That's what the pickle jar is for."

"Have any of the other women in the county actually been here?"

"You are the first female non-employee to darken my door since I opened. I wish I could get them to come see that I'm not threatening their marriages, but fear-mongering is a powerful tool."

"Indeed it is."

Sasha stopped at my elbow and laid a huge platter of barbecue chicken in the middle of the table, then a basket brimming with baked beans, coleslaw, pickles, and cornbread in front of each of us. My stomach roared.

Bobbi Jo giggled. "Don't be shy. Dig in."

Sasha handed me a fork and I scooped beans into my mouth. They tasted like they'd been smoked, with just the right hint of sweet in the sauce.

"Oh, my," I said, smiling at Bobbi Jo.

"It's good, right?"

"Indeed."

It was all good. The cornbread was the kind of crisp on the outside and moist on the inside that can only be achieved with the right recipe and a cast iron skillet, and the chicken really was magical. The pickles weren't standard-issue, either. Sweet and hot, they were addictive. I emptied my cup of them in half a minute and Bobbi Jo offered me hers.

"My grandmomma's recipe," she said. "Dill, sugar, and jalepenos."

Stuffed, I pushed my plate away and turned back to my notes.

"So, what kind of money are you making here? And how much has the county benefitted from it?"

"We clear about a thousand a night on the weekends after everyone's paid, and probably two-thirds of that during the week," she said. "That's twice what we made when we opened, and it goes up every month. I paid five grand in taxes last month."

"Seems a shame you can't have that money going to your hometown."

"I buy everything I can from Mathews. All the vegetables we serve in the summer come from the county. The baskets are from a local weaver. I'm trying."

I jotted that down.

"It was nice to meet you, Bobbi," I said, putting my notebook away. "I have to pitch this to my editor, but I'm sure it will fly. Do you have a card, just in case I have more questions when I start writing?"

She stood with me and pulled a business card out of her hip pocket. "Thank you."

"Thanks for talking to me. And feeding me. I'll be in touch."

She turned toward the kitchen with a wave and I watched her go, impressed with her business savvy and her dedication to the town.

It didn't occur to me to ask her about moonshine until I was halfway back to Mathews.

10

The last of the daylight faded as I reached the turn to the freeway, the budding trees disappearing into the night. My cell phone buzzed as I flicked my turn signal on, and I stopped in the turn lane to fish it out of my bag. Parker.

"Hey, are you still in Tidewater?" he asked.

"Just now heading home," I said. "What's up?"

"I'm at Tony's, and Ashton asked me to call you. She wants to talk to you. Can you turn around and come by here?"

Hot damn. Maybe I'd built up good karma, working while I was sick.

"On my way," I said, swinging the car back onto the main road.

I hurried across the bridge, my chat with Bobbi Jo coloring the island in a new light. Five grand a month in tax revenue. And all those guys going into the club every night. It seemed like the perfect save for a place that could use some recession-proof income. Shame it didn't work.

Stopping outside the crowded gate to the Okerson house, I cringed when three mics appeared in my face as soon as I rolled my window down. The press corps fired questions so fast and loud no one in the house could hear me on the intercom. I knew the look on the reporters' faces too well: they had been stonewalled by both families all weekend and were getting desperate. From the questions I got, they thought I was Sydney's mother.

Did I look old enough to have a teenage daughter? I decided to brush that off with the darkness as an excuse.

I grabbed my cell phone out of the cup holder and called Parker back.

"I'm trapped at the gate, and the wolves out here are hungry," I said.

"On it," he said. "Try not to let anyone in with you."

As the gate inched open, I glanced around the media throng. "A person would need titanium cojones to sneak onto Tony Okerson's property. Especially today. But I've seen stranger," I said. When the gap was wide enough to slide my car through, I gunned the engine, watching the rearview mirror as the gate closed behind me. "I don't think anyone hitchhiked."

"Good," Parker said.

I stopped in front of the house and clicked off the call. Parker stepped out the front door.

"Thanks for coming."

"Are you kidding? Thanks for calling. What's going on now?"

He swiped a hand down over his face, his fingers muffling the first part of his reply. "Ashton is...not well. She...well, I'll let her tell you. They loved your first write-up. They trust you, and not just because I said so. You earned it." He stepped aside and waved me toward the door. "Go on in. She's in the living room."

"You're not staying?"

"I have to go pick Mel up for dinner. If I leave right now I'll only be really late, not unforgivably late."

I nodded. "Thanks, Parker. Y'all have fun."

I turned for the door, but his voice stopped me. "Hey, Clarke? I'm not sure how you can help them, but they could sure use it if there's a way."

"I'll do my best."

He waved and walked toward his BMW motorcycle, strapping his red helmet in place and disappearing down the drive.

I opened the storm door, using a knee to keep the dog inside and grabbing his collar as I stepped around him. He pawed my shin and licked my free hand.

"Hey, boy." I ruffled the fur behind his ears. He whined and craned his neck to look out the door.

"He misses TJ." The comment choked off at the end, and I spun to find

Tony coming out of the study. He shut the door behind him, but I caught a glimpse of the far wall, dotted with trophy shelves and framed news stories.

"I'm sure he's not alone," I said.

"He is not." Tony cleared his throat and blinked a few times. "I owe you my gratitude for the story you did. A couple of the skeezier TV outfits have tried to make something out of nothing here, but everyone else seems to be following your lead, and I appreciate your help making this easier for my family to handle. Grant was right. Spin is everything."

I smiled, glad he thought I had helped.

"You spent your entire career building a practically untarnishable image, Tony. I'm ..." I sighed. "I'm just so damned sorry. And I hate that the press is camped outside your driveway while you grieve."

He shrugged his broad shoulders. "Goes with the territory. The NFL was awfully good to my family."

"Parker said Ashton wanted to talk to me?"

He waved toward the back of the house. "She's in there. Thanks for coming out."

"Anytime."

He turned toward the front door, pulling a leash off the hook next to it and clipping it onto the dog's collar. "We're going to get out of here for a while."

I paused to glance over the photos in the hallway: the girls, in matching dresses on first bikes, ponies, and the Dumbo ride at Disney World. TJ in various football uniforms, posing with the ball up like so many photos I'd seen of his father. His smile was always just a twitch away from a laugh, his eyes happy. I fished a notebook and pen from my bag and jotted that down.

I found Ashton on the sofa. At least, I was pretty sure it was Ashton. In the space of two days, she seemed to have dropped fifteen pounds, and she didn't have them to lose in the first place. She looked haunted.

The woman next to her had long, dark hair and hollows under her eyes that almost matched Ashton's. This had to be Sydney Cobb's mother.

The sliding doors on both ends of the living room's glass wall stood open, letting the sound and smell of the water inside. It was downright tranquil, save for the heavy sadness in the room.

I took a deep breath. "Mrs. Okerson?"

Ashton turned. "Nichelle!" She bounced off the couch with energy that so mismatched her haggard look it was creepy. Crossing the room in five long strides, she pulled me into a hug. "Thank you so much for the stories you did about my boy," she said, her words muffled by my shoulder and her sobs. "They're beautiful."

I patted her back and murmured thanks for talking to me, my eyes on the tears spilling down the other woman's cheeks.

Ashton let go of me and turned to her companion. "Nichelle, this is Tiffany."

"Sydney's mother," I said, stepping toward the couch and offering a hand.

"I was. I am," Tiffany's face crumpled. "Am I?"

I swallowed against a lump in my throat. The anguish on her face would haunt my dreams for weeks, I was certain.

"Sit down," Ashton said. "Can I get you anything?"

Sinking into the cushions opposite them, I smiled and shook my head. "I'm still full from dinner, but thank you."

A piece of driftwood on the end table caught my eye. "Heaven is a little closer in a house by the sea" it read, the letters burned across it in script.

I closed my eyes for a long blink, clicking out my pen. "Parker said y'all wanted to talk to me about something?"

They exchanged a look that radiated subtext. Uh-oh.

"You can't be mad at Grant," Ashton began.

"Mad?"

"He explained that you have a theory."

He what?

"Oh? Why should that make me mad?" I was impressed with my ability to keep my voice even. Grant Parker was a dead man. He did not come tell the parents I thought these kids hadn't killed themselves. I didn't have any more proof of that than the sheriff had that they did. What the hell did he think that would do, except cause pain?

"Now, we told him our theory first." Ashton put up both hands.

"Your theory?" Hang on. "Does it not match the sheriff's theory?"

"That's why we asked you to come. Our babies did not do this."

I hauled in a deep breath.

"What makes you say that?" I poised my pen.

"TJ was a happy kid," Ashton said.

Well, yeah. That's what I thought, but Sheriff Zeke didn't agree.

"Sydney was left-handed," Tiffany muttered, almost too quiet for me to hear.

My eyes snapped to her.

"Come again, ma'am?"

"She was left-handed. The note wasn't her handwriting. It was a good copy of it. Almost too good. But it wasn't her."

Hot damn. I scribbled down the new information. That was something I could work with.

"Did you tell Sheriff Waters that, Mrs. Cobb?"

"Of course I did. He smiled and said he'd take it under advisement." She looked up, her dark eyes windows to the gaping wound on her heart. "Look, Miss, we don't mean any disrespect. Zeke Waters is a good man, and he's a good sheriff. Fair. Sensible. But he thinks we're crazy. Maybe we are. But my Sydney did not write that note. And Ashton's baseball player friend said you didn't think the sheriff was right, either."

I sighed, keeping my eyes on my notes.

Parker hadn't told them anything that wasn't true. I knew he shared my suspicion about TJ, and now the girl's mother was sitting here saying her daughter hadn't written the suicide note the sheriff was using as his proof that her death was open and shut.

But what could I do about it? Either there was a bonafide serial killer in bitty little Mathews, and more lives were at risk, or someone had a vendetta against TJ and Sydney, and they were going to get away with murder.

I raised my eyes to meet Ashton's.

"Grant told me you've done investigative work on stories before," she said.

Seriously. He was at least looking at a swift kick in the ass. I did not want this woman thinking I could save the day when Zeke didn't want to talk about this and I wasn't at all sure I could get to the bottom of it.

"I have, but..." I searched for the right words. "Mrs. Okerson, this is a small town. It's an entirely different world than what I'm used to covering. I don't know anyone here."

"I understand that. I don't, either, really. Tony and I keep to ourselves. TJ was the one who had all the friends." Her voice broke and she curled her arms around her shoulders, like she could physically hold herself together. "Why would someone do this to my baby?"

Ashton buried her head in her knees and sobbed, and I pinched my lips together, studying them. I couldn't say no. These women were grieving the loss of their children, and had no one else to take their suspicions to. Monster exclusive notwithstanding, I had a personal reason for wanting to help, no matter how hard I tried to ignore it. Having the parents involved and on the record would help me get it right.

"I will do everything I can." I leaned forward, resting my elbows on my knees. "I'm going to need you to be completely honest with me."

They both nodded.

"I mean it," I said. "This won't be an easy conversation. You can't fudge facts to make the kids look good. Nobody's perfect, and if we're really trying to find a killer, you're going to have to start by telling me who had a reason to hate your children."

They exchanged a glance. Tiffany spoke first.

"There were probably lots of little girls who were jealous of Syd," she said. "She was a good girl, and a sweet kid, but everyone has their bitchy side, I guess. She wasn't best friends with everyone, you know?"

I jotted that down, catching Tiffany's gaze.

"Who was the girl they picked on?" I asked.

"I'm not sure I follow."

"There's one in every high school class in America," I said. "The pretty girls always have a girl they make fun of. Someone who wants to be part of their group, but doesn't fit in."

Tiffany appeared to consider that.

"Evelyn," Ashton finally said. "Evelyn Sue Miney."

I wrote the name down. "Tell me about her. Typical outcast?"

Tiffany shook her head. "Evelyn was Sydney's friend."

Ashton poked her gently in the ribs. "Tiff, she said we had to be honest. Evelyn and Syd hadn't been friends in a long while. And she had such a crush on TJ."

I kept my eyes on Tiffany as I put a star by the girl's name. A crush on the boy, a rivalry with the girl. Sounded promising.

"Evelyn and Syd were best friends when they were little girls," Tiffany said, dropping her head into her hands and sighing. "They did everything together. Evelyn spent as much time at my house as she did at her own. She couldn't have done this."

"Why weren't they friends anymore?"

"They just grew apart," Tiffany said.

The look Ashton shot her told me there was no "just" to it.

"When?"

"Last year. The summer before. I didn't notice at first, Syd was always so busy with cheerleading and her friends. But I started to notice I hadn't seen Evelyn in a long time."

"She's not a cheerleader?" I asked.

"No, she is. It's not that the girls are mean to her because she's not pretty. She's always been one of Syd's group."

"Until she started coming onto TJ," Ashton said.

Ah ha. I scribbled faster, underlining as I went. This sounded better the longer they talked.

"But TJ wasn't interested in her?"

"TJ was never interested in anyone but Syd," Ashton said.

I studied Tiffany, her face half-hidden behind unwashed hair.

"And Sydney didn't like her friend being interested in her boyfriend." It wasn't a question, because the answer was obvious.

"Who would?" Tiffany said. "She came home from a party last fall, and I'd never seen her like that before. She was sobbing and screaming at the same time. Evelyn kissed TJ. It crushed Sydney."

I turned to Ashton. "TJ didn't kiss her back?"

"He told us he pushed her down. He felt bad because he made her cry. He said they were talking while Syd went to get drinks and then Evelyn kissed him."

"So what happened to Evelyn?" Having been to high school, I had a good guess, but I needed them to say it.

"They froze her out of their group."

I nodded. Popular girl to social pariah overnight. It was worse, in some ways, than having never been popular at all.

"She emailed and texted TJ for months," Ashton said, and Tiffany and I both looked at her.

"Why?"

"It varied. Sometimes she was professing her love for him and telling him Syd would never be good enough for him." Ashton shot an apologetic look at Tiffany. "Other times, she said she was sorry and she didn't mean to kiss him and would he just talk to Sydney and help her explain? TJ finally came to me with it because he didn't know what else to do. He kept telling her he loved Sydney, that there was nothing he could do, and if she wanted to talk to Syd they needed to work it out."

"You said the other day that you studied psychology." I let the words hang in the air.

Ashton shook her head. "It's so hard to tell without talking to the person. But some of the messages I saw? She could be imbalanced."

Imbalanced enough to kill them? I didn't say it, but the looks on their faces said they were thinking it, anyway.

The boy I'd talked to in the gym flashed through my thoughts.

"What about Luke?" I asked.

"Luke?" Ashton furrowed her brow.

"There's a boy on the baseball team, another pitcher. I'm pretty sure the coach called him Luke," I said. "I talked to him when I went by the school the other day, and it was a weird conversation. Seemed like he didn't like TJ too much."

"Oh, the Bosley boy?" Ashton shrugged. "I don't really know him, and TJ never talked too much about him."

"He was the kid Sydney told me was mouthing off about TJ getting hurt last fall. How he would finally get his shot at baseball," Tiffany said.

I nodded at her. "The coach told me his dad was a baseball player in high school and does some major vicarious living through the kid. Puts a lot of pressure on him." I paused, a puzzle piece dancing on the edge of my brain. "Ashton, how did TJ hurt his knee?"

She tossed her hands up helplessly. "He fell. It happens. The grass was wet. He said his cleat slid right out from under him and he twisted his knee. Tore it all to hell."

"Do cleats slip?" It was an honest question. That was one kind of shoe I'd never had occasion to wear. "I thought the whole point of cleats was to give you traction."

"Tony said TJ's were too worn," she said. "That we should have bought him new ones. I didn't know."

I jotted that down. "Anyone or anything else that's stood out to you?" I asked.

"Not really. They were so happy. Sydney's been gone all semester. She should have stayed in Paris." Tiffany's face crumpled again, sobs shaking her shoulders.

"I think this gives me something to go on," I said, standing as Ashton moved to comfort her friend. "If only I could figure out how to get these kids to talk to me."

"Come to the street dance," Ashton said.

"The what?"

"Next Friday night, right in the middle of town. It's the welcome for the growing season. One of the biggest things the town does every year. Everyone talks to everyone. Dress in western wear and you'll fit right in. It's dark."

I smiled and patted her shoulder. "Perfect. Thank you."

She reached up and squeezed my hand. "No, thank you."

I let myself out quietly and inched back through the gang of reporters at the gate without literally steamrolling any of the competition. My thoughts raced for where I could find some help with the promise I'd just made.

It was time to suck it up and call Kyle.

11

I made it back to the freeway before I dialed Kyle's number. We'd been to dinner several times over the winter, and it was fun, getting to know him again. But I had blissfully not had to talk to him about work in months. And I didn't want to start again.

"Hey, you," he said when he picked up.

"Hey, yourself," I said. "You have a few minutes?"

"For you? Sure I do."

I checked the clock on the dash. Almost nine, and it would be another hour before I got back to Richmond. But I'd rather talk in person. I had a way better chance of convincing Kyle I might be onto something if I could look him in the face.

"Are you going to be up for a while? I'd kind of like to come by."

"Oh, yeah?" His voice dropped a full octave. "From dinner and drinks to booty calls? I mean, not that I'm complaining."

"For the love of God, Kyle. Way to jump to conclusions. Because a booty call is so me. I need to talk to you."

"I know I'm irresistible. Waiting for you to catch up." He paused. "Nothing? Okay. Talk about what?"

"I'll tell you when I get there."

"I'll open a bottle of wine."

"You're impossible."

I clicked off the call and spent the rest of the drive to Kyle's apartment mentally rehearsing five different ways to keep him from blowing me off. I stopped in front of his building still unsure any of them would work.

Tapping my foot through the ride up the rattly old elevator to Kyle's loft, I took a couple of deep breaths and tried to calm my jangled nerves. At least I didn't still sound like death.

He opened his front door before I knocked, a smile playing around his lips.

"I saw you park the car." He slid one hand into the back pocket of his well-worn jeans, flexing his impressive upper arm as he did so. My eyes widened at the way his red t-shirt hugged every line.

"You sure you just want to talk?" he asked, watching my expression.

I cleared my throat and tore my eyes from his shoulders. "I'm sure." My voice hitched between the words.

"No, you're not." He grinned. "But come on in."

He waved me toward the big olive sectional that dominated the living room space, disappearing into the kitchen and returning with two glasses of white wine.

"Kyle." I tried my best to sound like I was giving him a warning, but wasn't sure it worked. Dammit, he looked good.

"No means no. Got it." He handed me one glass and retreated to the corner of the sofa with the other. I put three cushions between us, just in case, and sat down, kicking my copper Manolo peep-toes to the polished wood floor.

"What are you into now?" Kyle's smile went from sexy to intrigued as he studied me over the rim of his wine glass.

"Why do I have to be into anything?"

"Because you're sitting way over there. Which means you didn't call and invite yourself over at ten o'clock on a Saturday night because you're lonely. So you're working. I know you."

I laughed. "I guess you do." I took a deep breath. "I've been following this story out in Tidewater," I began.

"I've been reading it. Teen suicides."

"Well..." I drew the word out. "I'm not so sure about that."

"Oh, yeah?" He sipped his wine nonchalantly, but his ice-blue eyes were interested. "Why not?"

"The whole thing has seemed off to me since the first time I went out there," I said. "Why does a kid like TJ Okerson kill himself?"

"It happens more often than you'd think," Kyle said. "Especially with kids involved in sports at that level. It's a lot of pressure."

Just like Aaron. And Sheriff Zeke. Was all of law enforcement so jaded?

"I thought about that. But I don't think the Okersons were putting crazy pressure on TJ. His baseball coach doesn't, either. And Grant Parker from our sports desk is good friends with Tony Okerson. He says no, too."

"Girl trouble?"

"The girl is the second victim."

"I saw. I'm saying, maybe it was guilt? They fought, he killed himself, she couldn't live with it?"

I sighed. Kyle was a great devil's advocate. "The parents say no. That's actually my strongest argument. I just came from talking to both moms. They say they don't buy it. The girl's mother says the note the sheriff is pinning his 'suicide' label on wasn't in her daughter's handwriting."

He set his glass on the table and leaned back into the deep cushions. The expressions playing across his face said he was trying to figure out how to convince me I was wrong.

I raised one hand when he opened his mouth. "I get it. You think I'm nuts. But can we consider, just for a second, that I might not be?"

He raised one eyebrow. "I'm reluctant to encourage you. You have a history of getting yourself hurt."

"Only when I'm right," I said. "Which, can I just point out, I was last time. And you didn't believe me then, either."

"Nicey, I'm not sure what you want me to do about this even if you are right. Which I'm not conceding. This is so far from my jurisdiction your dead kids might as well be in Constantinople."

"I'll get to that in a second." I needed to ask him about the moonshine, but I was pretty sure he was going to palm that off on the ABC police, and I'd gotten nowhere there. If he believed me about the kids, he'd want to help me with the moonshiners. "For now, can I just bounce this off you? You're Captain Supercop. I need to know if I'm missing something."

"It sounds to me like you're seeing something that's not there, not missing anything. Of course the mothers don't want to believe their children took their own lives. I don't have kids and I get that."

"Stop judging and just listen for a minute," I snapped. The words were sharper than I intended, but he was making me regret calling him in the first place. The mental tug-of-war between that irritation and my apparent inability to ignore the sliver of his toned abdomen I could see where his shirt had ridden up was making me testy. I gulped my wine and tried to steady my voice. "Sorry."

"You have the floor." He spread his hands, staring at me with a casually curious look.

"Thank you. So, the mothers say there was a girl. Another girl. Who was creepy-stalkering TJ and hated Sydney."

He tipped his head to one side. "You know anything else about her?"

"She's a cheerleader at the high school. Used to move in the same social circle, but she got blackballed last year when she kissed TJ at a party."

Kyle's hand moved to his chin, raking over the bristles of his barely-there auburn goatee. "Being demoted to social outcast is a powerful motivator for a high school girl. But it takes a certain kind of person to be capable of murder."

"I know. And I want to talk to this girl, but she's not exactly going to sit for an interview with me, especially if she did do something. Which is where you come in." I widened my eyes and smiled earnestly.

Kyle blanched. "I can't go out to Tidewater flashing my badge and haul a teenage girl in for questioning. Are you kidding? I'll end up in a manure truckload of shit over that. I don't care how cute you are." He smiled, shaking his head. "Stop looking at me like that."

I sucked my cheeks in and batted my lashes, and Kyle laughed.

"I'm not asking you to question her," I said seriously. "Not officially. But there's a big town street dance next weekend. I want you to come with me. Help me chat up the locals. In that kind of a setting, people will talk, right?"

"Like, on a date?" He leaned forward, putting himself in arm's reach, and let his eyelids drop halfway.

I sipped my wine. Oh, why the hell not? I wasn't committed to anyone. Joey was hot in a different way than Kyle, and I liked him a lot, but there were no promises on the table. Besides, I had never once in my twenty-nine years played the field. Maybe I should ask Parker for pointers.

"Sure."

"Yeah?" He grinned. "All right. I don't know how close we'll be able to get to teenagers without looking fairly creepy ourselves, but I'm game."

"We're younger than most of the people who play teenagers on TV," I said.

He chuckled. "I don't feel old. You ever wonder how the hell we got to be almost thirty?"

"Dude, a reporter mistook me for Sydney Cobb's mother tonight," I said. "I've wondered about nothing since."

"You don't look a day over twenty-one." His eyes locked on mine, a sexy smile tugging at the corners of his lips.

I leaned toward him, my hair falling into my face. Kyle reached up and brushed it away, his fingers trailing electricity across my cheekbone. His touch was thrilling and familiar at the same time. Like coming home to fireworks. I leaned my cheek into his palm, and he drew the pad of his thumb across my lips. My breath stopped.

"Nicey." He slid toward me.

I let my eyelids fall. "Kyle," I whispered.

The couch cushions shifted as he leaned in. Just as my cell phone erupted into the theme from *Peter Pan*.

My eyes snapped open. Kyle slumped into the sofa and let his head fall back, his breath coming like he'd been for a run. I knew the feeling.

"What?" I grouched at the phone, yanking it from the side pocket on my bag. "Oh, shit."

"What?" Kyle's head popped up.

"Hey." I put the phone to my ear.

"You sound better," Joey said.

"I feel better." And a little like a jerk. I shot a guilty look at Kyle.

"I think I might have a friend who knows a guy who knows something about your moonshiners. But you're not going to talk to him alone. When are you free? I'll set it up and come along for the ride."

"Really?" I grinned. Kyle's eyebrows shot up, and I tried to calm myself.

Talking about going to a meeting with the Mafia in front of the ATF. I had some titanium cojones, too.

"Who is that?" Kyle mouthed.

I shook my head. Good Lord, what a can of worms. I turned my attention from the hunky guy on the couch to the one on the phone.

"I'll make time on Monday or Tuesday. I'm going with Parker to TJ's funeral, but that's all I have in stone right now. Er. You know what I mean."

"I'll call you tomorrow?"

"I'd like that."

"Sweet dreams."

He hung up and I turned back to Kyle, the spell broken. "Tell me what you know about moonshine."

He laid one arm along the back of the sofa and sighed.

"Why?"

"That's my other theory. I think TJ was drinking it the night he died. I'm pretty sure Sydney was, because I saw the jar in the stuff the cops retrieved from the scene. They said it was near her. I did some reading, and it seems improperly made moonshine can kill people."

"It can. That's one of the reasons it's illegal to sell it unregulated. People think the government just wants their cut of the money. But the laws are there to keep people safe, too."

"So how is it that people still get away with making and selling it in the twenty-first century?"

"Funnily enough, the same kind of crafty evasion that has been in place for a hundred years. That, and there are aspects of the law that protect them. Or that they hide behind. For example: agents can go right up on a still, but if it's not running, there's nothing we can do. Moonshiners know that."

"But why not stake them out?"

He shook his head. "First, that's expensive, and a lot of resources going into cracking what's usually a small operation. We have a budget just like everyone else. Second, it's harder than it sounds. Most of that stuff is made out in the country. You can't scratch your ass without everyone in three counties knowing. An unmarked sedan full of strangers with crew cuts? They'll keep everything shut down until it rusts before they'll run a still if we send a team out there. The best way to work moonshiners is to get undercover. But that takes for-bloody-ever. It's hard to get those folks to trust new people."

"But what if that's how these children died? What if more people die if you don't do something? Is it worth the money then?"

"Possibly. But slow your roll, Lois. There's also the whole business of placing an agent undercover. You're talking more money, time away from the guy's family. An operation like that can take months—hell, years—to infiltrate. And, it's not my jurisdiction unless it's crossing state lines. It's an ABC police matter unless I can prove that. "

"Of course it is. That's like, the one police agency in town where I don't know anyone. I don't suppose you have a friend over there who might talk to me?"

"I haven't been here long enough to make any good friends over there, but I know a couple of guys. I can vouch for you and see if they'll give you a few minutes. Does it have to be on the record?"

I bit my lip, considering that. It would help. Especially with new cops I didn't have a history with. Not everyone is a solid source. Ashton Okerson's gaunt face flashed through my thoughts. I wanted the information more than I wanted an attributable quote.

"I'd prefer it, but if the only way you can get them to talk to me is to tell them it's not, go for it."

He nodded. "Are you even considering the possibility that you're wrong about this?"

"About there being moonshiners in Mathews? Nope."

"Nicey." His voice had a warning edge.

I sighed. "Yes. But what if, Kyle? What if there's a moonshine outfit poisoning kids? What if one of these jealous little creeps spiked their drinks with something? The open-and-shut doesn't feel right. And no one else is listening to these people. Hell, even Aaron White at the PD told me it was probably nothing more than what it looks like. They deserve to know why they're burying their children. So what if I'm wrong? I'm out a few evenings and a couple of Saturdays. But if I'm right—if *they're* right—how could I ever close my eyes again if I don't try to help?"

His face softened. "You have a good heart. It's one of the things I've always loved about you. But you know you can't get emotionally invested in every case. You'll burn yourself out."

"I don't. But this is different." My voice broke, memories I'd held at bay for two days crashing through my defenses.

"I know, honey." He reached across the sofa and grabbed my hand. "Have you even talked to your mom?"

"No." I bit my lip, telltale pricking in the backs of my eyes a warning that tears were coming. I closed my eyes against the flood, but they fell anyway. I pulled in a hitching breath. "I keep hoping she won't read it. It's April. Weddings are dropping from the sky. She barely has time to eat."

"Probably a good thing." He stroked the back of my hand with his thumb, and I fell across the cushions, burying my face in his shirt and sobbing until the tears were gone. Kyle stroked my hair and made soothing noises at intervals, but mostly he just held me and let me cry.

When I finally sat up and dragged the back of one hand across my face, he was ready with a tissue box and a smile.

"I figured this would get to you," he said.

"Then stop giving me shit and help me." I wiped my eyes and blew my nose. "Parker asked me to help. Their parents asked me to help. I can't let it go, Kyle."

He nodded, a long sigh escaping his chest. "I guess I knew that when you called."

"So you're in?"

"However I can be, but I'm not sure how much that is unless you can prove the moonshine is leaving Virginia." He held my gaze, his mouth pressed into a tight line. "Just because the parents don't see what the cops see doesn't mean this is the same story, Nicey."

"Maybe. But my mom was—is—" I threw my hands up. "What if it is? No one would help her. Well, except for your dad. I will always love him for trying. But what if we can help the Okersons?"

He squeezed my hand. "Whatever you need."

I smiled and returned the pressure on his fingers, wincing at the damp circle on his shirt. "Sorry about that." I waved my other hand toward the spot.

"Eh. It'll wash." The look in his eyes was so sincere I almost lost it again.

"Thanks, Kyle. I've tried so hard to not remember. To make this be just a story."

"We all have cases that get to us, honey. But you have to watch yourself. You're not helping the Okersons if you get yourself shot by a pissed-off redneck who doesn't want to lose his moonshine money."

"Noted." I stood and turned for the door and he followed, leaning on the frame as I stepped into the hallway. I said goodnight, then spun back and pulled him into a hug, landing a soft kiss on his stubbly cheek.

"It's nice to have you around," I whispered as his arms tightened around me.

"It's nice to be here," he said into my hair.

I stepped away and opened the gate on the elevator. He was still watching when I disappeared toward the lobby.

12

Sunday passed in a blur of cold medicine, minestrone, and *Friends* reruns, punctuated by phone calls. Parker was first up, confirming plans to go to the funeral and thanking me profusely for "What you did for Ashton." I resisted the urge to jump his shit for telling them I suspected anything in the first place. He'd had a lousy enough week without me yelling at him.

I called Bob around lunchtime to pitch him the story on Bobbi Jo's roadhouse, which I had decided was a much more fitting term for a place boasting degreed dancers in sequined bikinis than "smut joint." He laughed for five minutes and gave me a green light. I dozed off and on all afternoon, and by the time Joey called at ten to seven I felt almost energetic.

"You have a handle on your schedule yet?" he asked.

"I'm free anytime except tomorrow afternoon," I said, trying to ignore the memory of how Kyle's arms had felt around me—and the double-edged sword I was walking. The only way Kyle could bust the moonshiners was if they were exporting their product. And the most likely way Joey would have a friend who knew the moonshiners was if the guy we were going to meet was providing the transportation. It seemed unfair to get them to talk to me and then set the ATF on them. And selfishly, I wanted Joey and Kyle as far apart as I could keep them, for a multitude of reasons.

"How about Tuesday evening?" he asked. "We might even grab dinner, if you feel like it. I want to talk about those fantasies you mentioned the other night."

My stomach flipped. "I have no recollection of that." I cleared my throat. "But dinner sounds nice. And thanks. This story is a big deal to me."

"I recall enough for both of us. And no problem—this could be a big boost to your career if you're right. There's certainly enough of a spotlight here."

"It's not just the spotlight," I said softly. "I really appreciate your help, Joey."

"Getting you a source is easy. Keeping you out of trouble, I worry about."

"It's not like I go looking for it."

"You do sometimes."

"Not on purpose."

"Uh-huh."

A smile playing around my lips, I thanked him again and hung up, reaching for my laptop. Writing something non-tragic held a special appeal after the hollowed eyes that had haunted my dreams all week.

With menu items including a C-cup barbecue chicken breast and only "full racks" of ribs available, a roadhouse in Gloucester County is pulling in customers as much for the food as the show—and drawing the ire of a nearby church ladies' auxiliary.

"We managed to keep this place out of Mathews proper, but then they came right across the line and opened up here," Dorothy Scott, head of the First Baptist Church of Mathews Ladies' Auxiliary, said. "And we don't want our men's minds poisoned."

Scott and a friend have been frequenting the roadhouse's parking lot, snapping photos of license plates and using online sources to make sure the wives of the club's customers know where their husbands are spending their free time.

One of those customers tried unsuccessfully to run the women off Saturday, then defended the establishment when that didn't work.

"It's not like anyone's naked in there," he said, refusing to go on the record. "It's art. Like the ballet."

While there are dancers in the club, owner Bobbi Jo Ramsley said she opened it with an inheritance from her grandfather because the local economy needed a boost, and pointed out the sequined bikinis her dancers wear and the pickle jar she keeps on one end of the stage for tips as evidence of the strict hands-off policy she enforces.

I sent the story to Bob Sunday night. He loved it (he told me twice on Monday morning) proclaiming Bobbi Jo's menu item names brilliant and talking up a field trip for some of the single guys on the staff.

Still grinning, I went back to my desk to grab a file I needed for the staff meeting and found a copy of the morning's front page spread open across my desk. My advance on TJ's funeral in the bottom corner of the page was marked up in red pen. My smile faded.

"Here's what you need to learn," I read from the margin before I stuffed the paper in the recycle bin.

I avoided Spence's glare through the staff meeting, pretending I hadn't seen his little love note. Shelby watched him stare daggers at me with interest, bouncing her knee impatiently. I was sure she couldn't wait to corner him and commiserate.

Bob dismissed everyone but me and Parker, watching the rest of the staff file out before he asked Parker to shut the door. I steeled myself for a lecture about rising above office politics, figuring Spence had been bitching to him, too.

"You two square on the Okerson funeral today?" he asked.

Phew. I nodded, glad I was wrong. I might not have asked for this story, but I wasn't letting it go now. Spence could get over himself.

Parker nodded.

"I want this as an exclusive until it hits the racks in the morning," Bob said. "Everyone and their brother will be calling looking for a comment about it, but they get nothing 'til our story is in print." He glanced at me. "You feeling better?"

"Finally, thank God. I just have to finish the antibiotics they gave me," I said.

"Good. You've been on top of your game so far, and I want it to stay that way."

I exchanged a look with Parker.

"Bob, there's more to this story than you know," I began.

Bob leaned his elbows on his desk, shooting a glance between me and Parker.

I looked at Parker and sighed, opening my mouth and cringing in anticipation of the fallout. Bob waffled between loving the results and hating the process when I played detective.

"I don't think TJ killed himself," Parker blurted before I could.

Bob's eyes widened. "Now, Grant, I know this was your friend's son—" he began.

"I don't think he did, either," I interrupted.

My editor sat back in his chair, steepling his fingers under his chin.

"This has always been a hard thing for you to write about, Nichelle. I remember when that kid last year was bullied on the Internet, you were depressed for weeks while you worked on that."

"But I didn't ever question what the cops were telling me, did I?" I pulled in a shaky breath. "I'm trying to keep personal feelings from clouding my judgment here, Bob. Harder than you can imagine. And this doesn't feel right to me. It's too easy, and it makes too little sense."

"She's right, chief. I thought the same thing before she ever said a word to me. I've known TJ since he was a baby. His parents are like family to me."

Bob looked at me. "And the cops say what?"

"The sheriff is waiting for the tox screen to come back showing painkillers and alcohol so he can close the file. He's more worried about copycat suicides than he is about whether or not the obvious answer here is the right one."

"Given that there's already been one of those, I'd say he's got good reason for that," Bob said.

"Parker got me an exclusive with the mothers Saturday night. Both of them." I picked at a piece of lint on the arm of the chair, peeking at Bob through my lashes.

He put a hand up. "Don't tell me. It's a conspiracy. The girl was murdered, too, right?"

I swallowed a laugh at the skeptical look on his face.

"I'm poking around."

"Dancers. I like the dancers. Write more about them." He sighed, burying his head in his hands.

"I think there's a moonshine operation out there that might be poisoning people," I said. "Or people poisoning the moonshine, maybe. Either way. Illegal booze, dead kids—it's an impressive headline."

Parker coughed over a laugh and Bob peered at me from between splayed fingers. "Moonshine? Are you serious?"

"As a naturalizer nurse's shoe."

"Your friend at the ATF is helping you with this, I assume? The one who has a gun?"

I rolled my eyes. "Getting shot wasn't fun. I don't intend to repeat that experience."

"I want you to chant that at the mirror every morning while you do your makeup. Mantras bring about positive self-change. I heard it on Oprah once."

"Oprah is never wrong." I nodded, and Bob rolled his eyes.

"Hey, who am I to argue? If you're right, it'll be a hell of a story. But digging for something in a town that tiny won't be easy with all the TV cameras hanging around."

"The networks will clear out this evening," I said. "They're not interested in anything beyond TJ's funeral."

"Most of them, probably. But Charlie's been out there, too, and where you go, she'll go."

"I'm not advertising what I'm working on, and the families aren't talking to anyone else."

"Just be careful," he said. "And if you're looking for a murderer where the cops aren't, you better have it dead to rights before you bring it to me. You can't accuse someone of murder in the newspaper when there's no police report."

I nodded understanding. "Not planning on it. In a perfect world, the cops will come on board when I find something compelling enough."

"I know you'll make sure we have it first if you take it to them," Bob said.

"Of course."

"And the funeral is priority one today."

Parker checked his watch. "Speaking of priorities, if I'm going to file my column before we leave, I should get to work on it."

"And I need to call Aaron about a couple of police reports," I said. "The trials I'm missing to go to Mathews might have to wait 'til tomorrow, but I'll do my best to track down the lawyers and get an update in tonight. It might be late."

"We can hold Metro 'til nine-thirty before the guys downstairs get pissy. The drivers make overtime if we're any later than that, and Les will pop his hair plugs right out when he comes back if we let that happen, so if they're not in by then, they don't go."

"Yes, sir." I stood and saluted, clicking the heels of my classic black Louboutins together.

"Get to work." His voice was gruff, but he smiled.

Back at my desk, I flipped my laptop screen up and logged into the PD's online reports database. Armed robbery at a fast food joint on Southside. No fatalities, at least. I snatched up the phone and called Aaron, thankful for an easy story to get out of the way.

"You find any moonshine?" he asked when he picked up.

"Empty jars, so far," I said. "But I see the folks at Burger King on Hull found a guy with a gun last night."

"Two guys. One white, one black, ski masks, gun. Went in after midnight, ordered the staff to the floor, emptied the registers, and left."

I jotted that down. "Anyone get you a good description? See a car?"

"The manager said the guys weren't big. Five-eight to five-ten, a hundred and fifty or so pounds. No hair or eye color noted. They jumped in the back of a nineties sedan. Gray or white, possibly a Honda or Nissan."

"You have a sketch?" I asked as I wrote.

"Nope. Not enough to go on."

"We'll put it in Metro. Maybe someone saw something. Is Crimestoppers offering a reward?"

"The standard one."

"Thank you. This is an easy write-up, and I needed it today."

He chuckled. "I had very little to do with that, but you're welcome."

"Just try to keep things quiet around here this week, huh? This thing in Tidewater is getting more tangled by the day."

"You sound like you're feeling better, anyway," he said.

"Thank God for small favors."

I wished him a good week and hung up, rifling through the tea-stained papers on my desktop for the one I'd scrawled the ABC police officer's phone number on.

I crossed my fingers as I dialed, and smiled when the guy picked up on the first ring. I introduced myself and his voice went from congenial to guarded.

"Aaron White at the Richmond PD will vouch for my trustworthiness if you want to call him," I said. "I got your number from him, actually."

"Aaron's a good guy," he said. "But it's his job to talk to reporters. It's not mine."

"What if we're off the record? At least at first?" It wasn't my preference when dealing with a brand-new source, but I needed an in at the ABC police and he didn't have any more reason to trust me than I did to trust him.

"About what?"

"I'm working on a story that has ties to moonshiners," I said. "I would really love to know a little more about how the ABC polices that part of the illegal trade."

"Very carefully," he said.

I picked up a pen, not because I wanted to quote him, but because I didn't want to forget anything.

"Meaning?" I asked.

"Meaning moonshiners are a tricky business. It's practically a culture unto itself."

"Are there any active investigations into the manufacture and sale of illegal moonshine?"

"About fifteen, spread from the mountains to the beach and everywhere in between. We busted a group of bachelor businessmen with a still in their basement in Alexandria last year. Trial is coming up on that one, actually."

"So it's not just a country thing anymore?"

"Hardly. There are people who make the stuff all over the state. Though there are only a few operations with wide enough distribution for it to warrant our time and money."

"Any of those pushing their product across state lines?" I asked.

"I'm afraid I can't comment on that."

I tapped the pen on my notebook.

"Can you tell me if there's an open investigation in a little map dot called Mathews out on the bay?" I asked.

He paused. "I'm sorry," he said. "No comment."

Which was as good as yes. I put a star by that. I didn't know if Kyle had a way to find out what they were investigating, but it was worth asking.

After thanking the officer for his time, I hung up.

I fired through the armed robbery story and sent an email to our photo editor requesting a shot of the Burger King to go with it. Parker appeared at my elbow just as I finished proofing the article and got it ready to send to Bob.

"You ready?" he asked. "I want to get there a little early if we can."

I clicked send and closed my laptop, smoothing my black tank dress as I stood. "Since I don't fancy riding to Mathews on the back of your bike in this dress, I assume I'm driving?" I asked.

"I figured," he said.

I fished my keys out of my bag and turned toward the elevator, almost plowing into Spence.

"Teach her a little about writing sports on your way, Parker," he said.

"Lay off, Spence." Parker shook his head, putting a hand on the small of my back and trying to steer me around Spencer.

"Who plays infield between second and third bases, Clarke?" The words dripped so much sarcasm I was tempted to ask if he needed a napkin for his chin when I turned back.

Parker opened his mouth, but I laid a hand on his arm. "The shortstop," I said. "For the Generals, it's Mo Jensen, who hit two-ninety with thirty-five RBIs and only one error last year. Anything else, Mr. Jacobs?"

Spence rolled his eyes and stalked in the direction of Les's office. I sighed and strode to the elevator, Parker on my heels.

"I guess it might do Shelby some good to have a friend. Maybe she'll soften," I said, grinning at him as the doors closed.

He smiled. "I was all set to defend you and instead you shut him up," he said. "How'd you know that?"

"It was in your baseball preview last month. Things I read get stuck in my brain."

"Nice."

* * *

I drove to I-64 while Parker fiddled with the radio, a heavy sadness settling in the car.

"I'm sorry, Parker," I said. "This can't be easy for you."

"You can say that again. I'm sad. I'm worried about Tony and Ashton. And I'm pissed off, too," he said, running a hand over his face.

"At?"

"The cops. The kids. Just in general."

I paused, stealing glances at his profile. "So, when you went out there the other day," I said finally. "You were there for a while before you called me. And I know Ashton and Tiffany talked to me, but I'm wondering what they told you." And if it matched what they told me, but I kept quiet about that.

"I asked them what you told me to," he said. "About if there were kids who didn't like TJ."

"And?"

"Ashton said not really, at first, and then she told me a story about a cheerleader who had a crush on him. Said the girl texted him at all hours and some of the messages were 'I love you so much' and others were 'you prick, why don't you love me?'"

"They told me about her, too," I said. "That's definitely interesting."

Parker nodded. "You think a teenage girl could do this, though?"

"Have you ever watched a Lifetime movie?" I glanced at his puzzled expression and laughed. "Probably not. I don't know about this particular teenage girl, but is it theoretically possible? Abso-freaking-lutely."

"How do we find that out?"

"Well, I'm going to start by hoping the girl is at this big social event they're having Friday night and trying to chat her up."

"You always have a plan. Need help?" he asked, then snapped his fingers. "Oh. Wait. I think we're going to a play Friday night."

"Got it covered. Kyle's coming with me. But thanks, Joe Hardy."

The more I thought about it, the more I leaned toward the girl, just because the empty pill bottle and liquor pointed to someone conniving, someone who knew enough about TJ's every move to know he had a fresh bottle of pills in his pocket. Of course, that assumed there was foul play. I needed the tox screen to have a better idea of what I was dealing with. I couldn't see a cheerleader force-feeding a boy as strong as TJ a whole bottle of pills. But according to the sheriff, there were no obvious signs of trauma, so the blood test results had to hold the key.

I tapped my fingers on the steering wheel, my thoughts tangling up again. This whole thing was so damned convoluted. Every time I thought I had a new puzzle piece, it was just irregular enough that I couldn't find a place to make it fit.

"Was there anyone else Ashton talked about?"

"Not really." Parker shrugged. "She said she was sure he wasn't universally loved, but the girl was the only one who was weird."

I nodded. "Nothing about the boy from the baseball team? Luke?"

"I talked to Tony about him. He said that kid was jealous as hell, but he didn't mark him as a killer. Said the family is nice. Mom is the PTA president, Dad's super involved with the booster club."

Hmmm. "I don't know, Parker. I'm a total stranger, and he leapt right to 'I get to pitch now' with me like, the day after TJ died. That's a little narcissistic." But the M.O. didn't really fit with a jealous boy, in my opinion. I'd be more likely to go there with some kind of blunt force trauma, or even a bullet, being the cause of death. On the other hand, it would be harder to make those look like suicide.

"Tony said TJ told him Luke was really nice when he offered to take over for the second half of the football game after TJ got hurt. But TJ said he could still play, and the coach let him go back in. They talked some over the winter. Neither of them played basketball."

"Huh. Were they friends, then?" I couldn't shake the peculiar look on the boy's face out of my head, even as I asked the question.

"Eh. They hung out with the same kids, but in a town this size, almost everyone hangs out with the same kids, don't they?"

"They still have cliques. It's a high school. They're just smaller cliques."

I pulled off the freeway and turned toward West Point. Parker cranked up the stereo as I lost myself in this crazy, blurry puzzle. The tox results would really help. But Sheriff Zeke had no lab of his own and zero pull with the one in Richmond, so it could take weeks—hell, months—to get them back.

Kyle could maybe light a fire under someone on that front. I wanted to call him, anyway, and that was a better excuse than any I'd come up with. The pull I'd felt toward him Saturday night had knocked me for a loop, especially when I was so attracted to Joey.

I glanced at Parker when I turned toward the island, my throat tightening when I saw him staring out the window, tears flowing over his bronze cheekbones.

"I'm sorry," I said, patting his hand.

"It just..." His words choked off before he could finish the sentence, and I squeezed his fingers.

"Well and truly sucks. I know."

Yesterday, I'd talked to my mother for about five minutes. I rushed her off the phone before she could ask what I was working on.

* * *

I turned into the parking lot at the church, tall stained glass windows crafted with the kind of artistry you don't see anymore marking the century-old sanctuary.

A small handful of cars dotted the parking lot, but I recognized Tony's Land Rover.

I followed Parker through a side door and stopped by the back pew, studying the windows—there were twelve, depicting different scenes from Jesus's life—as Parker walked to the front and pulled Ashton into a hug. She fell into him, clutching his shoulder like a lifeline.

I walked back out to the welcome center and looked over the display Ashton had obviously spent days piecing together. There was a table full of TJ's favorite things, from his first little league trophy to his iPad and a handful of XBox game cases. His football and baseball jerseys hung from a makeshift clothesline. Another table was covered with photos. Baby pictures of him coming home from the hospital, grinning with his first tooth, sitting on Tony's Redskins helmet holding a football. Every birthday, up to him holding a set of keys and grinning from the driver's seat of a Mustang convertible.

"Sweet cartwheeling Jesus," I muttered, tears blinding me as I turned for the door. I'd seen so much tragedy in my career I'd be in therapy eight hours a day if I took it all to heart. But these people were Parker's friends. They were burying their baby, and didn't know why. I ran out into the sunshine and gulped air, silent sobs shaking my shoulders.

I closed my eyes for a ten count and took a slow, deep breath, wiping my cheeks before I spun on my heel to go back inside. I had one hand on the doorknob when three satellite trucks pulled into the parking lot behind me. The doors opened in unison and network-made-up Johnny Goodhairs in three-piece suits disembarked, carrying mics and racing for the best place on the lawn.

I slipped quietly into the church and strode past the photos and mementos, making a beeline for Parker when I spotted him sitting with Tony and an older couple in a hallway off the sanctuary.

I dragged Parker a few feet away. "Houston, we may have a problem," I said, pasting on a smile and hoping my waterproof mascara hadn't let me down.

A worried line creased his brow. "What's that?"

"The press is here," I said, the irony of me sounding that warning not lost on me. "Three network guys, already fighting for space on the lawn. All in dark suits. Want to bet on which one tries to slip inside the church first?"

He nodded and walked back to Tony, leaning over and murmuring to his friend. I hung back a few steps.

"Damned vultures!" an older man, who had that debonair look handsome men get when they age that always struck me as so unfair, exclaimed.

"Dad, they're just doing their jobs," Tony said, throwing me an apologetic look.

"This is a funeral, not a media circus," Mr. Okerson, senior, practically spat.

I shifted my weight, trying to blend into the floor. While Parker had asked me to be there, Bob had, too. And I was writing a story about the service. I didn't want to upset the family even more.

"Thanks for the heads-up, Nichelle." Tony stood and put an arm around me. "And thank you for coming, and for everything you've done for us. Ashton filled me in. I can't tell you..." His green eyes filled with tears and he paused. "If there's ever anything I can do for you, don't hesitate."

I nodded, trying to focus on the moment and the words and not the fact that Tony Okerson was hugging me. He wasn't a celebrity. Not today. He was a guy who was grieving a terrible loss, and I wanted to help.

"Y'all want me to go watch the door?" I asked.

Parker and Tony exchanged a look.

"Body combat or no, I think someone a little more intimidating might be better." Parker patted my arm.

Tony pulled out his cell phone. "Lucky for me, the same thing that makes them want to be here," he held up his hand, one Super Bowl ring glinting in the light, "gives me friends who are handy for intimidation. Excuse me for a second."

He walked back toward the sanctuary, holding the phone to his ear. Parker smiled and introduced me to Tony's parents.

"That article you did about our baby was just beautiful," Verna Okerson said, sniffling and squeezing one of my hands in both of hers.

"I'm so glad you liked it." My voice caught and she squeezed tighter.

We chatted, Parker checking the heavy stainless Tag Heuer on his wrist every two minutes, until Tony returned.

"Thank God, traffic was light." He glanced toward the Heavens. "There'll be two linebackers on the front door and one suitably-scary teammate on the other entrances in twenty minutes."

Parker and I watched as Tony showed his parents the display in the welcome center. Verna nearly collapsed looking at the photo table, and I turned away.

"I don't think I've ever been to a funeral with bouncers," I said.

Parker raised his head and grinned. "Welcome to professional sports."

"Sad, that they should have to worry about this today."

"It goes with the territory. Tony understands that. You want to be famous and have media coverage of the stuff you want them to cover, you have to manage them trying to get a piece of things you don't want them in."

I nodded.

People started to file in not long after Tony's friends showed up. I watched the back of the sanctuary carefully, but didn't see anyone who looked to be overtly recording anything. Most of the pews were packed with teenagers, their faces every variety of red and tear-streaked imaginable. I recognized a lot of folks from the school's faculty and staff, too.

Parker looked around. "I bet the whole high school is here," he whispered as the pastor closed the opening prayer.

I bet it was more like the whole town. Even Elmer was in a far right pew, looking somber in his starched gray shirt and shined shoes.

I scanned the crowd as the football coach took the podium and launched into a eulogy about what a hard worker and determined kid TJ was. He was followed by the baseball coach, the high school principal, and two teachers. I hung in there pretty okay until the pastor called Tony's name.

Parker's head snapped up as his friend made his way from the front pew to the red-carpeted stage. "How is he going to do this?"

"You're asking the wrong person."

Tony leaned his big hands on the sides of the podium and took a deep breath. "I came up here today to talk to you folks about who my son was. But now that I'm standing here looking at the faces of the people who miss him so much, I'm glad I made notes. My wife, Ashton, myself, and our parents would like to thank you all for being here." He picked up a few sheets of printer paper and held them up.

"This is what I had planned to say. And I apologize for putting him on the spot, but I wonder if I might ask my friend Grant Parker to come say it for me."

"Shit. I'm going to cry," Parker said.

"You'll be great."

Parker stood and made his way to the front of the room, swiveling heads following his progress up the aisle. I reached for the tissue box. As I turned toward it, my eyes lit on a young blond girl, lithe and pretty, shrinking into the end of the pew across and one behind from where I sat. She was wearing a black sundress, her slight shoulders caved over as she sobbed. By the time Parker started talking, her whole body was shaking.

Was this Evelyn the stalker? The description fit. Not that she was the only blonde in the place, but she was tall and pretty like Ashton said, and she was certainly more upset than the rest of the girls I could see.

Watching her saved me from losing what little control I had during Parker's impromptu eulogy, which started off with teaching TJ to throw a baseball and moved on to Tony's comments. The speech focused on the fact that TJ was a happy, helpful boy with a big heart who just happened to have a good arm. That's how Tony and Ashton wanted their son remembered.

"For the way he lived, not the way he died," Parker said. "We love you, Teej. We'll miss you every day."

Suspected-Evelyn sobbed hardest when Parker said the last words, and I dabbed my eyes with a Kleenex, keeping them on her.

I passed Parker the tissue box when he took his seat, then stood and sang along with *Amazing Grace* and *How Great Thou Art*. Bowing my head for the closing prayer, I couldn't resist stealing glances at the girl as the pastor's soft tenor carried through the church.

She was a hot mess by the time she stood to file out to the reception, which was through an annex in the community room. We lost her in the crowd, but I had a hunch I knew where to look.

"I'll catch up," I whispered to Parker, squeezing his hand. "I think I might have spotted stalker girl."

He raised an eyebrow. "She's here? That's brave, if she killed him, don't you think?" His voice was quiet, but loud enough to turn the heads of the people immediately around us.

"Parker!" I shushed him.

"Sorry," he whispered.

I ducked into the ladies room. There was a line of three women who moved through and did their business quickly, anxious to get to the smells wafting from the community hall. Nothing like a funeral to bring out the inner Aunt Bea in folks.

I leaned on the wall and watched the door that didn't open for three cycles through the stalls. When the room was empty, except for me, the blonde girl came out, her makeup smeared and face swollen.

She stepped to the sink, but spotted me and flinched before she managed to get cold water on her face. "I thought I was alone," she said, her voice hoarse.

"I didn't mean to startle you. I just need to wash my hands." I stepped to the sink. "I'm sorry for your loss. It seems like TJ was a great guy."

"He was the best. At everything." She sniffled, turning the water on.

"You were friends?"

"I—" she splashed water on her face, tiny droplets clinging to her lashes when she looked up at me. "Yes. He was special."

I dried my hands and put one out. "I'm Nichelle."

She shook my hand. "Evelyn. Nice to meet you." Bingo.

"It's very nice to meet you, too."

I followed her to the community hall, trying to make small talk about school and getting nowhere. When the doors opened, she slipped inside with her head down, muttered a goodbye in my direction, and scurried to a corner like a mouse in a roomful of emaciated lions.

"Nothing going on there," I muttered, watching her grab a glass of iced tea and sip it as she played with her hair.

"Where?" Parker asked from behind me.

I turned and found him holding a Dixie plate piled high with fried chicken, ribs, half a dozen kinds of casserole, and three biscuits.

My stomach growled. "Do you have a hollow leg, or something?" I asked as he shoveled cheesy hash browns into his face.

"Good metabolism, I guess." He shrugged. "What'd you find in the bathroom?"

I nodded toward Evelyn. "It's her. The girl Ashton was telling me about the other night. She's torn up. You should've seen her when you were talking. Nicely done, by the way. Not a dry eye in the place."

"Thanks. I guess. So, you think she's upset because she thought she was in love with him, or because she feels guilty?"

"No way to tell. I tried to talk to her, but I struck out." I watched from behind Parker or the corner of my eye, trying not to be too obvious. Evelyn stayed by the drink table, toying with a napkin, her eyes darting around the room. I followed them and found that they lit often on two groups of kids who stood in circles, whispering and shaking heads, or laughing.

"Jesus, they might as well point," I said.

"Who?" Parker asked around half a biscuit.

"The kids who are milling around talking about that girl."

"It's high school. You expect something different?" He swallowed.

"I guess I've tried to block it out." I turned for the buffet, wanting to snag a piece of chicken and some banana pudding before Tony's former teammates demolished everything.

I picked up a plate and had just grabbed a chicken leg when an indignant cry came from my elbow. "You!"

I flung the chicken in the air when I jumped, watching it fly end-over-end toward a group of large men in dark suits. It seemed to defy the laws of physics, taking forever to cross the room. Just when I cringed and started to cover my face as it flipped toward a huge expanse of bald head, one of the guys grinned, snatching it out of midair. He took a bite and waved at me.

"Nice hands, Petey," someone behind me called.

Something to be said for tossing chicken in a room full of professional athletes, I guess.

"Can't let that secret recipe go to waste," Petey replied, taking another bite.

I spun toward whoever was so annoyed at my presence and found myself staring at a broad white hat. I looked under it and discovered Miss Dorothy from the roadhouse parking lot showdown. Oops.

"Hello, Miss Dorothy." I smiled my best I-have-no-idea-why-you're-mad smile.

She did not bite. "I cannot believe you wrote that..." She sputtered. "That...you defended that..." She pinched her lips together and balled up her fists, taking a deep breath. "How dare you call that house of smut anything but what it is," she shouted.

The chatter around us fell silent. I kept my eyes on Dorothy, but felt every other cornea in the place on me.

"My job is to tell both sides of the story, which is exactly what I did," I said calmly, keeping the smile in place. "If you disagree, you're welcome to submit a letter to the editor. The email address is on our website."

"And we all know how handy Miss Dorothy is with the Internet, don't we, boys?" The booming voice came from my left and I bit the inside of my cheek to hold in a giggle, turning toward Amos. He nodded in my direction.

"Nice. I even reposted it on my Facebook. So my wife would see it." He shot Dorothy a pointed look. "I suggest every man in the county do the same," he bellowed.

I smiled a thank you. "I appreciate that, but I don't think this is the best place for this conversation."

"I'm sorry I didn't let you quote me, now." He winked.

"Well I'm sorry I did," Dorothy stomped a foot. "You were right, Amos, you tried to tell me she'd make me look a fool, and I should have listened."

I glanced around for reinforcements, my eyes lighting on Tony, who looked on with as much interest as he could muster.

A navy-pinstripe-suited arm appeared around Dorothy's shoulders. "Is it at all possible, Miss Dorothy, that you made yourself look a fool?" the pastor asked. "We had this discussion a month ago, and I believe this is just about what I told you would happen. Well, minus the Richmond media attention."

I had to cough to cover that laugh, and wouldn't have won any Oscars for the performance. Bob had texted me earlier to tell me the story was at seventeen hundred Facebook shares and climbing. And he'd had people tweeting it at intervals all day, so it was up to six thousand retweets by eleven a.m. The purple shade under Miss Dorothy's makeup told me it wasn't the right moment to mention that.

Dorothy squared her shoulders and shot me a withering look. "You tricked me."

"I don't think I misrepresented anything. I told you I was writing a news story, and I told you I was going to get the other side of it, and that's exactly what I did," I said gently. I didn't want the whole town making fun of her. "Miss Dorothy, have you ever been inside the club?"

"I would never." Her mouth gaped open, unable to finish the sentence, the color draining from her face.

"Is it murder if you give someone a stroke?" Parker whispered from behind me. I shot a heel back into his shin. "Ow." He hissed.

"I just think if you were to go inside the club, you might see it's not what you think. I found the ladies to be very nice. You might find the same."

"And some damned fine barbecue," someone hollered. A round of laughter and murmured agreement followed.

"Abigail did make the best sauce in the county," the pastor said, squeezing Dorothy's shoulder.

She snapped her mouth shut and shook her head. "I'd rather die."

"Better not say that around this bunch," Parker whispered. I kicked him again, turning my head. "Stop trying to make me laugh," I whispered sternly. "She really will have a stroke and it'll be your fault."

Dorothy tossed the general population of Mathews a final glare and stalked out of the room. A handful of other women scurried after her, and everyone else turned back to their food and conversations, drama forgotten.

I followed Parker to where Tony and Ashton sat, him alternately talking to people and trying to get her to eat, her staring at the wide expanse of white wall.

Parker laid a protective hand on Ashton's shoulder, but she didn't move to acknowledge it. The service was done, Tony's parents were watching the twins—those things had been her wind for days, and without them, her sails hung loose. She looked lost. And broken. It both wrung my heart and pissed me off, two emotions I wasn't sure I'd ever felt simultaneously.

My cell phone beeped a reminder, and I fished the prescription bottle out of my bag and shook an antibiotic capsule out, excusing myself to grab a glass of tea and swallow the pill. Tucking the bottle back into my clutch, I scanned the crowd for Evelyn, but didn't see her. Damn. She must have left while Dorothy was scolding me for telling the truth about Bobbi's club.

Stopping next to Parker, I spied Luke Bosley in the middle of a group of kids on the far wall.

"Lucky break," I murmured.

"What?" Parker asked.

I nodded toward Luke. "I need to borrow your baseball star power again, Parker."

"A football star isn't helpful?" Tony looked up at us.

"Not for this, I don't think," I said. "I'm so sorry. Excuse us for a second."

I grabbed Parker's arm and hauled him away.

"That's him," I said.

"Who?"

"The boy. Mr. I-get-to-play-now."

He nodded understanding, turning on the megawatt grin that made women who didn't know a slider from a swan dive read our sports page—and star-struck pitchers feel chatty.

Parker didn't even have to wave. He simply made eye contact. Luke pushed through a pair of girls who were giggling at his every word to pump Parker's hand as though Texas crude might spurt from his fingertips.

The girls frowned, and I rolled my eyes, hanging back a couple of steps so Parker could work his spell. In less than a minute, he had one arm around Luke's shoulders, leading him to the side door and a quiet courtyard. I followed.

"I was just a little kid when you played for the Cavs, Mr. Parker, but watching you pitch, and hearing my dad talk about your arm, was what made me want to be pitcher."

The way I'd heard it from the coach, a whole lot of nagging from his father was responsible for that, but okay.

Parker smiled a thank you. "I hear you're the one to watch for the Eagles now, Luke."

"You did?" Luke's eyes showed white all around the hazel. "For real? From who?"

"I have some friends out here."

Luke became very interested in his black loafers. "Mr. Okerson is your friend, huh? Your speech was nice."

"TJ was a good kid. I taught him to throw a ball when he was just a little guy."

"You said. I'm sorry for your loss, Mr. Parker."

"Call me Grant."

Luke's head snapped up and he smiled. "No, sir. My momma will pitch a fit."

Parker chuckled. "Lose the 'mister' at least. I'm getting an old man complex."

"Yes, sir."

"I thought you might like some pointers, if you're leading the team. The season is just starting. It's a lot of pressure."

Luke nodded. "I can take it." His eyes flitted back to his shoes, then to a statue of an angel behind Parker. "I wish it didn't have to be like this. Why did TJ have to be so good, you know? When he got hurt, I thought my chance was coming, but then he got better. Why—" He dropped his head back, staring toward the Heavens.

I held my breath, and it looked like Parker was holding more than that. Something resembling rage simmered beneath his understanding nod.

Was Luke about to confess? I'd seen stranger. And kids are often guilty of running off at the mouth. I stared, willing him to go on. He kept his eyes on the clouds.

The door that led back into the church opened, and a stout woman in a navy suit that had last been fashionable in nineteen ninety-seven stepped outside.

"Lucas Cameron, there you are." She shook her head and tapped her watch. "It's past time for your medicine. And you eating all this junk, too."

"Coming, Momma." Luke said. His eyes shot from her to Parker to me, and he blinked like he hadn't noticed me before and offered Parker a hand. "It was nice to meet you. Thanks for taking the time to talk to me."

"My pleasure," Parker said, doing an admirable job of holding his tone even. If I didn't know him so well, I wouldn't have been able to tell anything was bothering him. As it was, Luke was lucky to pull back unbroken fingers.

Luke moved toward the door and Parker stopped him halfway. "Hey, kid?"

"Yes, sir?" Luke turned back, squinting into the April sunshine and shading his eyes with one hand.

"You go to the party? On Wednesday night?"

"No, sir. I'm behind in history." He tossed a glance at his mother, who nodded a what-am-I-going-to-do-with-this-kid and waved him inside.

Parker turned to me when the door clicked shut. "Was it just me, or—?" He let the unspoken words hang in the air.

I shook my head. "It was not just you. Hell, my heart is still racing. I thought you had him. Nice, asking him about the party off guard like that."

"You buy it?"

"Nope. He answered too fast. My guess is mom told him he couldn't go, and since she was standing right there, he blurted the no. But is there another reason he doesn't want us to think he was there? Maybe. Sure seemed like he almost said something interesting before his mom came outside."

"That's not enough though, is it?"

"It's a hell of a start. He just passed Evelyn on my suspect list."

13

The lavender sky deepened to indigo outside the church windows as we chatted and cleaned up. By the time we got to the car, I was glad I'd already filed my "have-to" court copy for the day.

"I need to send Bob an update," I said, tossing Parker my car keys. "Can you drive?"

After climbing into my seat, I opened my email, hoping I had something from Kyle. Or Aaron. Anyone who could be any help with the moonshine angle.

I'd gathered empty cups and picked-over plates for an hour, turning Luke's dazed monologue over in my head. Was he feeling guilty about hurting TJ, or just glad his rival was out of the way? It was impossible to tell, backtracking through what he'd said. Evelyn had vanished during the great chicken brouhaha of Mathews County, and I figured she was glad Dorothy had made a scene because it got everyone's attention and gave her a chance to slip out. Having spoken to both of the kids, I was no closer to knowing if one of them was actually the killer. If there was a killer.

So my brain went back to trying to find cause of death. For the seventy billionth time in my career, I wished forensics labs weren't so overworked. Having tox screen results would be ever so helpful.

"How likely do you think it is that TJ got hold of a bad batch of moonshine?" I asked Parker, looking up from my email. I had fifty-seven new messages, but none interesting enough to read right then.

"He was training, but it was vacation." He trailed off and appeared to consider that. "I don't know. The pain meds make me think he wouldn't have had too much of anything."

"Well, we're assuming he took any of the pills. I mean, if he didn't take them all, like the sheriff thinks, what if he didn't take any of them?"

"Where'd they go?"

"Into the bay? Down the toilet? On the Internet for sale?" I paused, considering that. "Do pharmacies track lot numbers on prescriptions?" Maybe I could figure out where the pills went, if they weren't in TJ's stomach.

I opened my web browser and turned to my trusty friend Google for the answer to that. They did not. Damn.

Parker was quiet, lost in thought from the look on his face. We were halfway to Gloucester before either of us realized we'd missed the turn to the freeway.

"Sorry," Parker muttered a curse under his breath and jerked the car into the turn lane. I looked up from an email I was sending Bob—slowly, thanks to the spotty signal—and spied the sign for Bobbi Jo's club less than a football field up on the right.

"You want to go check out the roadhouse?" I asked, wanting to show him I'd been right about the place, and jonesing for a glass of Grandma Abigail's sweet tea. Calories, schmalories. That stuff was worth every apchagi it took to work it off. Plus, maybe I could get someone to answer a few questions.

He raised an eyebrow at me. "I don't need domestic drama."

"You're in my car, so they can't trace your plate. Anyhow, you're not married. And Mel would love this place. They have the best iced tea in Virginia, hand to God."

"Why not?" he asked. "I bet I'm the only guy with a date."

"I bet I'm the only customer with better shoes than the dancers."

The parking lot was fairly full, for a club on a Monday evening. I followed Parker inside to find it just as packed as I'd seen it on Saturday. Miss Cirque du Soleil was hanging upside down on the pole and Parker's eyes widened. I scrutinized her attire, making sure my story hadn't been skewed by the fact that I liked Bobbi.

"See?" I spun to Parker with a triumphant grin. "Not only is she wearing a bikini top, it's taped in place! Otherwise, her boobs would be falling out of it every three seconds with all that flipping. Does anything about that sound indecent to you?"

"There's not much indecent about her." He tore his eyes from the stage and shook a dazed look off his face. "One word to Mel and I'll never talk to you again, Lois."

"Whatever. Have your secret." I rolled my eyes.

"Nichelle!" Bobbi's voice came from behind me and I turned, then stumbled back into Parker when she tackle-hugged me, crushing my ribs. She was strong for a teeny little thing.

"Hey there," I said when I could breathe.

"Your story rocked," she stepped back and grinned. "Look around. It's Monday. Monday! There are guys I've never seen in here, both from the county and not. Some of them even said they'll bring their wives for dinner. You are my very own personal Annie Sullivan."

"Not sure how much of a miracle worker I am, but I'm glad someone liked the story. Miss Dorothy nearly caused a food fight at a funeral today with her disapproval."

Bobbi waved Parker and I into a round booth on the far wall and called for a waitress. "Bring them whatever they want," she said. "On me. Nichelle, honey, hold that thought. I have a couple things to do on the floor here, and I'll be right back to join you."

I ordered a pitcher of tea and a C-cup, and Parker asked for a beer and a double-D (a half rack of ribs, plus the chicken). That was some metabolism, all right.

The waitress sashayed off, but was flagged down by another table before she made it three feet.

Parker watched the scene with feigned disinterest, but I choked back guffaws at the way his eyes trailed to the girls every thirty seconds, no matter how hard he tried not to watch them.

"Even with someone like Mel at home?" I asked. "Men really are all hopeless."

"Nothing personal," he said. "I think it might be biological. Survival of mankind, and all that."

I watched our server, who was on her third table since she'd taken our order and had a sea of them to cross between us and the bar. I stood.

"Enjoy the show. I'm going to get a glass of tea before my throat completely dries out."

If he answered, I didn't hear him.

Four whistles and a pinched ass later, I leaned on the polished walnut bar and waved to the pretty redhead who was mixing drinks faster than I could type. She nodded a hello at me and held up one finger before she drained the contents of a shaker into a glass of ice and added it to a tray.

A tall man in jeans and a red plaid button-down was next in line, and she leaned across the bar and asked for his order a second time when some of the guys started hooting. I looked to the stage and found a new dancer in a black bikini with silver sequins and a pair of precious open-toe silver stilettos with bows at the ankles. Maybe the dancers did have better shoes.

I turned back to find the bartender pulling a mason jar full of clear liquid from under the counter. She poured three fingers of it into a highball glass, screwed the lid back on, and stashed it back out of sight. Captain flannel tipped his white straw cowboy hat, dropped a few bills into her tip jar, and took his drink back to a table full of guys.

Hot damn. My eyes stayed fixed on the spot where the jar had been, Bobbi's comment about buying everything she possibly could from local folks running through my head on fast forward.

"Honey, what can I get you?" The bartender's pitch was high and irritated, like she'd asked the question more than once.

"Sorry." I smiled. "Just a glass of iced tea, please."

"At least you're easy," she smiled, filling a tall glass with ice and grabbing a pitcher.

"I know a couple guys who would disagree with that," I said.

She put the glass on the bar and I downed half of it in one gulp. Seriously. Like liquid crack. She refilled it. "It's all about finding the one who's worth it," she said. "Not easy to do when you work in a place like this."

"This place is fairly tame when you think about what it could be," I said.

"Bobbi runs a tight ship, no joke." She picked up an order chit and turned to grab a couple of bottles, pouring both liquors and some sour mix into a clean shaker. "But still. When this is what you see of men all day…"

"I hear you," I said over more hooting, thinking about the glassy look that had even come over Parker. I could imagine a girl would get jaded pretty quick. I scanned the crowd for our waitress, who was now across the fifty-yard line, but stopped at another table, and turned back to order Parker a Sam Adams.

Glasses in hand, I stepped away from the bar, the mason jar bouncing around my thoughts. I stole a look at the cowboy and his friends. They were all drinking beer, except him. He tossed his glass back as he watched the show, setting it on the table empty. I stared, halfway wanting him to slump over and solve the case for me, then feeling like I was going straight to Hell for having such a thought. He kept laughing and talking. I watched for so long one of his buddies noticed, and the guy turned and winked at me when his friend elbowed him and whispered something in his ear. I felt my cheeks heat and smiled, scurrying back to my table to gather Parker's jaw from the floor.

"What is it with y'all?" I asked as I sat down. "I know you've been to racier places than this, and you can look at a real live naked woman that you can touch anytime you damn well please."

He ran one hand through his perfectly-tousled blond hair. Every strand fell right back into place. "I think you need testosterone to understand, because I have no explanation for you." He sipped his beer and smiled. "Thanks."

"Our server is juggling seventy tables. I think Bobbi was understaffed for the crowd that turned out tonight."

"Your story was spot on." He caught my gaze with his green eyes. "I know you wondered after the old bat made a scene this afternoon, but this place is cool, on many levels. You did a good thing here. Stop worrying."

I smiled. "Thanks, Parker. You're a pretty good friend, you know it?"

"I'm good at everything. It's the price of being me."

"Modest, too."

"Honesty is much more endearing than modesty."

"You are too much." I drained my tea glass.

"That's what she said."

He caught me flat-footed with the last and I snorted iced tea when I laughed. Ouch. Tea trickled out my nose, my eyes watering because it burned. I ducked my head and groped for a napkin. "Jesus, Parker."

"I don't think I've made a girl snort anything since the sixth grade." He handed me a tissue. "I feel accomplished now."

"So glad I could be part of it."

He opened his mouth to say something else just as Bobbi fell into the booth beside me.

"Damn, I'm going to need to hire more servers if this keeps up," she huffed. "Running drinks is tiring."

"This is busier than you expected to be tonight, then?"

"Ohmigod, yes," she said. "We usually get about fifteen regulars in for dinner on Mondays, maybe two of whom could give a damn about the show. The girls have been after me to close on Monday nights for weeks, because they don't make much in tips. I was thinking about it, too, but I don't think I'll get any complaints tonight."

"No complaints from this corner." Parker smiled and offered a hand.

"I'm sorry, y'all—Grant Parker, Bobbi Jo, Bobbi Jo, this is Parker. He's a big fan of yours."

"Well, my grandaddy was a big fan of yours," she said. "I don't suppose you'd sign something for me? A napkin, or a menu? Made out to the club. I'll start a wall of fame."

"Anything you want." He smiled.

She trailed her eyes over him in a way that said Mel might not appreciate what she wanted, and I jumped back into the conversation.

"I'm glad the story helped," I said, trying to figure out how to ask about the moonshine without being too obvious and coming up with nothing. I took a deep breath and hoped my brownie points for pulling in so much business would stretch that far. "Hey, Bobbi, when you said the other day about buying local stuff," I toyed with the salt shaker, "does that extend to the liquor y'all serve?"

She stared for a minute. "I'm afraid I don't know if I follow you."

"I think you do," I said. "I think I saw a mason jar pop out from under the bar when I went to get my tea."

She sighed. "There are things that are different out here than they are in Richmond."

"And there are companies that produce moonshine that is regulated by the ABC," I said. "I have a hunch that's not the kind you're serving. I also have a suspicion that some backwoods shine might have been involved in the deaths of a couple of kids out here."

"TJ Okerson and his little girlfriend? Everyone says it was suicide," she said, her eyes widening.

"Listen, I don't want it getting around town that anyone thinks it might not be, and the sheriff decidedly disagrees with me," I said. "Until the tox screens come back, no one knows anything for sure, but there was moonshine—the local, unregulated kind—at both of the scenes, and I'm wondering if there was something wrong with it. A bad batch, maybe. Or a couple of spiked jars."

"Well, if the batch was bad, why isn't anyone else sick?" Bobbi asked.

"I don't know," I said, my eyes flitting to the big guy in the red shirt, who was still fine. "Maybe someone put something in it. But to find that out, I have to find out where it came from. I hear there are three stills that run on the island these days. Do you buy from all of them?"

"Just one. I've known the family forever. Went to school with the guys. They look a little scary, maybe, but they wouldn't hurt anybody."

"Do you mind if I have a look at the jar you have?"

"If I lose my ABC license, I'll have to close down," she said.

"I'm not looking to print where I got this particular information," I said. "I just want to see if it's the same kind."

She shrugged. "Sure."

The waitress set food in front of us just as Bobbi stood up.

"You two enjoy your dinner," Bobbi said. "I've got work to do, anyway. Just come over to the bar when you're through."

She excused herself. Parker bit into a rib and chewed thoughtfully, smiling at me as he swallowed.

"This is good barbecue. Hey, don't take this wrong, but are you sure the moonshine thing isn't just an interesting side story? I've met you. Poking into criminal crap that people don't want you nosing around in is kind of your schtick."

"I'm not sure about anything," I said. "The more I think about this, the more convoluted it gets. All the what ifs and possibilities are enough to give me a headache. I mean, start with the most obvious one: what if the sheriff is right?"

"I don't think so."

"But you're too close to the story to see that clearly."

"Are you? You told me you thought something was off from the get-go."

I chewed a mouthful of beans while I considered that.

"I did. I do." I sighed. "But, I have my own baggage with this story, Parker."

"I caught that when we talked to Bob this morning. You feel like sharing?"

I shook my head. "Way too long a story for a place this loud and crowded. But I've been playing devil's advocate with myself, trying to figure out if I'm projecting into this case, and I really don't think so. Trouble is, the puzzle is entirely too blurry for me to see what's going on if we're right and the sheriff's wrong. Some days, I miss good old-fashioned homicides. Smoking guns and open and shut cases are way less stressful."

He finished the ribs and moved on to his chicken. "Seriously, what is in this sauce?"

"Crack?" I grinned. "I think it's in the tea, too."

"Maybe. Anyway. I don't know how you do your job and stay off antide-pressants. And I know you've caught shit from Bob before about some of your detective stories. But I'm with you on this one. Something's not right, and we seem to be the only people who give a damn about that. I'm really glad I have you in my corner."

"I'm not sure how much good I'm doing you. I can't figure which end is up, but something's definitely weird."

I wolfed down the rest of my food and another glass of tea and stood. "I'm going to go check out the local firewater. Be right back."

"Don't drink it," he called as I turned.

Check. I'd never tried anything stronger than a whiskey shot at a frat party once, and that made me sick.

I spotted Bobbi behind the bar, trying to help keep up with drink orders, and waited at one end until it looked like she had room to breathe. I waved, and she crooked one finger and raised the walk-through on the far end.

"I can trust you, right? You didn't make us look like smut peddlers in the paper, despite what Dorothy told you." She offered an uncertain smile that didn't quite reach her eyes. "This place is everything to me."

"I get it. I really do." I squeezed her hand. "These children were everything to their parents, too."

She nodded, pulling the jar from its hidey-hole and handing it over. "I've never heard of it making anyone sick," she said. "I mean, other than normal, hungover sick."

I turned the jar over in my hands. It didn't have a label.

"The one I saw at the bridge had a label on it," I said. "Does this ever have one?"

"The Sidell boys say that's stupid, because it makes it traceable," she said, shaking her head. "But I know some of them do. I've seen more moonshine than you can shake a tree limb at."

I looked sideways at her. "You grew up here," I said. "The sheriff said the kids have parties on the beach and at the bridge all the time."

Bobbi Jo laughed. "What else are they going to do?"

"Are there always a lot of kids?" I leveled a serious gaze at her. "Could you kill someone without being noticed?"

Her eyes widened. "I've never had occasion to wonder about that. I suppose it depends on how you went about it. Is it loud enough to mask gunfire? No. Someone would call the sheriff. But could you drown someone, or strangle them, maybe? If you were strong enough and got them away from everyone, sure."

I unscrewed the cap on the jar and smelled the contents, totally clearing what was still blocked of my sinuses. I shoved the jar and lid back toward Bobbi, my eyes watering again. "People drink this?"

"Never understood it myself, but it's a time-honored tradition. That's why I keep it. A lot of the guys who come in won't drink anything else."

"Maybe it burned off all their taste buds years ago." I swiped at my nose.

She laughed. "Could be. My granddaddy ran moonshine back in the day. Had the fastest car in ten counties. You know that's how NASCAR got started, right? Moonshine runners souping up their cars to outrun the law?" She screwed the lid back on the jar and stashed it.

"I heard that. This place is full of interesting history." I smiled. I liked Bobbi, but more than that, I respected what she was trying to do for her hometown, and the creativity with which she'd gone about it.

"My grandaddy used to tell a story about John Lennon coming into town once," she said. "He and Yoko wanted a retreat where no one would bother them, and they bought a place on the bay. A historical landmark with a mill that dates back to the revolution and was used to grind grain for Washington's troops."

"You're kidding. John Lennon lived in Mathews?"

"Well, no. He was killed before they got the house renovated. It sat empty for years, and the story goes that Yoko gave it to charity. The charity sold it to the current owners. But it's a fun bit of trivia."

I nodded, filing that away. I might be able to fit it into a story in passing, or maybe look it up and do a sidebar if I ever figured this mess out.

Bobbi stared at me for a long second. "Do you really think someone murdered those kids? I can't remember the last time there was a murder in Mathews."

"That's because it was before you were born," I said. "I checked. I know it doesn't happen out here very often. And I'm not really sure what I think. All I know is my gut says there's something funky, and I seem to be the only one who thinks so. Funny, I usually hope I'm wrong when I'm doing stuff like this, but here, I'm not sure what to hope. The whole situation is just sad."

"That it is. TJ was a good kid."

"You knew him?" The way most folks seemed to feel about newcomers, I was a little surprised by that.

"My boyfriend is an assistant football coach at the high school. I wish I could've gone to the service today. I was going to, but then things went bonkers here and I couldn't get away."

I nodded. Everyone really did know everyone else. I kind of thought that was better in theory than in practice.

"Thanks for your help, Bobbi."

"It didn't look like it was much help," she laughed.

"Do you know who else makes moonshine? The jar I saw had three x's across the middle of it."

"That came from the Parsons place," she said. "They're on the island itself, and very—you ever see *Deliverance*?"

"I have." I raised my eyebrows. "I'm not sure I want to meet the living version."

"Probably best to stay clear unless you're packing," she advised.

Fabulous.

I dodged pinching fingers that had been through another round of drinks and found Parker downing the last of his beer, all the food baskets empty.

"You find what you were looking for?" he asked.

"Of course not. It couldn't be that easy. There's moonshine, but it's not the same kind Syd had. Moreover, Bobbi says the dudes who make the one Sydney drank are bad news."

"The kind of bad news that means you might get hurt messing with them?"

"But also the kind that means there might have been something wrong with the damned alcohol. So I really want to check that out. But I like breathing."

"What about your friend—the federal agent guy? Can he help?"

"I don't know. I'm working on that." Kyle would be a good person to have along. Except, of course, that he would never agree to let me tag along to a call like that. And what if he got shot chasing a lead I took him? I'd never get over that.

"You ready to get out of here?" I asked.

"Anytime you are," he said. "We're not telling Mel where we had dinner, right?"

"Mel will not give a rat's ass about you watching girls dance around in bikinis. But whatever you say."

He dug a few bills out of his pocket and dropped them in the pickle jar on the way out. "Just the same," he said.

My cell phone binged as we stepped outside and I pulled it out. I had seventeen texts from Bob.

"WHERE ARE YOU?" The most recent one read, all caps.

"Shit. That's never good." I flipped my scanner on when I got in the car, but it didn't pick up Richmond feed out there.

I dialed Bob's cell.

"What's wrong?" Parker started the engine.

"Don't know." I held up one finger.

"What the hell have you done?" Bob demanded when he picked up.

"I was covering the Okerson funeral all afternoon, just like you told me to," I said. "Didn't you get my email?"

"Of course I got your email," he barked. "And I don't appreciate you playing coy with me. Nichelle, this was supposed to be an exclusive. And you always play your investigative stuff close to the vest. So why the hell did the *Post* just tweet a teaser for a story questioning the suicide claim?"

I caught a breath and held it. "I have no idea."

"I'm supposed to believe that?" he asked. "How could they have gotten it? You, me, and Parker are the only people who know about it."

And Bobbi Jo. And the Okersons. And Sydney's mother. And Joey. And Kyle. But I didn't think it pertinent to mention that.

"The sheriff?" I asked. I couldn't imagine why he'd tell another reporter something he'd been vehemently denying to me all week.

I heard a female voice in the background. A distinctly whiny, high-pitched voice that hit my ears like railroad ties on a chalkboard. Shelby. I couldn't understand what she said, but Bob's voice tightened more, if that were even possible.

"They're running it tomorrow morning. I want something from you by nine. And I need the funeral write-up, too."

Crap. Since that was an exclusive, I'd planned to send it in after I got home.

I checked the clock. "Bob, it's seven-fifteen."

"And I am holding the front for copy I expect to have in my email by nine. Nichelle, I—" He stopped. "I don't want to believe you leaked this to the *Post* to try to impress them. I think I know you better than that. But you better hope you have more than they do, and that they have some other source. Because Andrews has gotten an earful of your D.C. ambitions this afternoon, and he's not happy."

Dammit. The publisher back on my case was not what I needed.

"Bob, I would never—"

"I told him that. Do not let me down."

"Yes, sir." I hung up, my mind frantically spinning through what I might be able to do with what I had in an hour. And what I should give up and what I should keep quiet.

"What gives?" Parker asked when I slung the phone into the dash.

"The *Post* has a story on possible foul play in TJ's death," I sighed, digging for my notebook. I paused. "Tony played in D.C. Do you think he might have talked to someone?"

Parker shook his head. "Not likely. I went through things with him. He promised he wouldn't talk to anyone but you. But I don't know that for a hundred percent."

I chewed my lip. "I don't want to intrude, but is there any chance we can go there and I can borrow a computer to write a story? Bob wants mine on the web tonight."

He laid on the gas and headed for the island. "They won't mind. And maybe someone else looking at it will wake the sheriff up?"

I nodded as the fields, nearly swallowed by the night, blurred past the windows. I wanted someone to take my theory seriously. But I also wanted the story to myself. Would it be good or bad if I beat the *Post* to this headline?

14

We fought through the media circus at the gate and I huffed out another aggravated sigh.

"I should learn to keep my mouth shut, and maybe the universe will quit feeling it necessary to prove me wrong," I said. "I was just telling Bob they'd all take off after the funeral. I bet they got ten miles outside town before the tweet from the *Post* hit and they turned right the hell around."

"I wish they'd leave Tony and Ashton alone," Parker said, steering past the cameras and through the gate, watching the rearview for hitchhiking reporters.

"That, too."

Inside, Tony handed Parker a Corona and swore to us both they hadn't talked to a soul besides me and their families. He even called both sets of grandparents and quizzed them. No one admitted to having leaked their suspicions to the press. Since the story wasn't up yet, I couldn't see what the Post had, so I was writing blind when I sat down, trying to pick what to reveal and what to hold back. I wanted to beat them. But I didn't want to give away too much until I had the whole story.

.   .   .

Two-time Super Bowl MVP Tony Okerson and his wife, Ashton, buried their only son Monday, both unconvinced that local law enforcement in Mathews County are correct in their assertion that Tony Junior took his own life.

"I know my son," Ashton said in a tearful exclusive interview with the Richmond Telegraph. *"My baby did not do this."*

Ashton holds a degree in psychology from the University of Virginia and said her son had none of the signs of being suicidal.

"He was a happy kid," she said, her husband sitting beside her and nodding agreement. "I've been over every detail in my mind, looking for what I might have missed, and there wasn't anything. TJ was not depressed. He wasn't bullied. He was happy."

I quoted the sheriff last, purely so I could tell myself the story was balanced. No reason to believe it was anything but what it looked like, he insisted. I left out the moonshine, because I knew damned good and well no one but me knew about that. I wondered as I read back through the story if Lyle was the one who'd talked to the *Post*. He'd been around all week, and his stories were good, peppered with the kind of local flavor and insider comments that an out-of-town reporter would never know to look for. I'd seen him at the funeral that afternoon, too. But why would he talk to them? He didn't seem interested in notoriety. He'd said he wanted everyone to go away and leave the town alone.

I fired through my exclusive on the funeral next, my mind still half on the *Post*. What if they'd talked to someone I hadn't?

Sitting back in the chair, I sent both stories to Bob at five to nine, then clicked into Tony's web browser. I pulled up the *Post's* twitter feed and found the tweet that ruined my evening. *"Was it really suicide? Why some suspect foul play in the #TJOkerson case, only in tomorrow's edition."*

What. The. Everloving. Hell?

I dropped Parker at the office a little after midnight and grabbed my cell phone as soon as he shut the car door behind him.

"Miller," Kyle said sleepily.

"I'm sorry I woke you, but I need a favor," I said hurriedly, pointing the car toward my house.

"Nichelle? Hang on." The line was quiet for a second and then he came back on. "Sorry. I'm here. What's up?"

I wondered for a split second why he'd put me on hold, then told myself I had no reason to wonder about such things. And I didn't like the bite of jealousy that came with the thought, so I flipped my attention back to my story.

"I need tox results on TJ Okerson and Sydney Cobb. Like, now. And the sheriff in Mathews has less than no pull with anyone at the lab. I'm hoping you have a friend there you can light a fire under for me."

"I might." The hedging tone in his voice sent one of my eyebrows up.

"You don't sound sure about that," I said.

"I guess I'm not sure you want me to work the angle I have," he said. "There's a biologist there I've talked to about a couple of cases. She's cute. Seems to like me."

I didn't like the sound of that one little bit. And wanted to smack myself for feeling that way. Kyle was a good guy. He deserved to be happy.

"If she can process the samples they have faster, take her to lunch or something," I said, trying to unclench my teeth as the words slid through.

"I'm not interested—" he began.

"It's fine," I interrupted. "Really. Sorry. It's late, I'm beat. I could really use that report. Thanks."

"No problem."

"Kyle? One more thing?"

"Yeah?"

"If you're going to go charm her, ask for a full panel. I'd bet my shoe closet Sheriff Zeke asked them to screen for Vicodin and blood alcohol content. I'd like to know what else is there, if there's anything."

"You got it."

I went inside and fed Darcy, then tried to forget about Kyle's friend the biologist and focus on how the hell the *Post* was onto my story as I pulled the covers over me.

* * *

Tuesday was spent dodging media calls, appeasing my neglected Richmond sources, and avoiding pissy glares from Spence and Bob both. Thankfully, the *Post* hadn't printed anything about the moonshine, but they had so much of the rest of it dead to puzzling and unclear that I was afraid it was only a matter of time. They quoted the sheriff as having confirmed that Ashton and Tony suspected foul play, but who tipped them off in the first place was anyone's guess.

Aaron had an arrest in Monday's armed robbery, and my friend DonnaJo at the prosecutor's office had a seventeen-year-old going up on a capital murder charge over a drug deal gone bad. I sat through the opening arguments, fighting to keep my mind focused on the trial. Speeding back to the office, I didn't bother to work up a lead for the trial day one, instead running mentally through everyone I'd seen in Mathews in the past week.

By the time I'd filed both the trial and the robbery arrest stories, most of the other reporters were unplugging their computers and heading home, the section and copy editors talking about space and layouts. I clicked into my Internet browser, setting my scanner on my desk and turning up the volume. Being as I was in Richmond, I didn't want to miss anything else coming out of the PD. All I needed was to get on Aaron's shit list trying to help the Okersons.

I checked the clock. It was only a little after five, and Joey wasn't picking me up until seven-thirty.

Google, don't fail me now. I pored over public records for Mathews County, trying to figure out both what was going on, and how the *Post* knew there was anything going on.

I got nowhere on either front for a good while.

Pulling up the property tax records, I searched for the name Bobbi had mentioned as running triple-X moonshine. The family owned a house on the island that had passed through at least four generations. Cross-referencing the address in Google maps, I stared at the aerial satellite view. Trees obscured most of the property, save a little chunk of the roofline.

I slammed my hands down on my desk, wondering if it was possible for me to catch a teensy break on this one, and the silver frame that held a photo of my best friend Jenna's children clattered to the desktop. I stood it back up, staring at their adorable little smiles.

Family.

Everyone knew everyone.

Hot damn.

I pulled the marriage records for Mathews County and checked the last name from the property records, following the family tree all the way to sheriff Zeke. He was second cousin to the Parsons boys.

His whole "that's ABC police business" number made so much more sense as I stared at the trail on my screen. Sure, he was right about that, but at least now I knew why he was using it as an excuse to turn a blind eye to an illegal booze operation in his town.

Of course, it also meant I needed to tread carefully and make sure I had the story sewn up, because accusing the sheriff's cousin of murder could piss off said sheriff. Which I did not want to do.

Still mulling that, I noticed the clock and slapped the computer shut, shoving it into my bag and running for the elevator. I wanted to touch up my makeup and swap my white silk pants and coral top with matching strappy Manolos for a sexy dress and my newsprint Louboutins before Joey arrived..

Luckily, it was still too cool outside for me to have sweated off much of my makeup, so touching up only took a minute. I stepped into the last shoe as the doorbell rang.

Fixing a smile on my face and pulling in a deep breath I hoped would slow my pulse, I strode to the door. We'd never been on anything that seemed so much like a date. I might as well have been sixteen, waiting for a boy to come pin a corsage on me for the first time. Well. Except that boy had been Kyle.

But when I opened the door, I forgot all about Kyle. Joey leaned against the frame, looking downright dashing in a light gray suit, the emerald of his shirt perfect against his olive skin. There went my pulse again.

"You look beautiful," he said, his voice soft and low. He handed me a single, long-stemmed violet rose and laid a soft kiss on my cheek. Jesus, he smelled good.

I turned for the kitchen, looking for a vase for the rose, and he chuckled behind me. "I thought we were going out?"

"I have to put this in some water," I said.

"You like it? It's nearly the same color as your eyes."

I smiled, spinning back to him. "I love it. It's beautiful. Thank you."

Stretching up slightly, I only meant to brush my lips across his. He pulled me to him, slanting his mouth over mine in a much more serious kiss. I melted into his strong frame. The flower dropped to the floor, dead teenagers and moonshine falling away as I buried my fingers in his thick, dark hair.

One thing about Joey: he's a great kisser. Major league caliber. One arm cradled my shoulder, the other tightening around the small of my back as his lips parted. I returned the urgency, lightning flashing behind my eyelids as his tongue slid over mine. Sparks sped across my skin as his hand trailed up my spine, molding me to him. My toes scrunched inside my shoes, and I moved my hands to his chest, pushing the fabric of his jacket back over his shoulders.

He pulled back a millimeter, his eyes half-lidded and smoldering. "We are going out, aren't we?"

I swallowed the "we don't have to," before it popped through my lips, leaning back in his arms and trying to catch my breath. Dinner didn't sound nearly as appetizing as it had a few minutes earlier.

"We should." I trailed a row of tiny, soft kisses along his jaw and laid my head on his shoulder, taking long, deep breaths. His hands moved to stroke my hair.

"You sure? I still want to hear about those fantasies you were talking about the other night."

I let my breath out by degrees, reveling in the moment. I loved the way his voice rumbled in his chest when he talked, deep and strong and safe. It was an easy leap to wonder how it would sound if we were more horizontal.

I closed my eyes, letting the fantasy play for a few seconds.

Joey's lips. His hands. The things he could do with those lips and hands.

Moonshiners. Dead kids. Grieving parents.

Dammit, the things I sacrifice for my job.

I squeezed him for another second before I harnessed every ounce of willpower and stepped out of his arms.

"Where are we eating?" I asked, straightening my fitted forties-inspired black Calvin Klein dress. Hopefully nowhere I'd want to consume more than a few ounces of food, because the dress was already breathe-shallow snug.

"Well..." He let the word trail, his dark eyes flicking down the hallway toward my bedroom.

My heart jackhammered a few beats. I better get a Pulitzer for this.

I knelt and picked up the rose, laying it on the shelf of beach glass behind me. "I'll press this," I said, not trusting myself to stay in the house a millisecond longer. I stepped around him and walked down the steps. He pulled the door shut and locked it, following me to the car and opening my door.

"What are you hungry for?" He flashed a grin as he slid behind the wheel of his sleek black Lincoln.

"You cannot possibly understand how not hungry for food I am." I smiled as we started driving. "But I have to get this story. Not only do I have Tony and Ashton, grieving and wondering, now the *Post* has everybody and their dog out there looking for a killer."

"I saw that this morning. What happened?"

I sighed. "I got a big head? I had the exclusive with the parents and thought I had the story cornered. But, you know, I'm not the only nosy reporter around. Apparently, the *Post* has some folks who are better at being nosy."

"You're good at what you do. You'll get it."

"I hope so."

I wondered how, watching the familiar storefronts pass as he turned into Carytown. "Where are we going?"

He took a left into the parking lot at a chic French cafe. "This place good?"

"They have amazing bagel things they make fresh every day from French bread," I grinned. "I've only ever been here for breakfast."

"I have it on good authority that dinner is great, too." He shut off the engine and rounded the front of the car to open my door, pausing when he saw the lines creasing my forehead. "You're worried."

"Bob is annoyed with me. The publisher thinks I told the *Post* about TJ, thanks to our copy editor."

"You wouldn't do that." He dismissed the idea without a second thought, putting out a hand to help me out of the car. I grabbed it and hung on tighter than I should have, grateful tears pricking the backs of my eyes.

I blinked them away, clearing my throat. "Thank you."

"You have more integrity than anyone I've ever met," he said, holding my hand as we crossed the parking lot to the cafe door. He turned to me as he pulled it open. "It's one of the things I admire about you. Anyone who really knows you knows it. Your editor is nervous about losing the story, not about you being a mole for the *Post*. He'll come around."

I smiled a thank you at the hostess as we sat down, reaching across the table to squeeze Joey's fingers. "I needed to hear that today. Thanks."

"Glad to help." He returned the pressure, the look in his eyes making it very difficult to avoid crawling across the table and kissing him again. But the way my pulse and emotions were surging, that would lead to other things. Things that, there in the cushy booth, would lead to jail. So I kept my seat and smiled, instead.

He let go and tapped the menu, and I quickly settled on the rosemary chicken and turned my thoughts back to my story.

"The *Post* might have someone smarter than me, but they don't have you. Tell me about the guy we're talking to."

He sipped his water, and I found it easier to focus on his words if I skipped my eyes around the art on the walls or the pressed-plate ceiling, only stealing glances at him every few seconds.

"He does transportation and sales for a moonshining outfit out of Mathews," Joey said. "We have some mutual associates. There are several dry counties in Maryland and North Carolina, and a couple in Virginia, too. There are also a lot more places than I would have expected where you can't buy booze on Sundays."

"I saw that online. But why is it a big deal? That's what I don't understand. People can't stock up on Saturday?" I pulled a roll from a heavenly-smelling basket the server laid on the table and scooped butter onto my knife.

"I guess some people end up with hooch emergencies? Or don't live near enough to a liquor store, maybe?" Joey slid a knife into his roll. "I can't imagine. But I'm just the customer today. We're looking to buy a case from him. It was a good excuse for a meeting. Not exactly an interview, but I think you can get some useful information out of him."

"I can. And it's a good reason to spend the evening with you." I grinned, and his face lit up in response.

"There's that, too."

The waiter set our food down in front of us. When he left, I glanced at Joey.

"Maybe if you have time, we could pick up where we left off when we're done buying contraband alcohol." I twisted the napkin in my fingers, slightly amazed that I was brave enough to say that. And I hadn't even had any wine.

"Yeah? Well, let's go get it finished, then." The corners of his full lips edged up in a sexy smile, and my pulse took off at a gallop.

Lord, let's.

I picked at my chicken, and objected when Joey handed the server a credit card before the guy had even brought the check.

"You're doing me a favor," I said. "The least I can do is buy you dinner."

"On our first real date? I don't think so." He shook his head. "Next time, we'll talk about it."

My heart pounded. "Deal."

"Does that mean we're dating, now?" His dark eyes were serious.

I stared at him, my thoughts whirling. I wanted to squeal and say of course and wear his class ring (or whatever the grownup equivalent of that was). But...how would it ever work? And there was Kyle. I couldn't brush off the fact that I had feelings for him, too. I just didn't know how deep they went.

"We're trying things out," I said finally, choosing words carefully. "I like you. Probably more than I should. And not just because you can get me exclusives with shady characters. But it's been a pretty long time since I've done anything like this. I'm not sure how it works, period. Let alone how it works with so many complications."

He nodded. "I understand that. And I'll take it. I like you more than I should, too. I've tried to be your friend, but I want more. We'll see where it goes?"

"I'd like that." About as much as I like breathing.

"What about your," he paused, clearing his throat, "federal agent friend?"

"I don't see where it's any of his business. At least, not the particulars of it." I twisted the napkin some more. "Kyle is complicated."

"I don't give up easily." Joey took my hand, trailing the pad of his thumb over my knuckles. "And I'm used to getting what I want."

My breath caught when his eyes finished that sentence before he spoke the words. "As hard as I've tried not to, what I want is you."

Oh. My. God.

The waiter appeared with the credit card slip and Joey signed it, then stood and offered me a hand. "Ready to get this over with?"

I took his hand and returned his smile. "I haven't wanted to get through an interview more since the serial killer I saw on death row five years ago."

15

The drive to Maryland flew, the woods lining I-95 blurring past the windows as we talked and laughed about everything from music and TV to politics. I knew Joey lived north of Richmond, but I'd never been sure how far north until he pulled into the parking lot of a fire-hollowed warehouse in a questionable part of Bethesda.

"This city is crazy," he said as he stopped the car. "Five blocks that way, there's a nice part of town."

"You're sure?" I looked around. "I'm skeptical, but I'll take your word for it."

"I live six blocks that way. It's nothing like this." He smiled. "But there are few places better to go when you don't want to be seen by anyone else."

I dug out a notebook and tried to concentrate on formulating casual questions for the moonshine salesman, but the smell of Joey's woodsy cologne mixed with whatever magical something made him so delicious kept my attention focused about a foot to my left.

I reached down and cracked my window, clicking out a pen. If we could buy Mathews-distilled moonshine here, it was going out of state. Which meant Kyle might be able to get a case opened at the ATF, and I might land the story of the year, and find a big chunk of my TJ Okerson puzzle, too. Assuming I was right about anything, anyway.

Priorities, Nichelle.

I repeated that on a loop in my head until an aging F-150 rolled into the parking lot. Joey moved to get out of the car, but paused when both doors on the truck opened.

Two large men, one in jeans and a Polo with a gleaming bald head and barber-close-shaven face, the other in overalls and a dingy wife beater with stringy hair and an untamed beard, met at the front of the pickup and nodded to us. Joey shot me a look, tense lines settling in his face, and pulled a small revolver from the low center console. He slipped it under his jacket without being seen through the windshield.

Shit.

"The driver is my guy. Bubba there, I'm not familiar with. You sit tight for a minute." He handed me the keys. "If anything goes wrong, lock the doors, crawl over here, and leave."

"I'm not leaving you," I said.

"I can take care of myself."

"So can I." I held his gaze, not blinking. "I'm not leaving here without you."

He sighed, turning his attention back to the surly redneck leaning on the hood of the pickup.

"Fine. I'm sure it's fine. Just sit here until I check it out."

He stepped out of the car and walked to the front bumper, talking to Mr. Clean before he turned to Bubba. If I hadn't been so worried, it would've been funny, watching Joey talk to this guy in one-strap overalls and flip flops who spit tobacco juice every other word.

Joey waved toward the car as he talked, and Mr. Clean nodded. Bubba scuffed a flip flop toe in the gravel and twisted his mouth to one side, staring at me through the windshield. I kept my expression neutral, difficult when I was pretty much scared to death.

Bubba nodded to Joey, and Joey backed toward my door, his hand hanging very near where I'd seen him stow the gun.

He pulled my door open and helped me out of the car. "Stay behind me, and don't ask anyone's name," he said out of the corner of his mouth.

"I'm not stupid," I hissed back, nodding acknowledgement at the other two men.

"Evening, ma'am." Mr. Clean gave me a once-over when I stepped to the front of the car. "I understand you're interested in something a little stronger than a martini this evening."

I shook his hand, not breaking eye contact and standing up straight. I top six feet in my good shoes, and I wanted to look as invulnerable as I could, considering my cocktail dress. The gun under Joey's jacket was comforting.

I turned my head and smiled at Bubba. He spit on the ground.

"Martinis are last season," I said. "We heard y'all have something with a bit more kick to it."

"Don't know why you'd think such a thing," Bubba said. "Selling unregulated alcohol is against the law."

I looked between him, his friend, and Joey, not sure how I was supposed to answer that.

No one offered any assistance, Mr. Clean studying the shell of the nearby warehouse outlined in the night between us and the nice part of town, and Joey laying a casual arm across my torso, scooting me behind him a little more.

"Well, if we've come to the wrong place, I guess we should all just take our wallets and head home," I said, staring Bubba straight in the face. "Sorry to trouble you. You're sure you don't know where we might come by some genuine Virginia corn whiskey?"

"D'I look like I'd know anything about that?" He delivered the line with such a serious look I didn't dare give him a straight answer. Joey erupted into a coughing fit until he could stop laughing.

"We were told y'all might," I said. "I'm sorry for wasting your time." I took a step back.

"And what if I do? How d'I know you ain't wearing a wire or something? A fancy camera? You don't look like any kinda moonshine drinker I've ever seen."

He stepped forward and Joey slid in front of me.

"Where do you think you're going?" Joey looked down at Bubba. His steely voice and the tension in the part of his profile I could see were enough to send chills racing up my arms. Double shit. Thinking he might have hurt people and seeing him do it because I was stubborn were two entirely different things.

I laid a hand on his arm and leaned close to his ear. "Calm down."

"We ain't doing no business here if I can't check her for a wire," Bubba said.

"Over my dead body." Joey's voice was low and dangerous.

"We can arrange that, mister." Bubba glowered, rocking up on the balls of his feet so he was eye-to-eye with Joey.

I tugged Joey's elbow. I wanted the story. But not badly enough to let anyone get hurt.

"Look," I told Bubba hastily, scooting around the hood of the car and spinning before him. "Maybe you know something about the laws of physics that I don't, but I'd have to give up chocolate and bread for a month to fit a wire in this dress with me."

He eyed me shrewdly and motioned for me to turn again.

"I s'pose," he said when I obliged, a glimmer of respect in his dark eyes. He turned and walked to the back of the truck. I heard the hinges screech a protest when he let the tailgate down, and he returned with a plain cardboard box. "What is it I can help you with?"

"Can I see one of those?" I asked.

He opened the case and pulled out a jar, loosening the lid and passing it to me. "The first sample is free," he said, his eyes narrowing again.

"I trust your quality," I said.

"I insist."

I stared at him, and Joey laid two fingers on my elbow. "You don't have to drink it," he said.

Bubba's glare said refusing could be more headache than I might get from the moonshine. I looked at the jar. The triple-X insignia matched the one from the scene of Sydney's death.

Bubba nodded toward the jar.

Shit. What if it was a bad batch?

I shot Joey a glance from the corner of my eye, Bobbi's mention of *Deliverance* fitting with the moonshiner in front of me. I'd read enough to know a smidgen wouldn't hurt me, even if the stuff was spoiled. No one else was even sick, right?

Catching a breath and raising the jar to my lips, I took half a sip, heat spreading through me as I swallowed.

I blinked back tears. "Smooth," I choked out around a short cough. Kids were drinking this crap? My mouth and throat burned like I'd had a fire-eating lesson.

Bubba glanced at Joey. "I don't think it'll take much," he said in a voice so low I couldn't swear under oath I heard him right.

Joey produced a roll of twenties, peeled off ten, and picked up the box.

"Nice doing business with you," he said. "I'll be in touch."

Bubba's eyes raked over my dress again. "Will you?"

I wasn't sure how to answer that, so I ignored it and spun toward the car instead. Stopping halfway to the door, I turned back. Joey paused next to me.

"What kind of market do you y'all serve these days, anyway?" I asked Bubba. "I mean, you said we're not your typical customer."

"Lots of dry counties around here." Bubba shot a stream of tobacco juice from between his teeth that arced a good six feet. "I'd rather have more customers like you." He grinned, Copenhagen-stained drool dripping into his beard. Sexy.

I closed my eyes for a long blink. "People in dry counties have cars, right?" I asked.

"Say they go over to a store or across the state line and buy a bottle of whiskey," he said. "The government tracks everything with satellites and computers, you know. A body gets pulled over by the law on the way home, in a dry county, and possession will get them a night in jail, maybe longer, and a record. Moonshine is delivered. It's cheap. And it's off the books. Or the grid, like you city folks say. We live off the grid."

"Y'all do a lot of business with teenagers?" I asked.

Bubba shrugged. "Enough. Very carefully. I ain't got no objection to kids having a drink here and there. I got four boys, and kids'll do as they please. But that's trouble if the ABC catches you selling to minors. They get pissy about that faster than anything else. You seen all the stings they been running in stores on the TV?"

"I have." Damn. That didn't help me figure out where the kids got the moonshine. Or who took it to the party. And I was increasingly sure that was the key to this whole mess.

"Why d'you care?" Bubba asked.

"I'm curious. Occupational hazard. Thanks for indulging me."

"Much obliged for your business, ma'am." He climbed back into the truck.

Joey backed me into the passenger seat of his car, stowing the moonshine in the back floor board and shooting Mr. Clean an icy glare as he rounded the hood. The guy raised both hands and shook his head, calling something I couldn't make out. Joey didn't turn back, sliding back into the driver's seat and spinning the tires on his way out of the parking lot.

"I'm sorry," he said tightly, stopping at a light and tucking the gun back into the console. "I wouldn't have brought you out here if I'd known there was someone tagging along with him."

"I would have managed to convince you to bring me," I said, trying to keep my voice steady. It was shaking, as were my hands and knees. Hello, adrenaline rush.

Joey glanced at me as he laid on the accelerator on the onramp for I-95. "No, you really wouldn't have. I don't know who that guy was, but I know just enough about all this to know these are dangerous people. You handled yourself well. Nice, pointing out your dress. Though I didn't much care for the way he started looking at you when you did that."

"Everyone went home with the same number of holes they arrived with," I said. "That was my objective. I'm sure his wife thinks he's adorable, but he's not my type."

He glanced at me. "What is your type?"

"It seems tall, dark, and a little bit dangerous works nicely." When I thought really hard about that, it kind of fit him and Kyle both.

"Good to know." The corners of his lips tipped up a little.

I picked up my notebook and spent most of the drive home recording the details of our transaction. Moonshine being sold out of state. Check. But how to tell Kyle that without telling him how I knew it? I didn't have an answer. I noted the label on Bubba's brand, pulling out my cell phone and checking the photo of the one Sheriff Zeke had found near Sydney's body to make sure I remembered it right.

Wait.

I zoomed the photo in and stared, then reached behind my seat and pulled a jar from the box.

"One shot wasn't enough?" Joey asked.

"Hardy har har." I stuck my tongue out at him, holding the jar we'd bought up to the map light.

The one from the crime scene was faded across the middle. The one in my hand was not.

Which might just mean Bubba had refilled his ink cartridge since last week. But what if it was a coding system of some sort? I jotted that down and underlined it, returning the jar to the box.

"The labels are different," I said.

"Different how?"

"The one Sydney Cobb was drinking had this Triple-X label. But it was all faded across the middle. These aren't."

"What do you think that means?"

I sighed. "Hell if I know. Maybe nothing. Maybe everything. Any idea how I can find out which?"

"Not off the top of my head. But I'll let you know if I think of something." Joey grinned.

He turned onto my street, and I laid a hand on his arm. "I appreciate your help. I know you didn't want to do this. But these folks in Mathews deserve to know what happened to their children."

"That's the only reason I agreed to it." He parked the Lincoln in my driveway and turned to face me. "There's not much that scares me. But the idea of something happening to you...I can't stand it." He raised my hand to his lips, brushing them across the back.

A cavalcade of butterflies took flight in my middle as I stared into his dark eyes. Whatever he'd done or not done, he was telling me the truth. Better than half a decade of dealing with some of the best bullshitters to walk the Earth had graced me with a good radar for lies, or even half-truths. Joey wasn't selling either.

He let his eyes fall shut and leaned to kiss me, and I put one finger across his lips. He flinched, confusion plain on his face.

"Come in," I said.

His eyes widened. "That the moonshine talking?"

"From half a sip two hours ago? Not even I'm that lightweight. I think I'll swear off the hard stuff, but I have a nice bottle of red in my wine rack." My voice shook again, with nerves instead of shock. "You feel like a nightcap?"

"I'd love one." He strode around the car and opened my door, pulling me close to him.

I felt my brow furrow at the bothered look on his face.

"What's wrong?" I asked. "You don't have to stay, if you don't want."

"Oh, I want." He flashed a tight smile before his face fell serious again. "What I don't want is for you to feel like you owe me anything. I took you to meet that guy because what you're doing is important. Not because I expect anything in return."

I laid my hands along both sides of his face, pulling it to mine. "Good. Because I wouldn't trade this for a news tip or interview if it meant a sure shot at the Pulitzer," I whispered, kissing him softly. "Let's go find that bottle of wine."

He turned for the door, one hand on the small of my back. By the time I got the lock opened, heat had spread from that spot through my entire core. I bent to scratch Darcy's ears, gathering minor control of my hormones.

Smiling, I directed Joey to the sofa and busied myself opening my splurge bottle of Chilean red. I gulped deep, calming breaths as I poured it into glasses, but sloshed a few drops onto the counter, anyway. What the hell was I doing? Joey was sexy, and gorgeous, and downright debonair. He struck me as the kind of man who did not lack experience in this area.

It'd been so long since I'd had a man in my bed that my side of the mattress sagged from disproportionate overuse. Aside from one short relationship in college, Kyle was the only guy I'd ever slept with. I'd spent years going on a lot of first dates, and I have a rule against sex on first dates. The resulting dry spell had turned into a drought. And I thought this was the way to end it? I hoped I remembered what to do well enough to avoid making a fool of myself.

Grabbing the glasses and feeding Darcy a biscuit to keep her quiet, I peeked into the living room. Joey was perched on the edge of my navy jacquard sofa, his fingers steepled under his chin and an unmistakably unnerved look on his face.

Thank you, God, for letting it not be just me.

"I had this at a party and bought a bottle the next day," I said as I walked into the room.

He jerked his head up and a slow grin spread across his face. I handed him his glass and pulled the clip out of my hair, letting it fall into its soft mahogany waves around my shoulders.

Sitting on the sofa next to him, I watched as he took a sip. "It's good," he said.

He reached across the cushion between us and laid a hand on my bare knee. I jumped and splattered wine onto the rug, but he didn't move. Neither did I, except to drain the rest of my glass in one gulp. I set it on the table and put my hand over his. Joey finished his glass just as quickly and put it next to mine.

"Really good." I wasn't even sure who said that. My eyes locked with his.

He wound his other arm around my waist and pulled me to him, his lips crushing mine for an instant before he parted them. He flicked the tip of his tongue into my mouth and I gasped, pulling him closer before he laid me back onto the cushions.

"Now can I hear about those fantasies?" he asked.

"They're sort of show more than tell."

"Show me."

I reached up and traced the line of his jaw with my fingertips, trailing them over his lips before I pulled his head down and kissed him. He moved his mouth to my throat, his tongue leaving a trail to the hollow, where my pulse threatened to pound right through my skin. He paused there, then planted a line of soft kisses along my collarbone to my shoulder, pushing the strap on my dress out of the way.

My fingers curled into his hair and I closed my eyes as everything but Joey disappeared from my radar.

He rested one hand alongside my head, pushing himself up easily and staring at me as though he wanted to memorize every freckle. I took a hitching breath. No one had ever looked at me quite that way.

"You know," he said, trailing the fingertips of his other hand in loose patterns on my shoulder, "you're not the only one with fantasies."

Holy Manolos.

"Good to know," I whispered, reaching up to flick open the buttons on his shirt. I worked the Windsor knot out of his tie and threw it, pushing the shirt open and running my fingers over the smooth skin underneath. I knew he was gorgeous, but the rock-hard lines under my fingers said he was in great shape, too.

"You want to know mine?" I pulled his shirt free of the waistband of his pants and pushed it back over his arms. He took it off and tossed it onto the chaise, and the way his muscles worked for the simple motions made my pulse pick up more steam.

"I'm waiting." He leaned over me. I propped myself up on my elbows and kissed him, sliding my tongue over his. He put one hand on the nape of my neck, then moved it down, unzipping my dress in a single motion. I wriggled my arms free and fell back into the pillows, but he stayed with me, never breaking the kiss.

"It sort of starts with you carrying me to bed," I whispered against his lips.

"I heard that part," he said, raising his head a touch and brushing one hand over the black satin of my bra. "But my fantasy starts with you asking me to."

"Consider yourself asked."

His chest jumped under my fingers with a sharp breath, and he lowered his lips back to mine. I lost myself in the kiss, sliding my hands to his bare shoulders. I moved my lips along the roughness of his jaw, pausing to swipe my tongue over his earlobe. The sound that came from his throat told me he liked that, so I did it again. He buried his hands in my hair, his breath speeding, then twisted and dropped to one knee next to the sofa.

He kissed me again before he stood and scooped me into his arms. My whole body shuddered.

A thousand breathless dreams.

And this was really happening.

We were halfway down the hall when the doorbell rang.

Joey froze. "You've got to be kidding."

I dropped my forehead to his shoulder, trying to catch my breath. Pressing my lips against his skin, I murmured a string of swearwords that would make Bubba the moonshiner blush. "Go away," I finished, bouncing my feet and turning Joey's face toward mine. "Where were we?"

"Wondering why someone's ringing your doorbell at twelve-thirty?" The soft look on his face dissolved into the tense lines I remembered from the parking lot.

I twisted my head toward the foyer. "Shit. You don't think Bubba followed us, do you?"

He sighed and set me on my feet. I grabbed for my dress and slipped my arms back into it, dropping another kiss at the nape of his neck as he turned back for the front of the house.

"If there's not a nuclear bomb in the house next door, I'm going to hate this person on principle for the rest of my days." I zipped my dress, moving toward the door.

Joey put a hand on my elbow. "Let me." He looked down. "I need a shirt."

Standing back, I admired the physique that had felt so nice under my fingers a few moments before. His shoulders were broad, the muscles rising into ridges where they met his neck. His biceps were defined and impressive without being veiny and scary. The twin divots at the base of his spine that just peeked over his belt hinted at a sculpted rear end and made my pulse race again.

"I'm not convinced you should ever wear a shirt again," I said, leaning against the wall.

He shot me a grin and ducked into the living room to retrieve his, pulling it on as he walked to the door. He peered out the trio of windows that lined the top and turned to me with a raised eyebrow. "It's a woman. Who looks nothing like Bubba."

What? My best friend, Jenna, was the only woman I could think of who would drop by unannounced, and if she was ringing my doorbell after midnight on a Tuesday, catastrophe was afoot. My stomach wrung as I crossed to the door.

I jerked it open to find a puffy-faced Ashton Okerson.

16

"Ashton?" I tossed a confused glance at Joey, who was leaning on the edge of the open door. He raised his eyebrows and I waved Ashton inside. "What can I do for you?" I asked.

"I," she choked on the syllable, dissolving into more tears.

I put an arm around her. "Come in," I said gently, ushering her to the sofa. I heard the latch click as Joey shut the door behind us.

I sat with Ashton, who buried her face in my shoulder and sobbed for a good five minutes. Joey stood in the doorway, a worried line running the length of his forehead. I thought about the questions I'd asked him about Tony and gambling, and felt a little sick when I considered that she might be about to tell me she did know why her son was dead.

When she finally sat up, I didn't think her own mother would recognize her swollen face.

"What on Earth?" I asked, locking my violet eyes with her blue ones.

"The sheriff," she spat, hauling in a deep breath and trying again. "He closed the case file. The coroner says TJ died of liver failure, and they've stopped looking. *If* they were looking in the first place. He's having a press conference in the morning, and I just...I got in my car and I drove and drove, and I finally asked Grant to send me your address. I hope I'm not intruding." Her eyes jumped to Joey and his half-buttoned shirt and she bit her lip. "I am. I'm so sorry." She moved to stand up, and I put a restraining hand on her arm.

"Not at all." I threw Joey an apologetic glance and he waved a hand, shaking his head in dismissal.

"I just didn't know where to go."

"Liver failure would track with a Vicodin overdose," I said gently, my brain switching gears. Did we have it all wrong? Had TJ killed himself?

"My son did not overdose on Vicodin," Ashton said, dropping her head into her hands and sobbing. "No one believes me. I know my baby. It's just not...there's no way."

I stared, my brain rewinding through years of repressed memories to my own mother crying almost the same thing.

"I believe you," I said.

Ashton sat up, sniffling, and I passed her a tissue box.

"Why?" she asked me.

I took a deep breath and closed my eyes.

"This happened to someone I loved once. Someone my mom loved," I began, glancing at Joey. Concern creased his brow and he crossed to the sofa, sitting on the arm and laying a hand on my shoulder.

"I guess it's always been part of the reason I do what I do." My voice cracked, and Joey's fingers sank into my shoulder, massaging the tightening muscles there. "No one believed her, either, and I saw so many things I thought I could help. Truth to find, injustices to expose. All the noble crap I tell myself when I'm chasing a story."

I took a shaky breath.

"Did you ever find out what happened to your friend?" Ashton asked.

"He was my mom's fiancee," I said. "And no. Nobody would listen. By the time my friend's dad did, it was too late."

"I'm so sorry. I know the feeling."

"I'm listening," I said, trying to smile. "Have you thought of anything else? Any other person who might have wanted something bad to happen to TJ?" I studied her carefully. Her swollen eyes told me nothing was off the table, and I was out of reasons not to ask.

"Is Tony into anything he shouldn't be? Or was he?" I asked, reaching involuntarily for Joey's hand and lacing my fingers in his. "Gambling?

Drugs? Anything that could make TJ a target for someone who's trying to hurt y'all?"

She shook her head slowly, her face a blank mask of grief and confusion. "Tony was one of the cleanest guys in the league. His whole career, he never took anything he wasn't prescribed. He never cheated. He's a homebody."

"No steroids?" My grip on Joey's hand tightened. Forgive me. "Nothing organized crime would have a hand in?"

"Organized crime? Like *The Godfather*? Jesus, no. Tony would never." No doubt crept into her raw voice as she spoke.

I leaned my head back on Joey's chest. A soft chuckle rumbled under my ear.

"That puts us back to locals. Most likely local kids," I said. "What links TJ and Sydney? Anything besides their relationship?"

Ashton shook her head. "They had classes together. It's a small school, though. They all have the same teachers."

"How long have they known each other? Y'all only moved to the island a year or so ago, right?" I asked.

"Yeah." She nodded. "They grew up together in the summers, but they didn't start dating til after we moved out there."

Oh.

"Did Sydney date anyone before TJ?" I asked, a thousand Lifetime movies playing in my head.

"I'm sure she did, but I don't know who."

"Luke Bosley?" The creepy cold look in his eyes haunted my thoughts.

Ashton sucked on her lower lip. "Maybe? I don't know."

"Can you find out?" I asked.

"I can ask Tiffany."

I twisted my mouth to one side. "Any chance she's still awake?" I didn't want to be a pain, but I had no help coming from the cops and precious little to go on.

Ashton sat back. "You think someone might have killed TJ over who he was dating?"

I sighed. "If I'm being flat honest with you, Ashton, I haven't the first damned clue what I think. I'm doing a lot of flying blind and grasping at very thin threads. But I've covered a lot of murder cases in my years at the crime desk, and sex and money are always at the top of the motive list. Since TJ and Syd didn't have any money, I'm betting on the former."

"They weren't having sex. They were thinking about it. We'd just had that talk, because he said maybe this summer, when she came back from France, they might."

I smiled. "I didn't mean to imply anything. Just that unless there's an honest-to-God psychopath running around out there, we're dealing with an emotional crime. And they tend to be motivated by things like jealousy. Especially in a population where hormones are raging."

She tilted her head to one side and stared at me for a long moment. "You're talking like it was a murder."

"Isn't that what you think?"

She pulled her iPhone out of her bag, her children smiling at me from the back of her custom case. All three of them.

"I didn't think I'd convince anyone of that," she said. "Thank you. If you'll excuse me for two minutes, I'll get your answer from Tiff. She can sleep another time. If she sleeps at all."

I smiled a thank you and led Joey to the kitchen.

"Wow." He leaned on the edge of the yellow-tiled countertop and folded his arms across his chest.

"What do you think?"

"She's telling the truth about the dad," he said.

"I thought so, too."

"I asked around. Couldn't find a story anywhere about that guy so much as taking a leak in an alley. Found a couple people who tried to get him into something, but they said they never could."

"They wouldn't care enough about that now to hurt his kid?" I asked.

"Not likely." He shook his head. "I like your theory, if you want my honest opinion."

"Thanks."

"And I like the way you were with her. You're a good person, Nichelle. She needs help, and you'll help her, regardless of whether there's anything in it for you."

"I would. The story is a nice bonus, but this became about a lot more than the story the minute Sheriff Zeke made up his mind. I can't sit here and do nothing while this happens again."

"And that's what I don't like." Joey fixed me with a Baptist-preacher stare. "The cops are out. The sheriff's closing the case and he's not going to help you anymore. Once the press conference is over, the rest of the media will likely disperse. Which leaves you trying to pin a murder on someone who was crafty enough to get away with it. If they're that smart, they'll figure out you're looking. Maybe before you figure out who they are. Which means you could get hurt. That, I do not like."

I shivered under his gaze, though it wasn't cold in the room. "I can't walk away," I said. "They did that to my mom. It broke her. She's never been on another date, and Randy died when I was fourteen years old."

A tear escaped my eye before I could brush it away, and he pulled me into a hug. "I'm sorry," he whispered.

"Thanks." I swiped at my face. "Just don't give me a hard time about chasing this one, and we're good. I appreciate that you worry." I kissed his neck. "But I get a pass this time."

"Be careful, okay?"

"Will do."

"Nichelle?" Ashton called from the hallway.

I squeezed Joey and walked back to the foyer.

"Tiffany said Sydney's only ever had one other boyfriend, the year before she started going with TJ. But it wasn't Luke. It was Eli Morris."

"Any relation to Coach Morris?" I knew the answer before she opened her mouth.

"His only son."

* * *

Joey walked Ashton to her car while I wrote down everything she'd told me.

"I feel bad, letting her drive home," he said when he came back in, flopping down on the couch. I glanced at him from the corner of my eye, trying to focus on my notes and not how unbelievably sexy he looked. Stubble shaded his jaw, and his shirt was still untucked and half-unbuttoned. No tie. Yum.

Ashton had sort of mucked up our moment. Now I had a story to write, hopefully an exclusive until the sheriff's press conference. But since I wasn't any closer to figuring out how the *Post* had gotten the inside scoop, I wasn't sure of that, so time was not my friend.

"Yeah. I wish she'd stayed here. But she swears she'll be fine," I said. "I called Parker and he was going to call her husband and tell him she's on her way."

Joey nodded.

I put my notes down and reached for my computer.

"You have work to do?" he asked.

I scrunched my nose apologetically. "I really do. I want to get this up on the web early, so I need to get it ready and send it to Bob. He'll post it online at the crack of dawn. And maybe he'll be less annoyed with me as a bonus."

"He's not really mad at you," Joey said. "We covered this already."

"All the same, I'll feel better when he's fully back in my corner. I've been taking shit from the sports editor all week, and with Shelby filling in for Les, I can't handle anyone else gunning for me."

"What's wrong with the sports editor?"

"He's pissed because Parker asked me to take this story. Really has his panties in a bunch. It's creepy, because Spence has always been a super nice guy, and he's gone all stalker boy on me this week." I paused. "You don't think the *Post* got their story tip from him, do you?"

Joey frowned. "Couldn't he lose his job over that?"

"He could. At the very least, Bob would put him on leave. But someone who works for us had to have told them. I didn't run anything about it, and the families haven't talked to anyone but me."

"But to be fair, it's a small town," Joey said. "Everyone knows everyone's business out there. So someone else could have told the reporter from the *Post*."

"Maybe. But Bob and Rick thought it came from me, which means they have good enough reason to think it came from our newsroom."

"Why would the sports guy do that?"

"It gave away my exclusive before I was ready to run it, and got me in hot water with the bosses as a bonus. Anyone who's worked with me for ten minutes knows that's the surest way to get to me."

"I suppose it's possible." He shook his head. "I'm sorry."

I pondered it for another three seconds before I stood to walk him to the door.

"I don't have time to be worried about who Spence is talking to right now. Dead people first. Asshat sports guys later."

He stopped at the door and turned to face me, pulling me into his arms. "Where do I fit in?"

I kissed him, teasing the tip of his tongue with mine. "Wherever I can shoehorn in a stolen kiss or three," I said. "I'm sorry about tonight."

"Don't apologize. Your story is important right now. I'll wait. You still have plans for Friday?"

"Yes. I had to bail on Jenna, too. I'm going to a street dance in Mathews." A dance I had a date for. Oy. Why couldn't things just be easy?

"I see."

"Enjoy your dance. Be careful." He smiled, opening the door before he put one finger under my chin and planted a soft kiss on my cheek. "I'll call you."

"You'd better." I closed the door behind him and watched him walk down the steps, wishing the evening had ended differently. Damn Zeke Waters and his craptastic timing.

"All right, Darcy. Let's catch us a murderer, shall we?" I asked the dog, going back to my computer.

I thought about trying Waters, but didn't want to piss him off. It was coming up on two.

TJ Okerson's death has officially been ruled a suicide by Mathews County Sheriff Zeke Waters, the boy's mother told the Richmond Telegraph *late Tuesday.*

"They're closing the case file," Ashton Okerson said, sobbing.

Ashton said the sheriff told her and her husband, three-time Super Bowl champion quarterback Tony Okerson, that the coroner said TJ died of liver failure.

That, along with the empty prescription bottle of Vicodin found at the scene with TJ and the evidence of alcohol consumption at the party he was attending, was apparently enough for Waters to rule out foul play and close his investigation. Waters wasn't immediately available for comment early Wednesday.

The Telegraph *reported yesterday that the Okerson family doesn't believe TJ took his own life, and Ashton said in this exclusive interview that the coroner's report doesn't change her feelings about that.*

I finished up with the sheriff's prior comments about the simplest explanation usually being the right one, and teased the press conference he was planning for the following day. I sent the story to Bob with an explanatory email and closed my computer at three-fifteen.

Darcy took longer than usual about doing her business when I let her outside, barking at the pitch-dark back corner of the yard until I stepped outside in my bare feet to carry her back in the house before she woke up the entire Fan.

"Spring. The rabbits come back. Yay."

Though most of Thumper's cousins that visited our yard were twice as big as Darcy, she had no qualms about letting them know whose territory they were on. I locked the door and made a mental note to get a new bulb for the light.

She growled at the door while I set my coffee cup out for the morning, then gave up and followed me to bed.

I closed my eyes thinking of Joey's kisses, trying to keep my mom's anguished sobs and Randy's easy smile from haunting my dreams for another night. Ashton and Tony would end this with an answer if it was the last thing I ever did. I might not get the one they wanted, but I wasn't giving up.

17

I sidestepped, punched, and *ap-chagi*'ed my way halfheartedly through body combat the next morning, what I knew about Mathews High occupying way more of my brain space than the workout.

TJ was a good kid by all accounts: happy, popular, and in love for the first time. No history of mental illness or depressive behavior. Not a damn thing there added up to suicide.

The sheriff was determined to rule it such and move on, but he also had a cousin who made black-market moonshine. And TJ might have been drinking it. Sydney had likely been drinking it. Except her jar had a faded label. I still had nothing for that.

I added Zeke's name to my growing mental suspect list. I didn't really think he'd hurt the kids, but I was surer by the minute that he was turning a blind eye to whoever had. I'd worked cops and courts long enough to know good ol' boys' networks run deep.

Then there was Evelyn. Instinct (and every true crime novel I'd ever read) said the M.O. in this case made it likely the killer was female. I could hardly wait for the dance Friday night. I just needed to corner her. If the tears I'd seen at the church Monday were guilty ones, it'd take about five minutes of grilling her to get a full confession and probably a blood sample.

Luke would be a tougher nut to crack. For me, anyway. He'd almost spilled something, I could swear, to Parker at the funeral reception. My plan was to have Kyle butter him up with compliments about his pitching. He definitely liked the limelight.

Ashton had added someone else to my list with her phone call the night before, too. Eli Morris was Sydney's ex. If the kids all moved in the same circles, chances were good he was at the party where TJ died. And jealousy is a powerful motive.

But no matter which way I turned the puzzle pieces, the liver failure was the stubborn one.

Boys have more of a tendency to be violent. Some kind of poisoning spoke of a woman's hand. But how did twiggy little Evelyn force-feed a boy TJ's size and strength enough pills to cause his young, healthy liver to shut down?

Oh, shit.

I ran out of my class with five minutes left, leaving messages for Tony, Ashton, and Parker before I got into the shower. I hadn't asked to see TJ's medical records before, but what if there was something else going on with the kid's liver? Something that would make it easier to kill than your average teenager's? I didn't know what that could be, exactly, but it was worth looking into. How many helmets to the torso had he taken in his lifetime?

Leapfrogging ahead and assuming that was the case, was I looking for someone who knew that? Or was it an accident?

So many questions.

And Bob's half-smile when I walked into his empty office for the morning news budget meeting with my hair still wet told me he wanted answers.

"That was a good piece this morning. It's already on the web and it's pinging around the Internet like a celebutante sex video."

I grinned. "Well, good. I think." I dropped into my customary high-backed orange velour wing chair. "Your face says I'm not totally off your shit list."

"There's a lot going on here this week." He sighed, slumping back in his chair. "Do I think you fed the *Post* a tip? No. I know you better than that. The story is everything to you. Just like it was to me. I also know this one has a personal tic for you, and you're not going to let it go. To be honest, I had my reservations when Parker told me he was asking you to take it. I gave him the green light because I knew you'd do a good job with the suicide story, show the family respect, and for his sake, I was hoping everyone else would follow your lead. It didn't ever occur to me that it would turn into a one-woman murder investigation."

I opened my mouth and then snapped it shut. "Bob, these people—" I began.

He raised one hand. "Deserve to know what happened to their kid? I know. I agree. Go get it. But for the love of God, watch yourself. Moonshiners and murderers and God knows what, and there are miles of woods and water out there that would be really good for hiding a nosy reporter."

"Point taken."

His eyes told me something was still bothering him, but the rest of the staff began to trickle in, and he shrugged helplessly and sat back.

Eunice came bearing a platter of something that smelled heavenly. I reached under the foil and came up with a square of cornbread speckled with cheese and sausage.

"You're like the evil diet fairy," I said, biting into the still-warm breakfast bread and grinning at Eunice. "I bet I'm putting back every calorie I burned at the gym this morning."

"You might be surprised," Eunice helped herself to one, and pushed the tray toward Bob. Since he'd had a heart attack not even twelve months before, and was on a strict low-fat, low-cholesterol diet, I frowned at her as I swallowed.

"My sister's been doctoring Grandmomma's recipes to make them more waistline-friendly, and I made this with fat free buttermilk, egg whites, turkey sausage, and low fat cheddar."

It tasted sinful. But it was healthy?

"I retract my previous statement." I grinned. "You are the best kind of diet fairy." I snagged another square and passed one to Bob before the rest of them disappeared.

"We do enough sitting in front of computers around here," Eunice said. "If I can trick folks into eating healthy, I'm doing a favor for my fellow man, right?"

"And a much appreciated good deed it is," Bob said around a mouthful of food.

Bob started the meeting and ran quickly through the copy highlights for the day. Halfway through sports, my cell phone buzzed a text from Tony: "Got your message. Call me."

Spence paused, turning slowly to me. "Do you need to take that? Don't let my little section rundown keep you from stealing a story from anyone else this morning."

"Spence, that's enough," Bob said.

The rest of the section editors squirmed in their seats and focused on the photos and front pages dotting Bob's walls. I met Spence's glare with one of my own, biting my tongue.

Bob switched to the business editor.

Studying my notes to avoid Spence's go-straight-to-Hell looks and everyone else's curiosity, I tapped the heel of my pearl-rimmed, black Nicholas Kirkwood sandals on the floor through the rest of the meeting. When Bob threw us out with his customary, "my office is not newsworthy, so get out and find me something to print," I popped to my feet.

"Nichelle," Bob said. "Hang out."

I twisted my mouth to one side. "I have a text that needs attention. Can I come back?"

He nodded. "Go on, but we need to talk."

Yes, we did.

I half-ran to my desk, grabbing the phone before I sat down to dial Tony's number. Please, Lord. A tiny break.

He picked up on the third ring, and I barely let him get the "hello," out before I blurted my question.

"Was there something wrong with TJ's liver?" I asked. "Something that might have made it fail easier than it should have?"

"I don't know," Tony sounded hesitant.

"You don't know? How can you not know if your kid had liver problems that might have killed him?" I tried to rein in my frustration. "I'm sorry. I'm not—look, I can't imagine how hard this is for you, but you two seem to be pretty involved in what's going on with your kids. The coroner says liver failure. Ashton swears he didn't kill himself. If his liver was compromised, it might help me figure out what happened to him."

"I didn't push him," Tony said. "He played because he wanted to."

"Even though he was hurt?" I guessed.

"He took a nasty hit in football game his freshman year," Tony said. "Broke a rib. And it damaged his liver. The doctors said it was a miracle it still functioned. That's why I know he wasn't drinking too much, and why I'm sure he didn't OD on Vicodin."

"Why the hell did they prescribe him Vicodin if he had liver trouble?" I asked, scribbling down his comment, which made very little sense.

"They didn't, at first. But every other kind of pain medicine there is made him sick. He can't play baseball if he can't eat."

I nearly choked on the "so then don't play," offering a sympathetic silence instead. What makes sports the be all and end all of everything for some folks, anyway?

"TJ was careful about drinking. Never more than one or two, and not usually during a playing season at all. And he would never have taken Vicodin with booze. He knew better. He treated his body well. Taking good care of yourself is how you last through a long playing career."

Considering Tony's revelation, my brain careened off in another direction. As much as the memory of Ashton's swollen face haunted me, what if I was projecting?

"Tony," I began, clicking my pen in and out and searching for words that wouldn't sting. "If TJ knew that, about the booze and the painkillers, well..." I sighed. "Wouldn't that be a pretty effective way for him to commit suicide?"

Tony was quiet for so long I wondered if the call had dropped. "I suppose," he said finally. "But my son did not do this. I know it as sure as I know my passing record. Ashton said you believed her."

"I did. I do. I think. Every time I think I've made sense of part of this, the floor drops out from under me again."

"That, I really do understand," he said.

I tapped the pen on my notes, mulling my suspect list. "Would any of the other kids have known about this? The thing with TJ's liver?"

"I honestly have no idea," Tony said. "I don't know why they would, but maybe he might have told someone. Why?"

I jotted that down. Another blurry piece for my Mathews puzzle. "Just trying to find a thread to grasp today." I was quiet for a minute, Ashton's raw voice from the night before echoing in my ears. "Hey, Tony—did coach Morris know about TJ's liver?"

"It happened before we moved here. I don't remember ever mentioning it specifically, but the coaches look over the kids' medical records. So probably. But I'm not sure."

And if the coach knew, maybe his son did, too? I kept that to myself. It was thin, but maybe it would lead somewhere.

I thanked Tony for calling and disconnected the line before dialing my favorite coroner.

Ten minutes on the phone with Jacque Morgan, a senior medical examiner who shared my love of great shoes and claimed to be eternally grateful that I'd shared my eBay secrets with her, didn't get me much. Except that Vicodin overdose usually presents as suffocation.

"Everyone's different, though," she said. "People's bodies react differently to different substances. And I didn't work that case, so I can't tell you anything for sure."

"Who did work it?" I asked.

"Drake Carmichael. But the official statement is all he's cleared to release. They made that very clear at the staff meeting they called this morning."

"If the kid's liver was weak?" I asked, trying to sound hypothetical.

"It might fail before the lungs," she replied. "Again, not my case."

I thanked her and hung up, my watch telling me I needed to get on the road if I was going to make it to the press conference. I wasn't sure if I hoped Tony and Ashton would be there or not. I wanted to talk to Sydney's parents, too. Whatever had happened to the kids was linked, so digging around one was bound to help out with the other.

Throwing a glance at Bob's office, I pondered how mad he'd get at me for skipping out and decided he'd be a lot madder if I was late to the press conference and missed something. I'd catch up with him later.

I punched the button for the elevator, wondering if I was setting myself up to crash into a dead end.

* * *

Snagging the seat next to Lyle when I got into Mathews city hall, I pulled out a notebook and pen before turning to him.

"Have a nice weekend?" I asked.

"I've seen nicer. But at least no one else died." He shook his head. "I'm ready for all these TV cameras to disappear, I'll say that."

I glanced around. There were a dozen camera crews and a handful more reporters in the little council chambers. Charlie stood to my right, directing her cameraman to the extra footage she wanted. CNN was behind her, the Newport News stations scattered around the perimeter of the room. I scanned the faces of the seated reporters, but I couldn't tell the *Post* from *USA Today* based on sight.

Lyle cleared his throat. "In fairness, I have to tell you, you did a good thing with that story you ran on Bobbi's club. She's a great gal, and Dorothy Scott has been so ridiculous about this whole thing it's embarrassing. It needed to be printed. I know Zeke was glad to be rid of the conflict."

I nodded a thank you and considered asking him about the sheriff, but decided against it. Yet, anyway. I had some guys at the Richmond PD who skated the line between friend and source, and I knew working in a small town, Lyle was more likely to have a strong relationship with Waters. Since he used his first name and a fond tone when he spoke of him, I guessed it wasn't a strong hatred.

"Why didn't you run it?" I asked.

"My managing editor is Mr. Dorothy, Junior," he said, smirking.

"Damned if this isn't Mayberry come to life." I shook my head. "I grew up in Dallas and went from there to Syracuse to Richmond. But everyone really knows everyone out here."

He chuckled. "I don't think too hard about that. They all know each other's business, too. If I ruminate on that, I'll decide my life's work has no point."

"Local grapevine beats the paper?"

"More often than not."

I nodded understanding, and we both faced the front of the room when Waters stepped to the podium there.

He thanked everyone for coming and stood up straight, playing to the CNN camera behind Charlie.

"This has been a difficult week," he said. "For these two families, who could not be with us today, and for all of Mathews County. We are a big extended family, here, and tragedy hurts everyone. TJ and Sydney were bright young people with promising futures, and the entire community is poorer for their loss."

I scribbled, and Lyle held up a voice recorder.

"That said, I have the coroner's report here on TJ's cause of death." Waters waved a folder. "The autopsy revealed that he died of liver failure. That, coupled with evidence we found at the scene, has resulted in his death being officially ruled a suicide." He cut his dark eyes to me. "Despite what you might have read in the paper."

I rolled my eyes, but kept taking notes.

"This case is closed. And while we've enjoyed having you folks with us, we understand that you'll want to be on your way."

I looked up when he said the last, suddenly pondering Lyle's earlier comment.

Having the media underfoot wasn't fun for cops, or local reporters, certainly. But the "don't let the door hit you in the ass on your way out" didn't jive with the "we are family" crap they were throwing off, either. Bobbi had said her business had picked up some even before my story ran, with all the camera crews in town. Elmer said the same thing. And the cute little bakery where I'd stopped for coffee had a line of press people out the door and halfway down the block. Everyone was yakking about apricot scones, which I didn't get to try because they made them fresh every morning and were sold out before I made it to the front of the line.

The media was good for the local economy, which Bobbi said had been hurting.

So why did the sheriff and Lyle want everyone gone so badly?

And why hadn't Lyle ever done a story on the moonshiners? I mean, if I lived out here, it'd be the first thing on my must-get list.

I shot him a sideways glance. His eyes were trained on Waters, who'd just opened the floor to questions.

"Was there ever a reason to suspect foul play in this case, sheriff?" Charlie glanced at me as she asked that. So much for "let's go get the sports guys."

"We did our due diligence in the case, but our findings point to suicide," he said. "As I said earlier this week, the simplest answer is usually the right one."

I snorted softly, and the sheriff glared. I'd covered some pretty damned convoluted things in my time, and this was ranking up there with the best of them. I could not make myself buy his line.

Raising my hand, I returned his unblinking stare. He called on every other reporter in the room first, answering questions about the size of his department, the discovery of the body, and everything in between, before he nodded to me. "Miss Clarke?"

Slowly, I lowered my arm. "Do you have the tox screen back?"

I knew damn well he didn't. Aaron had cases in Richmond he'd been waiting on tox results for over two months on. And I'd heard nothing from Kyle about it.

"We do not."

I could have heard a Tic-Tac drop. I wondered if I was killing my exclusive, but I knew from the looks he was shooting my way that he was pissed and wouldn't talk to me outside a crowded room where it would be conspicuous for him to ignore me. "So, you don't know what caused the liver failure?" I asked.

"There was alcohol present, and an empty bottle of narcotics in the boy's pocket." Waters focused on CNN again. "As you well know."

I opened my mouth to say that wasn't exactly scientific evidence, but he picked up his folder and nodded to the crowd.

"If y'all will excuse me. Thank you for your time."

He disappeared out the side door while the gallery muttered, scribbled, and looked at me.

"You know he's probably right," Lyle said, looking around at the cameras.

"I know he thinks he is." I pinched my lips shut. I didn't trust Lyle anymore. Nodding a goodbye, I slipped out before Charlie could get her cameraman gathered up and follow.

* * *

Stepping into the *Star Wars* battle scene that is a high school passing period, I managed to navigate to the office unscathed, save for getting my toes crushed under a rolling backpack that was apparently carrying the entire library. I scurried under the sign marked "Administration," shutting the heavy door on the noise in the hallway.

The secretary I'd met the week before smiled when I looked up from examining my shoes. No damage, unbelievably. I didn't remember getting to class being so obstacle-ridden. I shook off the feeling of age that came with the thought and returned Norma's smile.

"How are you, honey? Those articles you did about TJ were nice," she said. "I can't believe his poor momma and daddy think somebody killed him. So sad. But I hear the sheriff has closed the case and ruled it a suicide. We half expected all the city reporters to be long gone by lunchtime. So what's on your mind today?"

I returned her bright smile. What was on my mind was that there was likely a murderer in the building. But I couldn't tell Norma that.

"I just feel so bad for the Okersons," I said, stalling. "I don't have any children, so I can't imagine what they're going through."

She fanned herself, dropping her hand over her heart. "I have two, and I don't want to think about it. I love those girls more than life itself."

"How old are they?" I asked, making small talk until I could find a way to ask her about Luke and Evelyn. And Eli, too.

"My oldest is twenty. She's a junior at RAU this year. And my baby is a sophomore here."

"You do not look old enough to have a daughter in college." I widened my eyes and waved a hand and she giggled.

"Why, thank you. Terry was just telling me last night how soft my skin is. Oil of Olay. My grandmomma was ninety-three when she passed and didn't look a minute over sixty in her casket. She swore by it."

"Terry? As in, Coach Morris?" I asked. She'd seemed sweet on him the first time we'd met. But didn't she say he was her sister's ex? Because...weird. Then again, how many single men in their early forties could there be in Mathews? Beggars and choosers, and all that.

"We've gotten closer here lately." Her Cover Girl True Red lips tipped up in a dreamy smile. "He's a wonderful man."

"He has a son, too, right?" I crossed to the counter and leaned casually against it.

"Eli." She nodded. "He's a talented boy. My favorite nephew."

Nephew. Stepson? A twinge shot through my head when I considered that for more than three and a half seconds, so I let it go.

"He goes to school here, too?"

"He's a junior. Straight A's. Drama club, baseball team. He's a good boy."

I smiled. "I'm sure y'all are very proud. Does he have a girlfriend?"

A dark look flashed across her face so quickly it could've been a trick of the light. "He's too busy for girls."

At sixteen. Uh huh.

I just nodded. "I know the feeling. Speaking of girls, do you know anything about Sydney Cobb?"

She shrugged. "Not really. She was popular with the kids. Like her mother. Tiff and I were friends once. Syd didn't ever really get into trouble, so I didn't see much of her up here."

I nodded. "There was a girl at the funeral service Monday," I said. "Tiny, blonde, pretty. She was really upset. But I haven't seen her anywhere since. I'm a little worried about her, with everything that's happened around here. I mean, I went to a five-A school in Texas, and we only lost two kids out of my class in four years. To a car accident. Y'all are way ahead of the national curve, and the police swear suicide spreads through teenagers faster than a bad case of mono in a game of spin the bottle."

She tipped her head to one side. "Blonde, you said? Oh. Evie? I wonder if that was Evelyn Miney?"

I fixed an interested, but noncommittal, expression on my face.

"I bet it was," she continued when I didn't say anything. "She had a thing for TJ. Everyone knew it. Kind of sad, really. I feel sorry for her. Lost her momma to cancer a few years back. And you know, I can't recall having seen her this week." She flipped a folder open and ran her finger about halfway down the paper inside before she turned a few pages and looked up at me. "She's been out of school all week. And her daddy goes away on business a fair amount." She pressed her fingers to her lips, reaching for the phone. "There's just been so much going on, no one bothered to ask why she wasn't here."

I watched, pinching my lips together, as she pulled off her clip-on earring and dialed the phone. Her expression went from worry to panic as she pressed the button in the cradle to disconnect. "She's not picking up."

She dialed again, only three keys this time, and I closed my eyes. Not another one. I felt a teeny bit bad for suspecting Evelyn. What if she'd just been sad about her friends? Just because they stopped talking to her didn't mean she wouldn't miss them.

I half-listened while Norma told the sheriff's dispatcher to send a deputy by to check on Evelyn, drumming my fingers on the desk and wondering about Luke. I had zero in the way of good excuses to ask Norma about him. Maybe I could get something from the coach, though.

"Does Coach Morris have a class right now?" I asked when she hung up. "I have just a few more things I'd like to talk to him about."

"No. He's at lunch. Probably in his office." She watched the phone like she could will it to ring.

"I hope she's all right," I said, turning back for the door. The hallway was silent, the kids all sorted into their classrooms.

"Me, too." Norma nodded.

I hurried down to the gym, hoping I wasn't about to have another dead kid to write about as much as I was hoping the coach would tell me something useful.

"Hello? Woman on deck," I called, poking my head into the boys' locker room. No answer.

I stepped inside, keeping my eyes level—just in case. "Coach Morris?"

I heard a clatter.

"Coach?" I walked toward the glass-walled office, but found it empty. Unease settled over me in a thick blanket as I walked the locker rows, looking for the source of the noise. "Hello?"

A metal-on-metal squeal sounded behind me and I nearly jumped out of my skin, grabbing the edge of a nearby bank of lockers to keep my balance as I whirled, images of ten zillion teen slasher flicks I'd watched with Kyle years before flashing through my head. There are few places creepier than an empty school.

I didn't see anyone behind me, but someone was in there. I put one hand on the locker and slipped my heels off, stowing one in my bag and turning the other stiletto-out in my hand. Creeping silently along the concrete floor in my bare feet, I peered around the edge of each locker bank before I scurried to the next, Kirkwood sandal raised and ready.

I was not getting chopped up and stuffed into lockers in a building full of people without a fight.

Soft footfalls sounded around the corner that led to the door. I held my breath, leaning back and locking my eyes on the doorway.

The door clicked shut.

I tiptoed to the little entry area, my hand on the cinderblock wall, steeling myself before I hopped around the corner, stiletto in the air.

The vestibule was empty, the door closed.

I sagged back against the wall and caught my breath. Something strange was going on in Mathews County.

I slid my shoes back onto my feet before I walked out into the gym. I found Morris crossing the basketball court.

"Hey there," he called, smiling. "Norma said you were looking for me. I must have passed you when I went to turn my attendance sheet in. She gets irritated with me for keeping it 'til the end of the day. I'm trying to do better." He grinned a goofy schoolboy-crush grin that matched her Coach-Morris-is-so-dreamy smile. It was like Peyton Place. With tractors.

"I just wanted to chat for a few minutes if you have time," I said, scanning the gym. "You didn't see anyone else in here on your way down, did you?"

He shook his head. "This is my free period. There shouldn't be anyone down here for another hour."

I nodded, keeping the fact that there had been to myself.

He waved me into the locker room, gesturing for me to have a seat in his office. I paused on my way, noticing the shiny locks hanging from the locker doors.

"Those weren't there last week," I said, turning a questioning look to Morris.

"One of the boys had some pills go missing out of his locker," he said. "I told them to bring locks in."

"What kind of pills?" My thoughts flashed to the empty bottle the cops found on TJ.

"Luke Bosley is diabetic," Morris said. "He takes pills to manage his blood sugar. His mother was ticked about having to pay full price for an early refill."

"Pills," I said, walking toward the office. "Not shots? I thought that was more common for adults."

Morris shrugged. "I don't know a whole lot about it. Luke's folks say it's genetic. Hit him during puberty. He handles it pretty well."

I sat down in a green plastic chair inside the office door, pondering that. Why would someone steal the kid's diabetes medication? Maybe teenagers knew something about getting high that I didn't. I smiled at Morris. His L-shaped metal desk rivaled mine in the piled-with-paper department.

Before either of us could speak, a gangly boy with dark hair and Morris's nose stuck his head around the corner. "Coach?" He turned warm brown eyes on me and smiled. "Oh, sorry. I'll come back."

Morris shook his head. "What do you need, Eli?" He took his seat and gestured to me. "This is Miss Clarke from the paper in Richmond. Miss Clarke, this is my son, Eli."

"I see the resemblance." I half-stood, holding a hand out to shake Eli's. "Nice to meet you." Resuming my seat, I crossed my legs and fished out a notebook and pen.

"I just wanted to ask you about tomorrow's lineup," Eli said to his dad. "It can wait."

"I haven't made it yet." Morris said, his tone holding an edge.

"What position do you play, Eli?" I asked before either of them could speak again.

"First base," he said. "Now, anyway."

I tried to be unobtrusive about writing that down, holding his gaze while my pen moved slowly over my notebook.

"That's an important position," I said.

"Better than left center field. I moved when Luke got pushed up to starting pitcher."

I held my eyebrows in place with effort, shooting a glance at Morris.

"Luke was a good first baseman," he said, defensiveness bleeding into his words. "He and TJ traded off the pitcher's mound and first. Eli's got good accuracy." He shot his son an affectionate grin, the tension in the room ebbing. "He's smart, too. Hasn't ever missed the honor roll."

"Syd helped me with math," Eli said, his voice cracking. "Even after we —well. Anyway. She was a good friend." He cast his eyes down, but not before I saw tears shining in them.

"I'm sorry for your loss," I said, unable to figure a way to shoehorn a question about his relationship with Sydney into the conversation without practically accusing him of murder. "Both of them."

His brow wrinkled briefly before he nodded. "Thank you."

I glanced between father and son, a nagging feeling I was missing something dancing through my thoughts. Staying quiet, I hoped one of them would fill in the blank. No one did.

"I hope y'all have a great season," I said finally, breaking an awkward, smiley silence.

"Thank you, ma'am." Eli nodded to his dad before he backed out of the office. "I better get to geometry. Nice to meet you, Miss Clarke."

I waved, then turned to Coach Morris. "Nice kid."

"Thank you. We're proud of him. What can I do for you today?"

"I just want to talk to you about the baseball team," I said. "Some of the other kids on it, how your season's looking without TJ pitching."

"Not as good as it was, that's for damned sure." He sat back in his chair. His face said there was something he wanted to add, but he didn't speak. I offered an encouraging smile, staying quiet.

"I saw your story this weekend, and the one in the *Washington Post*, too. Why do the Okersons think there's more to this than the sheriff does?" he asked finally. "Do you think they're right?"

Oh, boy. I twisted a lock of hair around my fingers, contemplating that. His face creased with worried lines.

"Why do you ask?" I countered, dropping my hair.

He sighed, running a hand over his face. "I've lived here all my life.

Most people don't even lock their front doors at night. Jaywalking and public intoxication are about the most serious criminal offenses we see. A giant snapping turtle made the front page last week, for pity's sake. I don't want to think someone killed this boy."

"But you do, don't you?" I asked softly.

"I don't know. I'm not a hundred percent convinced of anything. But I think Zeke is making a mistake, writing it off so quick."

"Why?" I clicked out a pen and flipped to a clean piece of paper.

"After you came here last week, I cleaned out TJ's locker and took his bag by to his dad. I didn't want them to have to come here and do that, but Tony said Ashton wanted his stuff back before the service." His eyes flicked to the window that looked over the locker room. "His football cleats were in the back, forgotten after that last game."

I froze when Morris's eyes came back to mine.

"Tony told me they were worn out after that game," Morris said. "I flipped them over when I put them in his bag, and they weren't worn out. They were filed down. Sloppily, too. I guess his dad didn't look that close. Somebody caused the fall that wrecked his knee."

I didn't even need to write that down, watching as Morris shook his head. "But why?"

I studied him for a moment. Everyone following the story knew the Okersons thought TJ didn't commit suicide. Morris looked genuinely torn up over the idea, but he seemed to believe it, too. And he might know something that could help me—as long as his son wasn't the guilty one. I just had to step carefully with my questions.

"Talk to me about Luke Bosley, coach," I said.

"No." He pulled in a sharp breath and closed his eyes. "My God. Do you think?"

"I don't know," I said. "Something seems off to me, and you said his dad puts a lot of pressure on him, right?"

"What do you want to know?"

"Does he play football, too?" I asked.

"Backup quarterback," Morris said. The tension in his face said this wasn't the first time he'd had this thought.

"And if TJ hadn't had access to the best trainers and therapists because of his father—if he'd been a normal kid—that injury would have ended his playing career." I raised an eyebrow at him. "Luke's the new starting pitcher, just like his dad wanted, right?"

Morris pinched his lips into a tight line, emotions warring on his face for a good two minutes before he spoke again. "Son of a bitch. We have to call the sheriff." He reached for the phone and I raised a hand.

"Not so fast. He's convinced he's done, and I don't think he'll listen. There's a dance Friday night, though, and I have a plan. Sort of."

"Can I do anything to help you?" he asked, his eyes on something behind my head. I turned to find a photo of the baseball team taken after the regional championship win the previous spring. TJ grinned from the center.

I turned back to him, wincing at the anguish that was plain on his face.

"I'm bringing a friend with me, and I want Luke to talk to him," I said. "You think you could help with that?"

He nodded. "These boys—I have a son, too." He cleared his throat, but the catch in his voice didn't diminish. "I see my players almost as much as I see Eli this time of year. You can't not care about these kids when you do this job. At least, I can't. This week has been a nightmare. I keep looking for TJ at practice, expecting to see him warming up his arm or helping a freshman get more drop on his curve." A tear hovered on his lashes for a long second before it fell. He didn't bother to brush it away. "He was a great kid. I can't imagine what his folks are going through. And if someone did this to him—well, if I can help you, count me in. I'll be at the dance. Just point me to your friend and I'll introduce Luke."

I stood and offered my hand. "Thank you, coach. I appreciate it. And I'm very sorry for your loss."

"Thank you," he said. "I know we're not the big city, but some of us really appreciate your help with this." Sincerity rang in every word. Man, I hoped Eli didn't have anything to do with this.

I smiled. "Let's tell the sheriff that when we're done, shall we?"

"I've known Zeke since kindergarten, and I play poker with him twice a month. You bet I will, ma'am." He tipped his Mathews Eagles baseball cap.

Ma'am. I vowed to stop on the way home for new eye cream. Smiling a thank you, I left him to his lineup and hurried back to my car before the bell rang again, checking my text messages and wondering if I could find anything else about Luke before Friday night.

18

The rest of my week sped by in a blur of routine crime stories, a murder trial, and sleepless nights spent in equal parts thinking about Joey (who had disappeared, save for the occasional text) and trying to fit the pieces of the Mathews puzzle together.

Bob warned me to stay under everyone's radar and give Spence and Andrews time to cool off, which I didn't see happening soon with Shelby yapping at them. I smiled and nodded and shoved office politics aside, mostly because I'd learned that Shelby will be Shelby, and I had bigger fish to fry than Spencer Jacobs.

By Friday night, I was fairly convinced Luke was my guy, and excessively grateful Kyle was taking me to the dance. A seasoned, superstar ATF agent could surely pry a confession from a pissed-off teenage boy. And arrest his murderous little butt, too. Leaving me to hand Tony and Ashton their answer and go back to my regular life. If I played it right, I might not even have to tell my mom about this one. She'd been crazy busy. If I told her she was off the hook for reading the week's copy, she'd probably send me flowers.

I left work a little early and took Darcy out for a game of fetch. She took off for the back corner of the yard and dug furiously at something in the dirt. I picked up her stuffed squirrel and followed, squatting to examine her find when I saw it wasn't a dead animal.

Cigarette butts. Unfiltered ones. I counted seven.

I looked over the fence. My neighbor was as granola as a person could get this side of Berkeley, but maybe he had a friend who smoked. Darcy's barking and snarling at that part of the yard Tuesday night flashed through my thoughts, though, and I kept my ears open as we played, locking the door when I went back inside. Someone had been out there. The knowledge was slightly panic-inducing, and there was less than nothing I could do about it. I locked the doggie door for added measure and jumped when Darcy barked.

"Sorry. I'd rather keep you in one piece," I said.

Kyle appeared on my porch at five-thirty on the dot, and I caught a sharp breath when I opened the front door. The cotton of his red button-down molded to his muscular shoulders like hot fudge over ice cream, the short sleeves outlining his impressive biceps with heart-stopping precision. His fitted jeans sported creases that could cut glass over perfectly worn-in Justin ostrich dress boots. But it was the black felt Stetson on his head that stuck the "hey" in my throat. You can take the girl out of Texas, but a sexy cowboy is still sexy in Virginia.

"Evening." He tipped the hat and winked and my knees forgot how to work. Jesus. I hung onto the door and tried to look casual.

"Evening, yourself. You look nice, cowboy."

"You look beautiful." He offered a hand and I took it, my fingers tingling when he laced them with his. It still fit.

I smoothed my smocked, prairie-print dress as I climbed into a white pickup, side-eyeing him as he started the engine. "You sell your Explorer?"

"Borrowed this for tonight. Just thought it fit a little better. And you used to like my truck."

I shook my head, crossing my feet carefully so as not to scuff my chocolate-and-turquoise cowgirl boots. "I'm a little too old to be won over by a pickup and a nice hat." Or I should be, anyway.

"I know you're not convinced we belong together anymore," he said, keeping his eyes on the road. "I'm not even sure I'm the only guy in your life these days. But even if I'm not, I'm the one who knows you best."

I sighed, watching his profile and feeling a subject change coming on.

"So, I've had an interesting week." I filled him in on my chat with Coach Morris, and brought him up to speed on Luke and TJ and Sydney—she was my sticking point, because I couldn't nail down a motive for Luke killing her. Which brought me to Eli Morris. Who seemed like a nice enough kid. But Parker had told me baseball scouts would watch a first baseman more than they would an outfielder, and that plus Sydney equaled motive. I considered Coach Morris. He'd appeared genuinely torn up, and willing to help. But it had occurred to me that he might be trying to push my attention off his son. I wasn't sure that was likely, but it wasn't unlikely, given the tangled mess this story had been.

"What if the girl did kill herself? Assuming you're right and there was any foul play at work here, of course," Kyle said.

I pictured Tiffany's sure expression, the pain in her brown eyes.

"Anything is possible, but I'm not willing to start down that road yet," I said.

He nodded. "We'll just see what we can see. What about the girl you told me about? Are we looking for her?"

I twisted my mouth to one side. I knew from a (very) brief call with (an annoyed) Sheriff Zeke on Wednesday that Evelyn was alive and well, just cutting class because she said she couldn't take the stares and whispers. Which was either really sad, or damned suspicious, and I'd been unable to figure out which.

"I'm not sure she'll show, because she's been a hermit since TJ's funeral, from what I understand," I told Kyle. "But I can't tell if she's holed up because she's sad or because she feels guilty, and I hear this thing is a big freaking deal to the kids out here. They don't have too many places to hang out besides the beach and the 7-Eleven parking lot. So I'm hoping she won't be able to resist. I'd really like to have a chat with her."

"I'm not about to walk into an underage serving zone, am I?" Kyle asked, turning the truck onto 161 as the sun dropped out of the sky behind us.

"I can't imagine. I mean, it's in a public street. On the other hand, the sheriff's cousins are local moonshiners, so I'm not a hundred percent on that. But don't go busting out your badge unless someone cops to the murder, huh? Underage drinking is ABC police business, right?"

"Strictly speaking. Did my guy there ever call you back?"

"Nope. I didn't think anyone liked me less than the FBI until I ran across those guys. I guess it's a good thing I've never needed them for anything past a press-release follow-up before." I glanced at him. "And a good thing I have friends in the right places these days."

"You want me for more than my badge." He winked.

"You know, part of my reservation comes from my rule against dating cops."

"There's a rule? Why don't you tell a guy? I quit."

I snorted. "You may not do that," I said. "Someone I know tells me rules are made to be broken, anyhow."

"I'm a cop. I'm not sure I'm comfortable with that."

"Well, they can always be changed. I'll call a special session and rewrite the law. Maybe."

He reached over and squeezed my hand. More sparks. "You have my vote."

I flipped on the radio and watched the fields speed by as Kenny Chesney sang about kegs and closets. He had a point. Being a grownup isn't much fun sometimes.

"You know," Kyle said, "me being a cop comes in handy for you on occasion. I have a surprise for you."

I waited for him to go on, but he just sat there, a smile playing around his lips.

"Are you going to share?" I asked.

He glanced at me from the corner of his eye. "I suppose you need time to prepare."

"For what?"

"The ABC has a guy undercover out here, working a moonshining operation. We're supposed to meet him at ten. It's all strictly off the record, but you said that was okay."

I stared for a second, then leaned across the bench seat and planted a kiss on his cheek. Even if I couldn't quote the cop, maybe I could find out what was going on with the moonshine. If the ABC agent was in with the right crowd, I might even be able to figure out where TJ and Sydney had gotten it. I grabbed a pen and an old receipt out of the console in the truck and scribbled questions for the rest of the drive.

I directed Kyle into Elmer's antique store parking lot and he marveled at the old-time feel of the converted gas station, even using some of the same words I had as he took my hand and helped me hop down from the truck. It was effortless to fall back to a level of normal with Kyle. But did I want normal and comfortable, or did I want exciting and unknown?

A rainbow of lanterns zigzagged the width of Main Street, which was blocked off at both ends of the square. A table full of tween-aged girls supervised by Norma from the high school office sat across the head of the street. I handed the tallest kid a twenty. "Two, please."

"Cute bag!" Norma said, eyeing my little brown leather "necessary objects only" evening pouch. The front was decorated with hand-sewn turquoise beadwork.

"Thanks," I said. "I got it a craft fair my mom dragged me to the last time I went home."

"It's nice of you to come," Norma said, handing me two printed card-stock tickets. I tucked them into my bag without looking at them.

"The Accidental Rednecks are playing," Norma said. "They're local, and they're real good. Don't leave without trying the barbecue. And the pie. My momma helps bake the pies."

I nodded, leading Kyle into the party. "Sounds great."

Food and beverage stations lined the sidewalks for half a block, hawking everything from fresh-caught seafood to funnel cakes and kettle corn.

We walked through picnic tables, complete with red-checkered table-cloths, toward the stage that spanned the far end of the street. The band was cooking, playing covers of classic rock and modern country. The half-block in front of the stage was the dance floor, dotted with couples (age range: pre-adolescent to geriatric, which I found all kinds of charming) either dancing with each other or swaying to the beat as they watched the show. I turned toward the drink stand, remembering the last of my antibiotics was waiting in my bag, when the singer flipped his collar up and the band played the first strains of "Are You Lonesome Tonight?" Kyle caught my hand, taking the bag off my shoulder and dropping it to an empty tabletop.

"Dance with me," he said, his blue lasers locked on my eyes.

Speechless, I followed him to the dance floor.

Everyone else fell away, and if I didn't know better I'd swear Kyle had paid off the singer to write a set tailored for us: we swayed, two-stepped, and boogied through a dozen of my favorite songs before the band took a dinner break.

"I think that's our cue to go eat, too," I said, breathless. "And to get some investigating done." I looked around at the darkness that crowded in from all sides, held at bay by the pretty lanterns, and checked my watch. "Holy cow. We've been here for over an hour."

I grabbed my purse and joined a dozen people waiting in line for drinks. Smiling at the pretty bartender I recognized from Bobbi's club, I ordered an iced tea and shook the last tablet from my prescription bottle, swallowing it and tossing the bottle in the trash. I scanned the dancers for Luke, or Coach Morris, or Evelyn, but didn't see any of them.

"Maybe everyone's getting food," I said, pulling Kyle toward the barbecue table, my stomach reminding me that I had skipped lunch to get my juvenile murder trial wrap-up done and ready to go on the web before Charlie got it on the air. "You hungry?"

"I'm always hungry," he said, wriggling a suggestive eyebrow.

I rolled my eyes. "Chicken. Toast. Pickles."

It all smelled heavenly, and I was slightly surprised to find Bobbi serving it.

"You ladies doing all the food service for the party?" I asked. "How'd you swing that?"

She grinned. "Thanks to you, I'm not nearly the leper Dorothy made me out to be for the past year. The mayor came in for lunch—with his wife —and they asked me to come cater the party when they got a load of Grandmomma's sauce."

I ordered myself a C-cup and Kyle a rack of ribs, and dropped a twenty in her tip jar when she refused to take payment for the food.

I'd put exactly three bites in my mouth when I spotted Evelyn lurking near the ice cream stand.

"She's here." I dropped my fork and stood, straightening my dress. "The girl. I'll be back. Wish me luck."

"At least finish your dinner," Kyle said. "She's not going anywhere."

I stared at her pink-rimmed eyes—which I suspected were crimson under her concealer— and guarded expression. "I'm not so sure about that," I said. "Sit tight for a few. I won't be long."

I wandered toward the ice cream stand, skipping my eyes around the crowd and trying not to look too obvious. Turning to glance behind me at just the right moment, I practically tripped over Evelyn.

"I'm so sorry!" I said over the music, righting myself and putting a steadying hand on her arm. "Are you all right? I should look where I'm going."

She nodded, a smile teasing the corners of her lips. "You didn't hurt me, at any rate."

I tipped my head to one side and studied her. "Don't I know you?"

"This is Mathews. Everyone knows everyone."

I smiled. "It seems. But I'm from Richmond. Oh, I know!" I snapped my fingers. "I saw you at TJ's funeral. In the restroom. You were quite upset. Are you feeling a little better? Ice cream always helps me." I nodded to the cone in her hand.

"I'm all right. I guess. Better than TJ and Syd."

Sydney's funeral had been the day before, her parents waiting for out of town relatives to get flights arranged.

"It's such a sad situation," I said.

"Syd was my best friend." Her voice broke. "For my whole life. Until last year. Stupid boys. Stupid me." She ducked her head and covered her face with one hand, tears dripping from her face as fast as vanilla-chocolate swirl dripped from her fingers.

I passed her a napkin from the holder on the edge of a nearby table.

"Thanks." She looked up, sniffling, and tossed the cone into a trash can. "I just want to talk to her one more time. To tell her how sorry I am. How much I wish I could make it right. How stupid I was."

"I'm sure she knew," I said. "That you were sorry, I mean."

She shook her head, hard, her wispy blonde hair flying. "No, she didn't. TJ was so cute, and he was so good to her. I just wanted someone to treat me that way. Stupid TJ. Why did he have to be such a good guy?" Her eyes narrowed as she spoke, her tone changing from anguished to angry. Huh.

I shrugged. "It's just the way some people are," I said. "I'm sure he didn't mean to be offensive with it."

"Of course he didn't. Syd was an amazing person. She deserved TJ. I didn't wish anything bad for her. It's just not fair. I miss my momma. My dad is—" she paused, hauling in a steadying breath. "Well, anyway. Syd's folks loved her like my momma loved me. She was an only child, too."

"So I heard."

"I just wanted to tell her I was sorry. Then she ran off to France to get away from me. From TJ and me, maybe. And I tried to tell her at the party when she came home, but she threw her drink in my face and screamed that she hated me." She dissolved into a teary mess, mumbling what sounded like "hated me" over and over between hitching breaths.

Christ on a cracker. I leaned on the side of the ice cream trailer and patted Evelyn's heaving shoulder. Maybe I was wrong about Luke. What if this girl had blamed TJ for losing her BFF and then lost her shit when Sydney humiliated her after TJ was dead? I felt bad, trying to comfort her while wondering if she was a murderer, but I'd have felt worse if I walked off and left her sobbing like that.

I watched the crowd as I pondered, spotting Luke on the dance floor with a pretty redhead in a fabulous pink cotton dress. I kept my eyes on him as they moved, shimmying to "Little Sister" before she locked her hands behind his neck and he laid his on her hips when the keyboard player tapped out the opening notes of "The Dance."

Evelyn cried herself out and looked up, wiping the concealer off her eyes as she did so. She looked like an extra from *Night of the Demons*.

"Thanks. Everyone around here has treated me like a dog since TJ died. Worse, really. Most people like dogs."

I tried to smile. "It gets better."

"People keep telling me time will dull the pain. But does it get rid of the guilt?"

I'll take loaded questions for four hundred, Alex.

"I meant, just life in general. High school can kind of suck. But it gets better," I said. "Hang in there."

"I'm trying." She scrubbed at her face with the napkin, her eyes falling on a cluster of pretty girls who were actually pointing at her as they cackled and chatted. "It was a big mistake, me coming here tonight. I need to go home. But you were nice, and I needed that. I haven't seen or talked to much of anybody since the funeral."

"Don't mention it." I thought about what I'd managed to glean from the conversation. She was at the party where Sydney died. "Hey, Evelyn? What was Sydney drinking that last night?"

"Freaking moonshine." She wrinkled her nose. "I heard her tell someone it was a gift. Somebody told her it'd dull the pain. She'd had half the jar when she got pissed at me. She was having trouble walking, but she still managed to hit me with the stuff. It stings when it gets in your eyes."

I nodded. "Thanks."

I watched her go, noting the way she slumped her shoulders, trying to make herself as small as possible. I'd walked through most of high school like that in an effort to hide my height. It looked like Evelyn was just trying to hide.

I spun back to the dance floor, looking for Luke, and found Kyle blocking my view. "Well?" he asked.

"Still don't know. She's got some anger and guilt around all this. And some daddy issues, too, I think, from the way she was talking." I knew Em would say that could mess a teenage girl up. "It's hard to say if she's upset for ruining her friendship with them and not having a way to fix that or if she feels guilty for killing them. Sydney was definitely drinking moonshine, though. Evelyn said she had half a jar before she flung the rest in Evelyn's face. Couldn't walk upright. And someone gave it to her." That sentence stuck in my head. We were dealing with something in the moonshine. I was as sure of it as I was my shoe size. That stuff would mask just about any kind of nasty taste I could imagine.

"That is a tough code to crack," Kyle said, turning and wrapping an arm around my waist, pulling me to his side. "You see the other kid you wanted to talk to?"

I looked up at him, liking my poisoned drink theory more as I considered Luke. "He was on the dance floor thirty seconds ago," I said. "He couldn't have gone far."

I searched the sidewalk on the opposite side of the street for Luke's blond head, and saw Coach Morris first. He waved, crossing quickly to shake Kyle's hand.

I introduced them, turning my most earnest smile on Morris. "Did Eli come with you tonight, coach?" I asked. "I'm wondering if he was at any of the parties last week. Maybe he saw something? Heard something?"

Morris shook his head. "He said he didn't feel like it. Hasn't been himself lately. He and TJ weren't exactly buddies, but he's torn up over Sydney. She was a special girl."

Crap. But interesting, too. Torn up, sad? Or torn up, guilty?

"I just talked to Luke," Morris said, glancing around. "It's been hard the past few days. I almost can't look at him. I can't believe he'd really want to hurt his teammate."

"We are still in America," Kyle said. "There's the whole 'innocent until proven guilty' thing."

"He tampered with TJ's cleats," the coach said.

"We think, anyway," I said, eyeing Morris. He was trying awfully hard to hand Luke to us on a platter. Too hard?

"Not the same as murdering someone. I'm not saying he's not capable of it, because causing serious injury to a rival is a bad sign, but if he'd wanted TJ dead why not call him out to the beach or the baseball field alone and just shoot him?" Kyle asked.

The coach fell silent. "I don't know. Maybe he wasn't planning to kill him."

"That would be way more likely if there were signs of trauma to the body that indicated a spontaneous method." Kyle looked around. "Nicey, you said tall and blond." He pointed. "That kid?"

I followed his gaze and saw Luke making out with the redhead in the shadows next to the barbecue stand. "That's him."

Kyle turned to coach Morris. "How about an introduction?"

"Sure thing," Morris said, waving for Kyle to follow him across the street.

I started back for the table, hoping Bobbi's chicken was as good cold as it was warm, when a voice behind me stopped my foot in midair.

"Who is that, and what does he want with my son?"

I spun to find the woman who'd come looking for Luke at the funeral, dressed in a purple broomstick skirt and a floral-print top.

She nodded to me. "You were talking to Lucas at the funeral the other day. With a different fella. Who's that one?"

I smiled. "He's a baseball fan. Coach Morris was telling us about Luke's arm, and my friend wanted to meet him. I hear this is going to be a heck of a season for the Eagles."

Her shrewd expression softened slightly. "It will be now," she said, her eyes flicking from me to Kyle and the coach, then back again.

I blanched, staring at her for a second with a smile pasted across my face, my brain in hyperdrive, shifting puzzle pieces.

How many stories had I read about moms who were willing to kill for their children? Okay, most of them were defending their wee'uns' lives, shooting intruders or occasionally taking out child molesters. But hell— what if I suspected the wrong Bosley? I turned my eyes to the scene across the street.

Morris tapped Luke's shoulder and introduced Kyle. Luke broke into a big grin and offered a hand, dismissing the girl with a wave. She backed up a few steps, staring daggers at the coach.

"He's a good boy," Luke's mother said from my elbow. "He deserves a fair shot."

I tried to keep my trap shut and failed. "Did he not get a fair shot at some point? The coach said he's been on the team for three years running."

"He should have been the star. But TJ was there. Not even from here, with his famous daddy and all their money. My husband was the most winning pitcher in Mathews history until TJ came here. Lucas was destined to start for the Eagles from the cradle."

"He's been a starter since he was a sophomore," I said. "I found that impressive."

She cut her eyes to me. "He should be the star," she repeated. "People wanting to meet him, shake his hand. Give him scholarships that will get him the hell out of this town. He's got a fair shot now."

She walked toward Kyle and my jaw dropped, my mind racing.

What did I know about Mrs. Bosley?

She was the PTA President. Which meant she was at the school as much as the teachers. Evelyn said someone gave Sydney the moonshine she was drinking. Which Evelyn probably wouldn't mention if the someone had been her.

I froze, digging out my cell phone and opening the photos.

There was Syd's moonshine jar. And there was a piece of paper in the bag next to it.

Bright green, like the one I'd seen in TJ's locker. I closed my eyes and pictured the party flyer. Concave, and crinkled up along one edge.

Like it had been wrapped around a jar?

Hot damn.

I clicked back to the county marriage records and searched for Bosley. I found that Simon Bosley had married Lily Sidell the year before Luke was born.

Sidell. Elmer and Bobbi Jo said the Sidell family made moonshine.

Quickly, I tapped every word into a note before they faded. Then I texted my best friend. "I need to talk to you," I typed. "Sorry again for bailing on girls night, but can we get coffee in the morning? Need a mom's perspective."

She texted right back. "Sure, doll. You find your murderer yet?"

"Probably. If I could figure out which one of these Looney Tunes it is," I replied. "Lesson from this trip: there's no shortage of folks with motive out here."

"Fun. Thompson's @ 9:30. Can't wait to hear. Miss you. Xoxo"

"Thanks. Miss you. Xoxo"

I looked up as Coach Morris and Norma slow-danced into my sight line, her short frame fused to his tall one. Her eyes were closed, her head resting just below his shoulder. His arms cradled the small of her back, and his feet moved to the music—but Morris's eyes were on Luke Bosley, an unreadable expression on his face.

I knew the feeling.

Tucking the phone back in my bag, I smiled as Kyle crossed the street toward me. I collapsed into his chest when he offered me a hand, the crazy week finally biting me in the energy stores.

"Hello, there," he said, squeezing my shoulders.

"I am so. Tired." I said. "Can we go?"

"If you're ready," he said, glancing at his watch. "We should head out to the woods to meet my ABC guy. And wait 'til you hear what I got from the kid."

* * *

Kyle passed the turn off for the freeway and drove for about a mile with the guidance of the high beams, then hung a right onto a narrow dirt road that barely cut through the woods.

I glanced at him, then at the pitch-black surrounding the truck. "We're meeting someone here?" I asked.

"It's hard to find places no one can see out here," he said. "We have to protect his cover, or we'll put his life in very real danger."

I nodded.

He rolled to a stop in a teeny clearing, and I spotted the outline of a pickup with no headlights on coming the other way. Kyle turned the brights off, the sallow glow of the low beams not making much headway with the darkness. He stepped out of the truck without turning off the lights, walking around to open my door and help me down. I blinked away fatigue as I stood up, turning for the front of the car.

The undercover ABC agent stepped into the light and I froze for a split second, tightening my fingers on Kyle's arm as a stream of tobacco juice hit the dirt in front of Kyle's borrowed pickup.

Bubba—the same Bubba I'd met Tuesday night in Maryland—called a "Hello," and I swallowed a "Crap hell."

I pulled a dose of composure out of the chilly night air and strode past Kyle, putting out my hand. Bubba's eyes widened slightly when I stepped into the light, and I started talking before he could open his mouth.

"Thanks so much for coming to talk to me," I said. "Nichelle Clarke, *Richmond Telegraph*."

Kyle put a hand on my elbow and then shook Bubba's proffered one. "We're strictly off the record here," he said.

Bubba gave me a once-over. "We'd better be." He raised an eyebrow. "You sure you're not wearing a wire?"

I pinched my lips down on a smile. "Absolutely," I said. "I didn't even bring a notebook. But I sure could use some background on what's going on out here."

"I understand you think moonshine had something to do with TJ Okerson's death," Bubba said.

"At the risk of sounding paranoid, can I ask where you heard that?" The *Post*'s story whirled through my thoughts.

"From Agent Miller, there," Bubba said. "Who has a lot of respect at the ATF." He held my gaze as he spoke and I fidgeted, dropping my eyes to my boots. Kyle chuckled and thanked him.

"I don't know for sure what to think," I said. "But I know there was moonshine present at both scenes. And Sydney Cobb was definitely drinking it. Can you tell me where the triple-X label comes from?" My voice shook and I cleared my throat, praying Kyle would think I was just nervous. I'm a lousy liar.

Bubba smiled. "I believe I can. That's the Parsons family. I've been working a sting inside their operation for eighteen months," he said, leaning against the hood of the truck. "I understand you've called half the guys in my division looking for a comment this week, but they won't breathe a word about an investigation with an undercover officer in place."

So that's why they'd been so sweet. "That's common policy."

He spit again. "We've got three stills. Parsons has a business front at the auto body shop on Main, and there are a couple of places serving the stuff. I'm days away from a bust. And now you have dead kids? Part of the reason I came tonight was to find out what you know."

"Not a lot," I said, lighting on the "places serving" part of that and worrying about Bobbi. But I had zero ways to ask about that without implicating her, on the off chance she wasn't already on his list, so I moved on. "Moonshine was there at both parties, and like I said, Sydney was seen drinking it. Half a jar, I heard. I've seen two different labels on it, though. The one Sydney had was faded across the middle. A different one I saw was not."

"Faded how?" He looked interested.

"Like the ink went to gray and then back to black."

"I've never noticed that, and I've seen about every part of their operation."

I put a mental star by that.

"You said they sell it out of a body shop? Do a lot of kids come around to buy it?"

"I wouldn't say a lot of kids. Some, probably. I know we get more old guys than kids."

"Did you ever see TJ?"

"Not off the football field."

Damn.

"Does the sheriff know you're working out here?"

"It's agency policy to coordinate with local law enforcement."

"That's not an answer," I said.

"It's the best I can do."

I resisted the urge to lean back against Kyle, keeping everything as professional as I could considering the waves of exhaustion crashing over me.

"You know the sheriff has cousins in the moonshine trade, though?"

"He does. So does everybody else around here, to be fair."

"Have you heard anyone say anything about the dead kids? Any reason someone might want them dead?"

"Not a word."

"How about the moonshine? Any complaints of a bad batch lately?"

"Not that I've heard."

Double damn. I sighed, wading through thick thoughts in search of another question. The funky label. He'd never seen a faded one, so where had it come from?

"Do the Parsons sell unlabeled jars of triple-X to anyone?" I asked, bracing a hip against the truck's fender to stay on my feet.

"Not often. There are a few folks distributing across the state who prefer unlabeled jars. It's not as traceable that way."

"Why label them at all?"

"Vanity? Underground brand recognition? I have no idea."

So someone could be buying them unlabeled and putting the faded ones on themselves. Which meant knowing about the auto body front didn't help me. But it'd have to be someone the moonshiners trusted, from what he'd said. Someone like Lily Sidell Bosley?

"Do you know who takes the unlabeled ones?"

"Not by name. It's not a big group of people."

I nodded to myself, then smiled at Bubba. I was out of questions, which flipped my focus to getting Kyle the hell out of there before Bubba brought up our first meeting. "Thanks so much for talking to me," I said, offering my hand again. He shook it.

"If my name turns up in the newspaper—" he said.

"I don't have your name," I cut him off. "And I would never compromise a police officer's safety."

"I don't suppose I gave it to you, at that." He dropped my hand, holding my gaze with somber eyes. "Do yourself a favor and be careful. These guys aren't the type you screw around with, and they don't like the things they've been hearing about you. I wouldn't be surprised if they'd done a little research on you, too. Like, maybe on where you live."

I shivered in the breeze and nodded, the unfiltered cigarette butts in the corner of my yard flashing through my thoughts. "I appreciate the heads up." Not that I could keep the Mathews grapevine quiet.

He got back in his truck and started the engine after Kyle thanked him and told him to leave first.

"Thank you," I said, turning to Kyle.

"It didn't exactly solve your puzzle," he said, wrapping me in a tight hug after Bubba was out of sight. "And I'm more worried about you than I was before."

"There are unlabeled jars," I said, laying my head on his chest. "The faded ink is the key to something, here. I just have to find out who gets the unlabeled ones. And then who gave it to the kids."

"You will." He turned and opened the passenger door of the pickup. "You're pretty smart."

The heel of my boot caught on the edge of the door when I climbed back into the truck, tossing me forward into the floorboard. Graceful as a drunkard on stilts, party of one.

"Did you sneak some moonshine when I wasn't looking?" Kyle slid behind the wheel and offered me a hand as I clambered up into the seat. His fingers closed on the bare skin of my arm and I froze for a second at the warmth that radiated from his fingers, thinking about dancing close to him, feeling his breath on my cheek and his hands on my back.

I smiled as I smoothed my skirt. "Yeah, no. Once was all the exposure to that I'll ever need. I think I wear heels so much, other types of shoes throw me off."

"Too bad. The boots look good on you, Texas."

He turned his head to check the mirror as he started the truck and I studied his jawline, shaded auburn with stubble around his goatee. I sat on my fingers to keep from reaching out to see how it would feel under them. "The hat looks good on you, cowboy."

He turned back and flashed a grin. "You always have been a sucker for a Stetson and a pair of good boots."

"That was a long time ago." I gripped the door handle and averted my eyes, giving in to some very nice memories for a moment.

"But it was good. And it could be again."

I stared out the window, thinking about how natural his arms felt around me. It really could.

"You were amazing tonight," I said, my eyes on his sure hands, guiding the truck around dark curves.

"So were you. We still make a good team."

"I suppose we do. Thanks for believing me. And thanks for coming with me."

"Anytime, Lois. Your instincts are good."

"Thank you." That was high praise coming from Kyle. "So, what'd you find out from Luke?"

"He's capable of it, I think, but the way he seems so contemptuous of TJ and the temper he seems to barely conceal, I'm not sure the lack of trauma matches."

"Liver failure." I'd been mulling that since Tuesday, and had nothing to show for it. "I can't figure it."

"It would track with a Vicodin overdose," Kyle said gently.

"Don't go back there. My instincts are good, remember?" I said. "Besides, the coroner I talked to said the Vicodin should have caused suffocation first." Except TJ's liver was already damaged. But I wasn't offering up anything that might raise his doubts.

"I just feel like you need a voice of reason."

Subject change. "I talked to Luke's mother for about twelve seconds, but speaking of crazy." I shook my head. "I'm wondering if she might not fly to the top of the suspect list."

"Oh, yeah?"

"She went on about how TJ had an unfair advantage and Luke was the rightful star of the baseball team, and that's been rectified."

He whistled. "Like the cheerleader thing, you think?"

I grinned. "Very much." I'd gone through a true-crime phase, studying cases and the media reports on them for a chunk of my adolescence, and the Texas cheerleader murder was one of my favorites. A mom had killed the girl who was her daughter's big rival for a spot on the squad.

"Would she have had access to TJ's cleats?" Kyle asked. "I mean, do we still think Luke filed them down if we think mom might have killed TJ?"

"I cannot figure a way she'd be in the boys' locker room alone for good reason, but I'm sure she knows where it is and could come up with an excuse if she had to," I said. "Which is a long way around 'maybe.'"

"You're chasing vapor here, you know that, right? You have a boatload of circumstantial evidence, but not a damned thing you can prove. Even if you are right. Which I'm not conceding just yet."

"Em agrees with me." I reminded him.

He was silent for a minute. "Yeah. And she's as good as it gets at criminal psychology. Every time I try to blow you off, I think about what you told me she said. But this is going to be tough to pin on anyone, honey."

"I like tough." I fell into silence as the dark fields outside gave way to freeway street lights. When he pulled off I-64 at the exit for my house, I sighed.

"Something about the moonshine could have caused liver failure, too," I said. "I know the jars I saw came from the Parsons family."

"I can't touch it if it's staying in the state. And the ABC is on it—you heard him, they've almost got enough for a bust."

"It's not. Staying in the state, I mean."

"How do you know that?" He pulled the truck into my driveway and turned to face me, his brow creasing. "I asked you about drinking it and you said 'once was enough,' too. What did you do?"

Dammit. Me and my big mouth. "I can't tell you." I fought to keep my voice even.

He held my gaze for a long moment. "I know this is important to you. But I can't look into it based on a lie, Nichelle. I'm walking a close line with getting in trouble as it is. I know a couple of guys who would say I've already put my nose too far in without an open investigation. If the wrong people decide that, I could lose my job."

"I'm not lying, and I certainly don't want you to lose your job." I fidgeted in the seat, groping for an answer. "People who wouldn't talk to you will talk to me. I promise you, I'm right. If that helps you with an excuse."

He studied every line of my face as I stared at him, trying to look earnest. I was telling the truth. Mostly, I just didn't want to tell him anything that would lead him back to Joey. I knew that was a bomb waiting for a trigger, but I wasn't looking to provide it.

"Did you go interview the moonshiners?" he exploded. "Do you have any idea how badly you could have gotten hurt?"

"But I didn't." I skirted the question, my breath coming faster. I tried to slow it. I didn't want Kyle to be mad at me.

He tipped his hat back. I turned toward him in the seat.

"I don't want you to get hurt." He reached for my hand.

"I don't, either." I squeezed his fingers. "I'm trying to be careful. Jeez, I've only been to Mathews by myself a couple of times."

He pressed his lips into a tight line, holding my gaze silently for a minute before he got out of the truck and came around to open my door.

My head swam when I stood up and I grabbed Kyle's arm to stay on my feet as the driveway wavered. He put one hand under my elbow and wound the other arm around my waist, concern furrowing his brow. "You okay?"

I blinked. "Wow. I guess my equilibrium is still off because of my cold."

He walked me to the door. I leaned back against the wall, ignoring the porch swing because of my unsteadiness.

"And here we are." Kyle's voice dropped. He rested one hand on the wall just above my head, facing me. I breathed the clean smell of his favorite cologne, his eyes holding mine.

My pulse quickened. "Who'd have thought you'd be walking me to the front door at the end of the night, like, ever again?"

"I could walk you inside, if you like." He tipped his hat back, leaning so close I could smell the cinnamon gum on his breath. He traced one finger along my cheekbone, and the light touch sent such a shockwave through me my knees buckled. Oh. My. God.

I closed my eyes and slid my hands up his chest to his shoulders, pulling him the rest of the way home. He brushed his lips lightly over mine, sending sparks skating across the back of my skull. My fingers dug in, pulling him closer, and I parted my lips and traced the line of his with the tip of my tongue. He wound one hand into my hair and deepened the kiss, his other arm sliding behind me and pulling me against him.

"Kyle," I whispered into his lips, trying to catch a steadying breath.

"Nicey," he murmured, kissing his way across my jaw to my neck. I shuddered at the electricity his goatee brushing my skin sent through me, knocking his hat to the floor as I clutched at the back of his head. His close-cropped hair was soft under my hands.

He trailed his mouth slowly up the side of my neck and returned to my lips, his tongue moving languidly over mine. The porch rocked under my feet.

"I need to go inside," I said, my breath coming so fast my vision blurred. When had Kyle gotten to be such a great kisser? Never mind. I probably didn't want to think about that. I was having trouble thinking about anything except wanting to lie down, and wanting to kiss Kyle some more. And how to reconcile those two things.

I fumbled a key out of my bag, handing it to him and leaning my head back against the wall, willing my pulse to slow.

It refused, a fine sheen of sweat frosting my skin in the cool night air. I gulped for breath as the lights in the house across the street wavered and then blinked out. From far away, I heard the door open. Darcy barked.

Then Kyle was saying my name with a don't-walk-out-in-front-of-that-bus urgency, and everything went dark.

19

I opened my eyes to the brightest light this side of the pearly gates, groaning and waving it away as I clamped them shut again.

"Nicey?" Kyle still sounded far away, and it was so bright. What the hell?

"Where are we?" I asked, not opening my eyes. "And who turned on the high beams?"

"The ER," he said. "And the nurses did. While they were hooking you up to machines and trying to get your blood sugar back up."

"My blood sugar? Why would it need to go up?" Everything seemed sticky and hard to analyze.

"Because you haven't eaten all day and we danced for an hour and a half?" he asked. "You passed out and your skin was so clammy when I picked you up, it scared the shit out of me. I thought maybe you'd been faking your recovery and you had pneumonia or something. But I brought you here and they said your blood sugar crashed. It was forty-two when they checked it."

I shook my head, slitting my eyes open against the bright light. "I have never once in my life had a problem with my blood sugar. Am I getting diabetes or something?" That sounded scary.

The door opened on the end of my question and a balding man with a lab coat, a kind smile and large, seventies-style bifocals answered. "You are not diabetic," he said. "But you do have to take better care of yourself. Agent Miller tells me you've been working even though you've been sick, and you don't eat properly. No case is that important." He checked an IV bag of yellowish fluid hanging over my cot, marked something in the chart, and had just turned back to me when the loudspeaker paged Dr. Gandy to the nurse's station. "Be right back," he said, darting out the door.

"Case?" I looked at Kyle, who was hunched over in a chair next to the cot, rubbing his temples.

He raised his head and grinned. "I might have flashed my badge and let them think you were my partner. They would've kicked me out to the waiting room, otherwise, and I didn't want to leave you back here alone."

I reached through the bedrail for his hand. "Thanks for looking out for me."

"Someone should."

"I do all right when I'm not unconscious."

He smiled. "Mostly."

"So. Blood sugar?"

"You said you were starving when we got food at the dance, but then you ran off to talk to the girl without eating, and I didn't see you go back to get your food. I assume from what the doctor said that you didn't eat it?"

I opened my mouth and then clamped it shut. "I got waylaid by Morris, and then talked to Luke's mother," I said. "And then I was so tired and we left."

"Another symptom of low blood sugar. So is being off balance and clammy skin."

"Well, hell. I didn't mean to."

"You need to stash a Powerbar in your purse," Kyle said.

The door opened again and a nurse came in. "There you are." She smiled. "Feeling a little better?"

"I think so." I glanced at Kyle, remembering suddenly what we'd been about to do when I'd passed out. "Compared to being unconscious, anyway."

"You need to remember to eat," she said, hanging a new IV bag and taking down the empty one.

"So I've heard. But this has never happened to me before. It's not like there haven't been plenty of days when I got busy and forgot to eat. So why now? Does this mean I'm going to get diabetes?" I had a hard time letting go of that worry. I hate needles.

"Not necessarily," she said. "Low blood sugar levels can be caused by a combination of things that have nothing to do with diabetes. Illness, poor sleeping habits, inadequate nutrition. Any of that sound familiar?"

I grimaced. "Maybe. But I'm a little freaked out because I've never had this problem before."

"Aging makes things in your body work less efficiently, as a general rule." She winked, noting the time on the chart and turning back for the door. "It only gets worse."

I rolled my eyes as the door closed behind her. "Aging. I'm not even thirty yet."

"I'm coming up on it quick," Kyle said. "I feel it some days, too. I can't lift as much at the gym as I could when I was twenty-four."

"I don't think I care for this getting older business." I plucked at the threads of the blanket across my lap.

"Beats the hell out of the alternative."

I sighed. "I always thought I'd be in a different place at thirty. Thirty was old. Dentures and walker old. Remember?"

"We were going to rule the world," Kyle said, squeezing my hand. "Have it all."

"Maybe we do." I said. "You're a bonafide hero—I mean, your career is shooting off into the stratosphere."

"I guess. I feel like it's been stalled lately. After my last big case, there's been a shortage of giant operations to run. I've been doing a lot of little one-off busts."

"You'll land another big fish soon. Aren't you, like, the youngest special agent big shot they've ever had, or something?"

"Haven't you, like, caught a couple of murderers and won some pretty impressive awards?" he countered.

"I guess."

"Thirty's not old. We'll pin that one on forty. 'Til we get there. We can move that line forever."

I smiled at the thought of turning forty with Kyle. Which gave me a warm-fuzzy and made me wonder again what the hell I was going to do about my love life. Such a massive mess required more brainpower than I had to spare.

"I know one thing: I wouldn't go back to being twenty-one for all the Manolos in the Saks warehouse. There's something to be said for that whole age and wisdom thing." I rolled my eyes up toward the bag of yellow fluid. "Is that the magic blood sugar juice?"

"I suppose." He sat back in the chair. "You seem to be feeling better."

"I'm sorry I ruined our evening."

"Eh. I'd be lying if I said I wasn't disappointed, but I'm more glad you're okay. Raincheck?"

"When the time is right." I closed my eyes. "I'm sleepy."

He kissed the back of my hand. "You rest."

I did.

The doctor pronounced me balanced and ready to go home at a few minutes after two, and Kyle delivered me there without further comment on our missed encounter. I knew him well enough to know that took immense self-control, and I kissed his cheek and thanked him for everything. I shut the door and fell into my bed, wanting nothing but to sleep off my crazy week.

20

Peter Pan flitting around the room wasn't usually part of the dream where I got offered a job covering the White House for the *Washington Post*—yet there he was, Tinkerbell hot on his heels.

Around the time the editor in my dream (who looked much more like Christian Bale than a newspaper editor ever actually would) began belting out *Second Star to the Right*, dream-me figured out my real-life phone must be ringing.

Groping for my cell phone, I cracked one eye enough to see that my bedroom was pitch-dark. Had I slept all day? I turned my head and groaned when I saw the clock. I hadn't even slept three hours.

"Money or shoes?" I mumbled into the phone, turning my head so I could hear. The only acceptable reason for this call was to tell me I'd won one of those things.

"Pardon?"

"Aaron?" I sat up and pushed my tangled hair out of my face. "It's four-forty-five. In the morning. On Saturday."

"You'll thank me when you've had some coffee," Aaron said. "I know you've been sick and I figured your scanner was off." Aaron hated working weekends and almost never called me at home. Which was the only reason I didn't hang up and dive back into my pillows.

"What's up?"

"I've got a hotel fire that will make a hell of a headline if you feel up to dragging yourself over here."

I shook the haze out of my head. A hotel fire? Andrews was still pissed at me, best I could tell. I needed all the brownie points I could get. "Thanks, Aaron. My scanner didn't even make it out of the car last night. I owe you one."

"Bring an extra cup of coffee. It's cold out here."

"Text me the address and give me twenty minutes." I clicked off the call and threw my sage duvet back. Darcy growled at me from her bed.

"I know. But what can I do?" I put my feet on the cold wood floor and wondered why I didn't have a rug for the bedroom.

Shuffling to the bathroom, I stretched out of sleep and pulled a pair of jeans and a heavy cable-knit sweater from the dryer that sat across from my bathtub. I scrubbed my face and brushed my teeth, yanking my hair back into a hasty ponytail since I didn't have time to wash it.

While Aaron's coffee brewed into a plastic Starbucks cup, I ran back to the bedroom and jammed my feet into a pair of lavender silk Manolo Blahnik sandals. An absolute eBay steal at less than two hundred dollars, because of a tiny pull in the fabric. A quick dot of clear nail polish, and it wasn't even visible.

Darcy raised her head, squinted at the overhead light, tucked her tiny face back under her paw, and resumed sleeping.

"Lucky dog," I mumbled, moving back toward the kitchen.

I put a lid on Aaron's coffee and punched the button to brew a cup for myself. The coffeemaker burbled, and I spooned half a can of Pro-Plan into Darcy's footed silver dish for when she got up.

I added a shot of sugar free white chocolate syrup and a little milk to my cup, then grabbed my bag and the coffee and headed for the car.

Flipping the scanner on, I listened for something about the fire, but it was eerily quiet. A hotel blaze should warrant a fair amount of beat cop and dispatch chatter, which meant someone had told them to shut up. Why? I checked my cell phone for a text with the address and my jaw dropped. Not just any hotel. The poshest hotel in town. I owed Aaron more than a coffee for the wake-up call.

Slamming the gas pedal to the floor accomplished two things: it got me to the grand whitewashed building with the knot of police cars and fire engines out front faster, and heated up the car a little quicker. By the time I got off the freeway, I was downright toasty, which was good since I was likely to spend the next couple of hours freezing my ass off. It would warm up quickly after sunrise, but early spring still carries winter's chill in the pre-dawn hours.

"Your coffee, detective." I presented the cup to Aaron with a flourish and he smiled.

"Thanks." He sipped it, staring at me. "You okay?"

"Do I look that bad?" I shook my head.

"You look a little peaked, as my momma would say."

"I managed to crash my blood sugar and earn myself a trip to the ER last night," I said. "I didn't get home 'til after two, and now here I am, awake and freezing with you." I looked around, spotting a gaggle of teenage girls in dreamy gowns and smeared makeup, huddled under a ratty wool blanket near the back of a fire truck. "What's going on, anyway?"

The front of the hotel didn't show signs of damage, and the firefighters milling about meant the blaze was under control. I hoped I wasn't about to get really irritated with Aaron for dragging me out of bed. But he knew what was news and what wasn't.

He grinned and shook his head. "Debutante ball meets Girls Gone Wild. The St. Mary's prom was here last night. Most of the kids got rooms, that being what kids like to do after the prom."

I nodded to the frocked group. "That them?"

"They've been begging us not to call their folks since I got here," he said. "Their boyfriends went on a drugstore run, and the girls had set up dozens of candles in the suite. Trying to set the mood, I guess."

"Wait." I tried not to laugh. "A bunch of teenagers trying to create a sex scene set fire to one of the most beautiful buildings on the eastern seaboard?"

Aaron nodded. "Told you."

"This will get blasted all over Facebook and Twitter," I said, a lead already whirling through my head. "And I need a few points with the big bosses right now. I could kiss you,"

"My wife probably wouldn't care after twenty-five years, but I'll take an owed favor." Aaron laughed. "I'm sure there'll be something I won't want to tell you sometime soon. You let it go when the time comes and we'll call it even."

I nodded. "Has Charlie been here?"

"Not yet, but she doesn't go on the air until six, and I'm pretty sure she sleeps with her scanner under her pillow," Aaron said. "She'll show."

As if on cue, the Channel Four van pulled up and parked right behind my car.

I watched as Charlie stepped from the passenger seat, her petite frame clad in a gorgeous camel wool peacoat and black pants, her makeup and blond bob flawless.

"Detective White." Charlie flashed a Colgate-commercial smile at Aaron. "Nichelle. You get bored out in the sticks?" Her tone was casual, but her eyes were way too curious. Scooping each other would always come first with Charlie and me. But I could live with that.

I grinned and shook my head. "No comment. Charlie, how is it that you don't ever have circles under your eyes? Are you a pod person, or something?"

"Just handy with a makeup brush, honey," Charlie smiled, arching an eyebrow at my ponytail and blotchy skin. "Lucky for you, you don't have to worry about the camera."

I rolled my eyes. "I got to sleep later than you did, I bet."

"Now, ladies." Aaron held up both hands in a peacemaker gesture. "Anyone want particulars on this incident?"

Charlie waved her cameraman over and handed Aaron a wireless mic. While he attached the unit to his belt and clipped the tiny microphone to his collar, I rummaged in my bag for a notebook and pen.

Charlie flashed Aaron a smile and he gave the camera a more official version of what he'd told me. "A group of teenagers started a small fire on the fifth floor with candles," he said. "The hotel's fire alarms alerted security, and the first crew from the Richmond Fire Department was on the scene in less than five minutes, containing the damage to three rooms."

"Was there any structural damage?" Charlie asked.

"The structural engineers haven't been here yet, but it doesn't look that way," Aaron said.

I jotted down his answer.

"Have any of the hotel guests been evacuated?" I asked. Charlie could dub the audio to put in her own transition and use Aaron's comment, anyway.

"Six other rooms on that side of the fifth floor were evacuated because of the smoke," Aaron said. "But the hotel had empty rooms to move those guests to."

"The Washington's historic decor dates back to the city's earliest days," Charlie said. "Was anything in the lobby damaged by smoke?"

"No," Aaron said. "And the hotel's management has assured us that at this time, there are no plans to close anything other than the affected rooms."

"Are the students being charged with anything?"

"I'm not taking them to jail, if that's what you're asking," Aaron said. "Whether or not they'll face charges will be up to the fire marshal and the CA." I jotted that down, the abbreviation for Commonwealth's Attorney still a teensy bit funny-looking after half a decade of writing about the Virginia prosecutor's office.

"Thanks, Detective," Charlie said, waving the cameraman toward the fire trucks that sat in the large circular drive in front of the hotel.

Aaron handed the microphone set back and nodded. "Of course."

She followed her cameraman to the fire trucks, grabbing a firefighter to interview.

"Why do I have a feeling there's something you're not saying?" I smiled at Aaron, glancing at the girls huddled under the blanket and wondering if they'd tell me anything.

"Because you know me too well?" He grinned. "Charlie didn't ask me what the kids were drinking. Or, planning to drink. But I have a feeling it might be of particular interest to you, since you were asking me about the ABC police and moonshine last week."

"No way." I stared at the debutantes. "These kids?"

"Teenagers are the perfect market for people making back-door booze. Everywhere, it seems."

"Did they say where they got it?"

"One of them has an older sister who bought it off someone in her dorm. They claim, anyway. But I ran the labels when the fire guys first handed it to me this morning. It's not a legal brand."

"It has a label?"

He nodded, turning around and opening the trunk of the cruiser. "Here."

We didn't need gloves because the kids had confessed to possession, making fingerprinting unnecessary. I took the full jar he handed me and turned it over. Triple X White Lightning.

"Son of a bitch." I tapped my foot, studying the label. It was faded across the middle, too.

"Look familiar?" Aaron asked.

"Indeed it does." I handed the jar back. "What are the chances you can have a lab analyze this stuff in some sort of timely fashion?"

"Why? They didn't drink it, and it didn't combust."

"Because the sheriff in Mathews has closed his investigation, which I know isn't your problem. This is what those kids were drinking, though. Someone poisoned them, I'm almost positive, but I don't know how. This label is weird, like the one on the jar the dead girl had. I want to know what's in it."

"Cause of death?"

I smiled. Aaron was a good detective. "Liver failure. The boy. The girl's isn't back yet."

"And you don't think the kid OD'd because why? That sounds like the most logical answer to me."

"I'm not even sure I have the words to tell you that," I said. "My gut says no. The parents say no. The coach says no. Good friend of mine who's a master shrink says not likely."

He nodded. "But the sheriff is done?"

"The sheriff has a cousin who's making moonshine." I shook the jar.

"A-ha." He chuckled. "Oh, the joys of small-town politics. They're not that different here, if you want to know the truth. People are just connected by friends and money instead of blood."

"Right? But I can't let someone get away with killing two kids because

Sheriff Zeke wants to turn the other cheek to the criminal branch of his family tree, either."

"No. That doesn't seem right. But are you sure the moonshine had something to do with it?"

I snorted. "I'm not sure of a damned thing. There's more nebulous crap around this story than the big bang, Aaron. I'm just trying to cover all the bases. There was moonshine at both scenes. I heard last night that someone gave it to the girl as a gift, and for all I know, they spiked it with arsenic. I'm pretty sure TJ's invite to the party he died at was wrapped around a mason jar, too. TJ died of liver failure. I know too much rotgut could cause that eventually, but he was so young."

I stopped.

Except TJ's liver was already compromised.

"What if he didn't know he was drinking it?" I asked, talking more to myself than to Aaron. "Could you mix this shit with anything that would mask the God-awful taste?"

"I'm sure if you put enough syrup or sweet stuff with it. But would he have had enough of it to do anything if someone mixed it?"

"I remember once when I was in school, the guys mixed up a batch of Hawaiian Punch and Everclear in garbage can. One of the cheerleaders got so sick she had to have her stomach pumped because they kept telling her there was no alcohol in it and she drank a ton of it. You couldn't really taste it."

"I guess if there was enough sugar, you could pull that off. Maybe. I'm not a doctor, but I bet you know one you can run that by."

"The Vicodin." I nodded, thinking out loud some more. "Taking it with alcohol—this kind of alcohol—with a damaged liver. Could that do it?" I'd been trying for a week to figure out how someone could have given TJ an overdose of painkillers, but what if they didn't? What if he just took one, and thought he was drinking fruit punch?

It made at least as much sense than any of my other theories, anyhow.

"Good luck," Aaron said. "Can't wait to read all about it. Just don't go jumping ship for the big city if you scoop the *Post's* guy out there."

"They've been quiet for a few days. But I'm sure if I can figure it out, they can, too. I have to be faster and make sure I'm right." I turned toward the fire truck. "Thanks, Aaron."

I took down the particulars of the hotel damage from the fire captain on the scene and managed to get a useable quote from the least-smeary-eyed of the girls just before a line of European cars arrived to collect them.

"We just wanted it to be a night to remember," she said. "That was the theme."

"Where did you get the booze?" I asked, trying not to sound urgent and looking around for Charlie.

"Candy's sister got it for us. From a friend in her dorm."

"Where does she go to school?"

"RAU."

I jotted that down. The last thing Richmond American University needed was more scandal. Three dead coeds in two years was quite enough. I contemplated calling the chancellor.

The girls were plucked up and ushered into cars, their parents cutting Charlie and me dirty looks. But she hadn't interviewed any of them on camera, and I wasn't using their names, so they'd get over it.

Back in the car, I cranked up my heater and headed for the office. It wasn't even six yet. I could get done, grab a nap, and still meet Jenna for coffee on time.

* * *

Young love gone awry led to thousands of dollars in damage when three rooms on the fifth floor of the historic Washington Hotel went up in flames in the wee hours of Saturday morning.

"We don't have an exact estimate on the damage yet, but there are a lot of antiques in this hotel," Richmond Fire Captain Keith Richeleaux said at the scene. "One of the rooms was mostly gutted, and two others sustained heavy damage."

Richmond Police Department Spokesman Aaron White said smoke damage forced the evacuation of four other rooms on the same floor.

"The structural engineers haven't been here yet, but it doesn't look [like there was structural damage]," White said.

. . .

I ended with the comment I'd gotten from the girl about wanting the night to be memorable. Once I'd read back through the story, I emailed it to Les, who had spent the day before acting shocked every time anyone commented on his full head of hair. I couldn't even make fun of him, I was so glad to have Shelby back at the copy desk and out from underfoot.

No one else was crazy enough to be in the newsroom at seven on a Saturday morning, though, so I got up and went to get more coffee from the breakroom. Walking back with a full cup, I nearly jumped out of my skin when Spencer Jacobs stepped off the elevator.

"Shit!" I gasped as the lava-hot liquid sloshed out onto my hand, switching the cup to my left and shaking the burned one.

"I'd say I was sorry, but I'd be lying," Spence said. "Karma's a bitch, ain't it?"

I rolled my eyes. "I think the most disappointing thing about this entire week, next to the tragedy of these children losing their lives, has been finding out that you are such a selfish prick. Have you stopped for three seconds to think beyond yourself and your ridiculous outrage about not being assigned this story? Which, by the way, you probably wouldn't write, anyway, because you don't write that much copy. So you've spent this whole time giving me shit because you didn't get to assign this story to one of your reporters? Really?"

I walked to the reception desk and set my coffee cup on the edge of it, grabbing a tissue from the box on the counter and wiping my hand.

"It should have been a sports story," he said. "You don't know that I wouldn't have written it. It's the kind of story that could make a career. Land me opportunities."

"You want to leave the *Telegraph*?" I blanched. "I had no idea."

"No one ever asks. Just because I'm a sports guy doesn't mean I'm not as smart as you are."

"I don't think anyone ever said that, either," I said. "I sure as hell couldn't keep up with all the numbers you guys have to."

"Why did you take this story?" His face looked pained. "It's the kind of break I've waited for for years. You have the spotlight around here all the time. Cops and courts are the meat and potatoes of news."

"Sports keeps the paper in business." I said. "I never knew you weren't happy writing sports. You seem to love it."

"I do love it. I want to do it for the AP. But I'm never going to get there with my ho-hum resume. Something like this Okerson thing could get me noticed."

I stared at him, my own goals of working for the *Washington Post* dancing around my head and melting at least part of my annoyance. "Why didn't you just come talk to me?" I asked. "If you hadn't been such a jerk, we could have found a way to work together on it."

"Because I'm capable of doing it myself," he snapped. "Why should I have to share a story that clearly falls under my beat with you? Wait. I know, because you're the editor's pet."

I bristled at that.

"If I'm the editor's anything, it's because I'm good at what I do. And the fact of the matter is that you have little or no experience dealing with cops, and this has become a sticky mess of a story. I appreciate that you have goals beyond this." I waved a hand around the newsroom. "But no one's goals are more important than the truth. Particularly when we're talking about a murder case the local cops are ignoring."

"Awfully convenient that the *Post* is the only other news outlet that knew about that." He smirked.

"You told them, didn't you?"

"I did not. I assume you did. As feet in the door go, a lead like that is great currency."

"I would never. This story is too important to me. For a number of reasons that have absolutely nothing to do with the *Post*."

"But scooping their reporter doesn't hurt anything. Which is why you're hanging onto the story."

"I'm hanging onto the story because I think I can help these people," I said, utter conviction in my voice. "I'm disappointed that the *Post* is poking around in it because I think it might be harder for me to do that with another reporter mucking things up." Every word true. I'd thought a lot about it, and the Okersons were more important than an "attagirl" from the *Post*. Which wouldn't turn into anything, anyway. Unless someone retired, no newspaper was hiring. "Thankfully, the TV folks seem to have dismissed it and gone on their way. Even Charlie hasn't been out there in a few days."

He shook his head. "No one is that noble. If you're right and this turns out to have been a murder, or two, even, you'll be the big superstar again. Keep it up, and the offer you want from the *Post* will come along sooner, rather than later."

"That's not what it's about," I said. "You ought to take a good look at what you want and why you want it, and turn that greedy self-involved speech right back around on yourself."

I picked up my coffee and turned back toward my little ivory cube as the elevator doors whispered open to reveal Shelby and Les, whose hair didn't look nearly as much like George Clooney's as he thought it did. He'd won the hair club equivalent of the booby prize on *Price Is Right*.

I scurried off before either of them could say a word, leaving Spence to bitch to them. They could have the "We Hate Nichelle Club" meeting out of my earshot, thank you very much.

They must've had quite a powwow, because it took Les an hour to kick back revisions on my fifteen-inch fire story. He wanted the room numbers that were affected and the number of kids involved. Picky Nitpickerson, but it was still better than answering to Shelby. She'd been a real pain in my ass for most of the week.

I dialed Aaron's cell and got the information I needed, wishing him a happy Saturday. I added two lines to my story and sent it back, clicking my computer off and closing it. I needed some better coffee and good sounding board. Between Thompson's and Jenna, I had them covered.

21

Jenna's eyes popped wider by degrees as I talked for half an hour. When I finally sat back in the chair with my white mocha, she shook her head, bouncing her reddish-brown curls, and winced.

"The mom, huh?" she asked.

"I'm just wondering about the psyche here. I'm going to call my friend Emily in Dallas as soon as it's late enough there for me to call on Saturday without pissing her off. She's brilliant, but she doesn't have any kids, either. You do. Could you see killing for them?"

"If someone was trying to hurt them? Absolutely. For a better spot on the baseball roster? You have to be a special kind of bat-shit to rationalize that."

I nodded. "That's what I thought, too. But she's the president of the PTA. She has access to the kids and the school, right? Someone gave Syd that jar of moonshine, and I think TJ's party invite came wrapped around one. What if they were gifts from Luke's mom? She comes from a family that makes the stuff, too." It occurred to me that the funky label on Sydney's jar might've been a brilliant way to throw suspicion, since Lily's family didn't make Triple-X. Then again, it might just mean I was wrong.

"Well, there are people who are just crazy," Jenna said. "But just to argue the other side for a second: Does Luke have any brothers or sisters?"

"I don't know. Why?"

"Only children get doted on more," she said. "I don't have time to be invested enough in my kids' stuff to kill people. Not that I'm saying all people with one kid are loons. But it might explain some of the extreme stuff she said to you. I mean, if she didn't do it. She's so into his standing on the team because he's her only kid and that makes him her whole world. I get that. Doesn't mean she's crazy enough to murder someone."

"Hmmm. And my go-to mom of one source is unavailable for this story."

"You haven't told your mom about it yet, huh?" Jenna's tone turned gentle and she laid one hand over mine.

"I don't want to, if I can help it. Like, I don't even want to go 'look, mom, I saved the day!' if I can manage to figure this out."

"Surely she's seen the reports on TV. It's been all over everything for a week. Until the day before yesterday, anyway. Now they're talking about the middle east and celebrity baby names again."

"She's been so busy I wouldn't count on it, and even if she saw something in passing, that's different than her knowing what's really going on here."

"Then there's the part where she'll worry about you playing Nancy Drew again."

"Well. There's that." I chewed a bite of my muffin.

"That looks amazing," Jenna said.

"I'd offer you a bite, but I spent half the night in the ER getting my ass chewed for not eating."

"What?"

"Apparently one of the joys of getting old. My blood sugar crashed. Busy day, no food, dancing with Kyle, blah, blah, hospital."

"First, I take offense at that. If you're old, I'm decrepit, and I don't feel decrepit. Second, take better care of yourself. Third, what's the blah blah in the middle of the evening with Kyle?"

I tried to smother a grin, but it didn't work.

"Did you?" Jenna's eyes did the white-all-around thing again. "That guy is smoking hot. And there's something about a cop, too. I think it's the big strong protective thing. Maybe I'm not as liberal as I think."

"I thought you said I shouldn't rush back into anything with him?"

"That was before I met him." She sipped her coffee. "Because...damn."

I giggled. "You should have seen him last night. Full on cowboy gear right up to the hat. I thought I was going to fall down when I opened the door."

"So?"

I sighed. "We probably would have, if I hadn't passed out. He is a much better kisser than he was ten years ago."

"Aw, Nicey!" She shoved the muffin at me. "Eat something."

"It's so complicated." I bit into the muffin. "He is hot. And he's so sweet, and he's trying to help me with this case. But then there's Joey. When I'm with him, I think I could find a way to make it work. He's really a great guy."

"Except for the whole criminal overlord thing." Jenna rolled her eyes. "Haven't you ever seen that movie? You can't marry into the mob. It even ended badly for Michelle Pfeiffer."

"He's not asking me to marry him. But he did say he wanted me the other night."

"Holy crap."

"Yeah."

"Did you sleep with him?"

"Close only counts in horseshoes and hand grenades, right? That's what Papa Jim always says." The older couple who lived across the street from my mom had adopted me into their brood of grandchildren when I was little, and he was full of fun one-liners. Like Eunice.

"Close?"

"He was carrying me to bed when TJ's mom showed up and rang the doorbell."

Jenna covered her face with both hands. "What a mess. Poor guy. Poor you! Even if I'm not all that sweet on him, you seem to be."

"It'll work out." I finished the muffin and set the plate aside, picking up my latte. "So, we do or don't think Luke's mother is the killer?"

She puckered her lips. "I think maybe. But from what you told me, she could just be a serious helicopter mom, too. Just because she doesn't care that the other kid had to die to make a spot for hers, doesn't mean she killed him, you know?"

"I wonder if that kind of attitude and pressure could have pushed Luke over the edge and made him do it?" I mused.

"That is one I'm not sure I want to touch. How a kid could do something like that. It's why I like hearing about your job, but I don't think I could ever do it."

I nodded.

"Did you figure out how they died yet?" she asked.

"Cause of death is supposed to be back on Sydney Monday or Tuesday, according to the sheriff. I have new theory about TJ, though."

I filled her in on what I'd come up with that morning.

"Sounds logical. But damn. Diabolical. Using the kid's weak liver to kill him? Then pinning it on him as a suicide? What the hell is the matter with people?"

"I wish I could figure that out."

We talked for two more lattes, then hugged goodbye.

"Thanks for your insight," I said.

"Happy to help." She checked her watch. "But I really have to go. Gabby has a soccer game and Chad gets pissy when I'm late. He has to coach, and keeping up with the baby makes that a little difficult."

"Kiss her for me and tell her to go get 'em," I said, grabbing my little leather evening pouch, which I still hadn't had time to empty.

"You get some rest. And some food. No gym today," Jenna admonished in her best mom voice.

"Yes, ma'am."

I shuffled into my house ten minutes later, scratching Darcy behind the ears when she pawed at my ankle and seriously considering going back to bed. Just as I turned for the hallway, my cell phone buzzed. I reached into the pouch to grab it, but my fingers bounced off pens and change and my MasterCard without finding the phone. I dumped the bag out on the counter and retrieved it, punching the talk button when I recognized the Mathews area code on the screen.

"Nichelle Clarke."

"Nichelle, it's Lyle at the *Mathews Leader*," the deep voice on the other end of the line said. "Listen, I thought you ought to know, we've got another dead kid out here this morning. I figured Zeke wouldn't call you, and I know how pissed I'd be if that happened to me."

My breath stopped, Evelyn's crimson eyes flashing through my thoughts. "Shit. Who is it?"

"Luke Bosley."

"Good God." I snatched up my keys. "Thanks, Lyle. I owe you one."

"Maybe it'll be good karma, or something. Zeke's still at the Bosley house, but he'll be at the high school to take questions from the local press in the auditorium when they wrap up there." Lyle hung up.

I reached to sweep the scattered mess on the table back into my bag when something caught my eye. I picked up the tickets from the dance the night before. The center of the type was faded on the right end of one. And the left end of the other. Not straight across the middle, like the moonshine labels, but similar. I stared at the two tickets for a long moment, my brain shuffling through the images of the labels. I ran a finger along the edge of one ticket. They were cardstock, with perforated edges all around.

Laying them back on the table, I switched them, lining them up end-to-end with the faded type touching. I spread my thumb and finger over the span of the mistake and then held them up, picturing the jars. It was about the same.

The tickets had been printed on the same printer as the labels. As part of sheet that fed through, and then was torn apart. Who would've printed both things? Luke's mother was the PTA president, but the dance wasn't a school-sponsored event. Still, she might volunteer for other things.

I shook my head, stuffing the tickets back into my bag. Luke was dead. No way his mother was responsible.

"What the ever-loving hell is going on here, Darce?" I grumbled, shoving a cup under the coffee maker and adding white mocha syrup and milk before I twisted the top on, snatched a pack of Pop Tarts out of the pantry, and stomped to the car.

There was something there. But, I was too freaking exhausted to see it, very possibly.

I hopped on the freeway, trying Kyle's cell. Maybe he could talk me through it. Straight to voicemail. I checked the clock and saw that it was after noon. Sleeping in? I left a message telling him I was on my way to Mathews and asking him to call me as soon as he could.

I tried Joey. No answer. I left him an almost identical message, then dropped the phone into the cup holder as I pulled onto I-64, thinking about the tickets and wondering how I could match the fault with a printer. There must be a few hundred in the county. When I got tired of pondering that, I called Emily.

"What's up, girl?" She asked in place of "hello." "I never hear from you more than once every few months, and here you are twice in a few days."

"I just miss you. Homesick, and all," I said.

"You don't, either. You're working on something you want my help with. You find out more about that dead kid?"

"There are now three dead kids," I said. "And I'm pretty sure this is not the suicide epidemic the sheriff wants to make it out to be."

"Cops see things in very black and white terms," she said. "That makes it hard for them to get past an idea once they've settled on an explanation."

"I really wish this dude would get past this. I think it's going to take a warrant to figure it out." I explained the similarity between the tickets and the moonshine labels.

"Huh." She was quiet for a minute. "So, whoever printed the tickets for the street dance printed the labels on the moonshine jars. But only the ones the kids had."

"Even the kids in Richmond, though, which is the weirder part. That brand is sold out of the back of the auto body shop on the edge of Mathews. The ABC has an undercover guy out there working on a county-wide sting. So how did it end up being sold out of a dorm in Richmond?"

"Did someone fake the labels?"

"And put them on a bad batch of off-brand illegal moonshine?" I asked. "I didn't think about it that way. Maybe."

"Or they're printing labels on two printers and it's a coincidence," she said.

"I don't trust coincidences," I said. "I've covered crime for long enough to know that real ones are few and far between."

"Good luck," she said. "For what it's worth, I'm on your side. I've been reading the coverage of this all week, and it doesn't line up. But the sheriff probably won't listen to me, either. You have any suspects?"

"Only a half a dozen or so," I said. "I actually had you on my call list this morning to ask if you thought one of the other pitcher's mothers was capable of doing this. But then her son turned up dead this morning, so there goes that one. No way that woman killed her own kid."

"How about the other kids at the school?"

"Well, the dead boy was my chief suspect. But there are a couple of others. A girl who had a crush on TJ, and a boy who used to date Sydney have moved to the top of the list."

"Romantic entanglements can be good motivators for teenage murderers," she said. "Either of those kids have a history of violence?"

"Not that I've heard about, and everyone knows everything in this town. I can't figure how the kid who's dead today fits with the other two as far as motive goes, though."

"It's not impossible for a first violent act to be a murder at that age. They don't yet fully comprehend the permanence of death a lot of the time. And you watch yourself. If you get too close to what's going on, you might find yourself on the wrong end of an arsenic toddy, too."

I thanked her for her help, wondering how I might be able to get a little more face time with Eli.

22

I pulled into the parking lot at the high school early, judging by the fact that there were only two other cars present, and neither of them belonged to the sheriff. No TV trucks, either. I smiled, thinking there was no way in hell Lyle had called Charlie. More brownie points for me, and not a one to spare with Spence hanging out with Les and Shelby for the day. Somehow the three of them conspiring to get me in trouble with Andrews seemed so much worse than Les and Shelby alone, even if I couldn't explain why.

I walked up the steps and found the front door unlocked. The sheriff must've had someone come open the school for the press conference.

Stepping into the foyer, my heels clicked on the tile floor eerily loud in the silence. I shook off the slasher-movie memories, the spring sunshine pouring through the doors helping.

I went to the auditorium, but it was locked, so I rounded the corner and peeked into the office. Norma sat in front of her computer, studying something on the screen through a pair of reading glasses perched on the end of her nose.

She looked up when I opened the door.

"Hey there! What brings you by here on a Saturday? I think I'm the only person in the building."

"Lyle called me," I said, furrowing my brow. "There's a press conference here today, right?"

"Oh, yes," she said. "Not for a while yet, though. They're still cleaning up at the Bosley place. I just don't know what's gotten into these children."

I shook my head. "You and me both."

"So sad. You're welcome to have a seat. I just have some data entry to catch up on. Everything's been so topsy-turvy here I haven't had time to do my job lately."

"Thanks." I sat down and pulled out my cell phone. I had a text from Kyle.

"Sorry I missed you. On with the lab. Your dead football player didn't take any Vicodin."

That's it? I stared at my screen.

"You're killing me! What happened?" I typed.

"Liver failure caused by massive Glucotrol overdose. There was a shit ton of it in his bloodstream."

Glucotrol. Luke was diabetic.

But Luke was also dead. And I didn't know how yet. What if someone had figured this out and killed him? But wait. Coach Morris said the lockers downstairs had shiny new locks because some of Luke's medicine was stolen. To poison TJ and make Luke look like the killer? Or did Luke say it was stolen because he lacked a better explanation for missing pills? Crap. More questions.

"You're sure?" I tapped back, my brain forging ahead a thousand miles a minute. If Kyle had the results, the sheriff would have them soon. Which meant so would everyone on their way in for the press conference, if he happened to run by his office first. And I still didn't know what the *Post* had or where their guy was getting his information.

Kyle's answer flashed on my screen. "They ran it twice. Elevated BAC and Glucotrol."

Ho. Ly. Crap. Somebody spiked the moonshine. With drugs, but not Vicodin. And if I hadn't asked Kyle to beg for a full screen, nobody would have known it, either. I tried to recall that conversation with Coach Morris word for word. Did he say what kind of medicine Luke took? Or anything else?

That Luke's diabetes was genetic. Did that mean his mother had it, too? But if it was her, why was her kid dead? I dismissed her from my list, focusing on who could have taken Luke's pills.

"Thank you! I'm in Mathews," I typed to Kyle. "Call you soon."

I took a deep breath and fixed a neutral expression on my face, looking up at Norma.

"I can't get over this thing with Luke Bosley. I was just talking to his momma last night."

She nodded, a sad look in her blue eyes. "Such a nice boy. He had problems, but you couldn't tell it. He was diabetic, you know."

"I heard that. Were there any other students here who had the same condition?"

Norma shook her head. "It's a small school."

I looked past her at the nurse's office, desperate to know what kind of medication Luke took. "Did Luke have to keep medicine here at school?"

"Sure he did. There's a bottle locked in the nurse's cabinet and probably some in his locker, too. Poor boy. He had to take pills, but then carry sugar in his pockets on the baseball field so if he got too low, he could get to it quickly."

Hot damn.

So the pills that had probably killed TJ were floating all over the school? But they belonged to Luke. I thought about Evelyn and Eli. It was a clever way to throw suspicion if the sheriff didn't go with the suicide story. But why hurt Luke? If the killer was setting him up, why kill him? To keep him from talking, maybe. What if Luke figured out they were taking his pills and confronted the killer? Or, what if he ran out of pills to take because they stole them?

I tapped "Glucotrol overdose" into my Google app and scanned the symptoms, trying not to picture TJ going through all the phases leading to death. Fatigue, dizziness, unsteadiness, clammy skin, fainting—I paused, reading them again.

All the things that had happened to me the night before.

Because my blood sugar had crashed.

I raced back through the events of the evening. I hadn't eaten or drunk anything that tasted off.

But I took a pill. Without really looking at it, I swallowed my last antibiotic.

About five hours before I passed out.

I scrolled down and checked the effective time.

"Someone poisoned me," I murmured.

"What was that, honey?" Norma asked.

"I—nothing, I'm sorry." I smiled. "Thinking out loud."

Who had I seen at the dance? Luke. His mother. Evelyn. Coach Morris. Most of the rest of the town. Even Dorothy had been there with her friends from the ladies' Bible group.

"I'm going to run to the little girls' room," Norma said, standing. "I'll be right back."

"Yes, ma'am."

She disappeared and I pulled a notebook from my bag, rummaging for a pen and coming up empty handed. Shit. I must have left it at home.

I got up and walked to Norma's desk to borrow one. Plucking a purple one from her Mathews Bait and Tackle coffee cup, I started to turn when my eyes fell on the corner of a paper sticking out of a manila folder.

No way.

I flipped the folder open.

The ticket paper.

She printed the tickets for the dance. Of course. She'd been sitting there selling them. I glanced at the nurse's dark doorway. She also worked in the school and had easy access to Luke's pills. And she'd told me her oldest daughter was a student at RAU. Puzzle pieces rained into horrifying order.

I glanced at the door, skirting the desk and wiggling the mouse. I sent the spreadsheet on the screen to the printer and held my breath.

It was slightly faded, right through the center of the page.

My heart pounding in my ears, I jumped to my feet and looked around for another exit, but didn't see one. I had a million questions about how and why, but right then the only thing I gave a damn about was getting out of that building.

I started for the door, but she came back in before I could go out.

"You need something, honey?" she asked, raising her eyebrows.

"Pen." I waved the purple one and smiled. "I borrowed one from you because I left mine at home."

"Help yourself," she said, resuming her seat. I watched her sit down and start typing again, at once terrified and fascinated. How could you murder a child--or maybe three--in a week's time, and just sit there and do spreadsheets?

I backed slowly toward the door, thinking if I could just get through it, I could run. I never took my eyes off Norma.

She stopped typing, her fingers hovering above the keys, but kept her eyes on the screen. Then she sighed.

"How long have you known?" she asked.

"Known what?" My voice broke between the words.

She turned slowly in her chair, a sweet smile on her face.

"Known it was me, honey." She opened a drawer and pulled out a black-handled revolver.

I dashed out the door before she squeezed the trigger, the explosion behind me making me run harder for the front door. The heel of one lavender Manolo sandal skidded on the tile as I rounded the corner into the main hallway. I caught my balance, sprinting over the inlay of the eagle just inside the foyer.

I fell against the front doors, but they didn't move. I jiggled the crash bar.

Locked.

"You don't think I'm that stupid, do you?" Norma called from the other end of the hallway.

I heard the gun cock. Figuring that was a rhetorical question, I dove for the nearest hallway, the shot zinging off the metal of the doors behind me.

My legs burned as I fled, not the first damned clue where I was going. Dark classrooms lined both sides of the hall, and it split into a T at the end, with lockers and more classrooms going one way, and a single door the other. Glancing behind me, I took door number two, saying a fast prayer and promising to give up chocolate for a year if the door opened. It did. I shut it softly behind me, looking for a lock, but not seeing one. A bank of high windows let in just enough sunlight to show me I was in the band hall.

I scanned the room for a hiding place, settling on a row of cubbyholes in the far corner that housed large drum sets and tubas. I pulled the tuba on the far end free, climbed in, and pulled the instrument in behind me.

Curled into a ball with my knees up my nose, I listened for Norma and hoped my breathing wasn't actually as loud as it sounded to me. How the bloody hell was I going to get out of this?

My phone! I wriggled an arm down my side into my pocket and got it free. It had full bars, but everyone I knew was two hours away.

Shit.

Wait. I'd called Tony on his cell phone to ask for a comment after the sheriff's press conference. When was that? Wednesday. I scrolled back through my recent calls until I found the one to a Mathews area code on Wednesday afternoon. "Thank you," I whispered. I punched talk as the door to the band hall opened. I dropped the phone into the curve of my lap, resting my forehead on my knees and trying to imitate a statue.

"Olly olly oxenfree." Norma's voice had taken on a manic edge. "Everyone out of hiding, now."

It sounded like she was walking through the room flipping over chairs and music stands. "I know you're in here, Nichelle," she called. "You can't hide forever. I managed to get TJ Okerson out of the way, for God's sake. I didn't spend a year planning all this so you could wreck it. Now just put on your big girl panties and come on out and face your fate."

A drum set crashed to the floor a few feet away and I flinched. Turning as far to the side as I could, I watched Norma's feet. When she got directly in front of my hiding place, I shoved the tuba with my right hand and foot, catching her off guard and knocking her over. She screamed—more indignation than pain, from the sound—and I heard the gun clatter against the cabinet across from us and fire. My cell phone bounced to the coffee-brown carpet as I scrambled to my feet.

Norma lay sprawled across the floor, but still had her grip on the gun. She swung it upward, and I dodged behind the end of the cabinet, snatching a trumpet off a shelf. She grunted, getting to her feet, and I called my biggest question.

"Why?"

"Why? You didn't get that with all the questions you asked me the other day?"

I replayed that conversation on fast forward.

"Eli."

"My Eli. He's such a good boy. So talented. He and Luke Bosley would have led the baseball team. But TJ came here and took everything he worked so hard for. Including his girlfriend. He's been so sad. Poor Terry couldn't figure out how to pull Eli out of his funk. A worried daddy is no good for romance."

"You killed TJ because you wanted to score with your ex-brother-in-law?" I couldn't stop the scorn pouring through my lips. "Jesus, lady. Have you talked to Jerry Springer's producers? You could have your own week."

"Keep talking. It just helps me aim better," she said. The gun hammer clicked back again and I tried to mentally count shots. One in the office. One in the hall, maybe two. And one into the cabinet. That left two or three bullets if she'd started with a fully-loaded gun.

She only needed one. She was six feet away.

I peeked out and she leveled the revolver and smiled. I reacted without thinking, hurling the trumpet at her head as hard as I could. It made a satisfying clang when it hit and she staggered backward and screamed, blood trickling over her left eye. Two points for the crime reporter.

The gun went flying, clattering into the dark reaches of the room behind her. She pressed a hand to her forehead and glared at me, turning for the gun. I stepped out and swung one foot up and around in a hooked side kick that caught her arm. She lurched away and squealed, a welp of blood appearing on her skin from my heel.

"Why Sydney?"

"She dumped my Eli for that boy," Norma spat. "She and that mother of hers. Always thinking they're too good for everyone else."

"I thought you said you were friends?"

"I said we were friends once. She married money. She's too good for me, now." The bitterness in her voice would've soured Eunice's creme brulee.

"And Luke was in Eli's way, too?" I guessed. "He was the easiest for you to get to with the Glucotrol, right?"

Norma shook her head. "I've known Luke since he was born. I would never hurt him. Annalynn over at the sheriff's office told her momma this morning that Luke shot himself in the head with one of his daddy's hunting rifles. God rest him. They put so much pressure on him. Word is, he left a note saying TJ and Sydney didn't have any worries anymore, and that sounded nice. Poor boy."

I didn't have time to fully process that before she stepped forward. I raised my hands, widening my feet into a punching stance. She paused by the desk, her fingers closing on the handle of a pair of scissors lying on the blotter. Damn.

"You can't make this look like a suicide," I said.

"Probably not, but I can make it look like someone else was responsible. Assuming anyone finds you. My cousin Sherman was none too happy about you asking questions about his moonshine, you know." She smiled. Just before she lunged. I dodged to one side, but she swung fast and winged my upper arm, hacking a jagged gash in my skin with the scissors. I yelped and grabbed for the wound.

"People will be here any minute," I panted, kicking a chair into her knees and smiling when she tripped over it.

"Why? It's Saturday." She jumped back to her feet.

"The press conference." I backed up another step.

"Is at the sheriff's office. I called Lyle and told him it was here. Right before I mentioned how sweet you were, and what a nice guy he is. I knew he'd call and tell you. If the Glucotrol I slipped into your purse last night worked, he wouldn't get you. If it didn't, you'd come running. I was right. I texted him that I was mistaken, and I'd sent you on your way. With Sherman to escort you." She grinned a too-wide-eyed grin that belonged in a horror movie. "You've been far too nosy. All the other reporters left town when Zeke closed the Okerson file. Not you. So many questions. I figure it's about time to make sure you never get this story to print."

She lunged forward again, swinging the scissors wildly, and I stepped back, stumbling over one of the music stands she'd knocked over. Hitting the floor, I shrank away from the crazed glassiness in her eyes as she hunched down in preparation to tackle me.

Every movement seemed to be through Jell-O, my eyes registered the action so slowly.

I bent one knee and whipped my lavender Manolo off, flipping it around so the heel pointed toward her and locking my elbows.

She couldn't stop herself.

I squinched my eyes shut.

She screamed, and something warm and wet trickled over my hand for an instant before she fell to the floor beside me, howling. I peeked through my lashes to find my stiletto buried up to the sole in the flesh between her chest and right shoulder. Ouch.

I scrambled to my feet, snatching the other shoe up as a weapon and kicking the scissors away from her hand. She stared at her wound, shock plain on her face.

"You stabbed me with a shoe."

"Technically, you impaled yourself on it trying to kill me."

Her eyes widened. "You bitch!" she screeched, pushing herself up with her left elbow. "I'll kill you!"

I backed toward my hiding cubby, spotting my phone on the floor and scooping it up just as I heard footfalls in the hallway.

"Nichelle!" Tony.

I cleared my throat, which didn't want to work. "In the band hall."

Turning my eyes back to Norma, who was frozen with terror, I smiled. "Fitting, I think. You go ahead and tell Mr. Okerson why his son deserved to die for being a good athlete. I'll wait."

Her face twisted into a mask of fury that didn't resemble anything human, and she grabbed a music stand and slung it in my direction just as the door opened, framing Tony and Coach Morris. I jumped backward, the stand thwacking into my ankle and sending a wave of pain up to my hip that I ignored.

"Are you all right?" Tony crossed the room in a half-dozen long strides, worry creasing his forehead as his eyes locked on my arm. I looked down to see that my sweater sleeve was a bloody mess, the gash deeper than I thought.

"Maybe I should sit," I said, slumping into a chair. "Somebody ought to tie Nutty McCrazy there up before she finds another weapon."

Tony stood over Norma, rage, sorrow, and pity warring over the planes of his famous face as she howled incoherently. He pulled one foot back, held it for a ten count, and then returned it to the floor.

"I've never hit a woman in my life."

"Start," the harsh word came from Morris, who was backing away from his new girlfriend with disgust plain in his eyes and tone.

Her eyes flew to him, her scream cutting off. "No. Terry, this was all for you. You and Eli. So we'd be together. Haven't I been good to you? Taken care of you? Helped you feel better? And Eli is so much happier."

"You," Morris floundered, his inability to process that flashing across his brow like a neon sign. "You murdered my favorite student so you could console your way into my bed? That's...There's not a word for what you are." He looked at Tony. "I. I can't. I'm so sorry, Mr. Okerson."

Tony nodded, a tear falling from the corner of one eye.

Morris shrugged helplessly, then turned on his heel and fled. "I'll get the sheriff," he called over his shoulder. "I can't sit here and look at her."

Norma burst into tears.

"There's a gun over there somewhere." I waved.

Tony collected it and sat down next to me, holding the gun on Norma with a clear give-me-a-reason set to his jaw. He winced at my arm. "You all right?"

"I've lost more blood. And I even had a tetanus shot last summer. So I'll live." I held pressure on the gash. "Plus, I've got one hell of a story to send in when I get patched up. Unless the *Post* has bugged the school, it's an exclusive, too."

He flashed a half-smile. "I think you earned it. Thank you."

"Happy to help."

23

Zeke brought the cavalry, offering me a grudging apology and refusing to look Tony in the eye as a team of paramedics extracted my sandal from Norma's shoulder.

The tall, silver haired medic bent over Norma grinned. "I thought I'd seen it all, but this is a new one on me." He offered my shoe to the sheriff. "You need this for evidence?"

"I don't believe I'll be prosecuting anyone over this," Zeke said.

The medic turned to me. "You want it back?"

I stared mournfully, trying not to look too closely at the globs of...I didn't want to know...that clung to the heel. "I love them, but I think they're done," I said. "Looks like I'll just have to shop for another pair."

Tony chuckled. "There's a way to look on the bright side."

A petite blonde medic examined my arm, asking me if I'd had a recent tetanus shot.

"I have," I said.

"You'll just need some stitches to close this up, then," she said. "We'll take you to the hospital in Gloucester."

"Oh, yay. Needles."

Tony grimaced. "I'm sorry you got hurt."

"I'm sorrier TJ did," I said.

He nodded. "I called Grant. He's on his way out here. I'll tell him to come to the hospital?"

"You didn't have to do that," I said. "I'm a big girl."

Parker was a good friend, but I wanted more than a friend right then. I couldn't commit to Kyle because I had feelings for Joey. I couldn't commit to Joey because he was a crime boss (well, that, and the fireworks that were Kyle's kisses). Emily would have a field day. I reached for my phone and texted them both. "So, I nabbed the killer. It's going to be a great story. Just a few stitches, and I'll call you later. Thanks for your help."

My cell phone pinged back with "What? How many stitches?" from Joey and "Where are you?" from Kyle, one on top of the other.

"Don't know yet. She got me with scissors," I tapped back to Joey.

"I'm in good hands. Call you soon," I told Kyle.

"Ready?" Tony asked, putting a hand under my elbow. "I told the medics I'd drive you. Didn't figure you wanted to share the ambulance with Norma."

"Thanks," I said. "You know, you're a nice guy. Why couldn't you have played for the Cowboys?"

He laughed. "It's all about money."

"Or sex." I cast a glance at Norma, strapped onto a stretcher and headed out the door with a silent stare on her face. "Almost always one of the two."

* * *

I sent Bob a short report for the web on Norma's arrest from the waiting room at the ER, where the triage nurse was less than impressed with my wound. Tony sat with me for half an hour, despite my objections. Parker ran in just before they called me back, and between his million-dollar grin and Tony's superstar status, the poor nurse trying to enforce the "family only" visitor policy didn't stand a chance.

"Just put him down as my brother," I told her as she blushed and stammered about the rules.

She smiled gratefully and nodded, leading me to a treatment room. Parker followed, and Tony hugged me gently before he left.

"Thank you. If there's ever anything I can do," he said.

"Do you know Troy Aikman?" I asked, only half-joking.

"As a matter of fact, I do."

"We'll talk," I said.

He waved as he walked out into the sunshine.

"So, can you write a story without sustaining mortal injuries?" Parker asked. "Bob is never going to let me hear the end of this."

"You? How many lectures do you think I'll get?" I pulled out my phone and checked my email. "See?" I asked, flipping the screen around to show off the "Excellent work. Now stop trying to get yourself killed," in my email.

Parker chuckled. "Thanks for helping them."

"Happy to." I took a deep breath, remembering Randy helping me learn to roller skate and smiling.

The stitches didn't even hurt as much, and the needles looked less scary. I wondered if I was becoming an old pro and didn't want to think about what that meant, so I dismissed it. Parker took me back to the school to get my car.

"I'm headed to Tony's," he said. "You want to come? Mel's already there. I left her with Ashton on my way to the hospital." His tight smile made me wonder what was going on there, but I didn't have the energy to ask right then. It couldn't be too serious if she'd tagged along to the Okerson's. I hoped.

"I'd love to, but I have work to do and sleep to catch up on," I said, ignoring the fifteenth text from either Joey or Kyle that had buzzed my cell phone in the past hour. I also had men to juggle. "Give them my best. Maybe next time. Especially if Troy can come hang out."

"He's a good guy," Parker said with a wink.

"Sure, rub it in, Mr. Celebrity." I grinned and waved as I climbed into the car.

* * *

I went back through my Mathews family tree file and found that Norma's uncle owned the auto body shop, and the triple-X white lightning still. A visit from Kyle, who showed up in the newsroom and refused to leave 'til he could escort me home, netted me the rest of the story.

"The ABC police have been working a sting on the three big stills in Mathews for over a year, like the agent said last night," he said, pulling Mel's chair into my cubicle. "I called him this morning to tell him what you're writing about, and the busts will all go down this weekend. They've got two sales fronts, three businesses that are serving it, plus manufacturing and interstate commerce cases. It's a huge bust."

I scribbled notes as he talked, already planning a sidebar story on the busts. And a call to Bobbi. It might not do any good, but it would probably help if she didn't get caught with it in the club. Joey hadn't known enough about it to be traceable, so I wasn't worried about him, for once.

I thanked Kyle and opened my laptop to start typing.

Mathews County Sheriff Zeke Waters arrested Norma Earlinger, 47, Saturday in connection with what the sheriff is now calling the double murder of Tony Okerson, Junior and his girlfriend Sydney Cobb, both juniors at Mathews High School.

"Obviously, the case has been reopened in light of recent developments," Waters said as he accompanied Earlinger to the emergency room after she was injured while trying to stab a Richmond Telegraph *reporter Saturday.*

Waters said the toxicity screen report on Okerson's blood came back from the state forensics lab Saturday, showing that the star quarterback for the Mathews Eagles died of liver failure caused by an overdose of Glucotrol, an insulin-stimulating medication used for management of type 2 diabetes. Earlinger, a secretary at the school, confessed to stealing the medication from a student's gym locker.

Lucas Bosley, a baseball teammate of Okerson's, was diabetic. He was found dead in his home Saturday morning, of an apparently self-inflicted gunshot wound. Waters said the death will be thoroughly investigated.

"There's nothing about this that doesn't suck," I told Kyle, sitting back in my chair as I finished the story with a plug for the suicide helpline. "Norma went off her rocker and killed TJ and Syd—and almost got away with it—using Luke's medicine. Which no one would have known if you hadn't pressed the lab to test his blood for something besides Vicodin and booze, so thanks."

"Anytime."

"But then Luke, who has parents who push him to the breaking point and a battle with depression he hides very well, buys the sheriff's suicide story. He figures if TJ and Syd did it, maybe it's not a bad idea. The medics said his mother told them he started a new antidepressant last week and was having wild mood swings. Crazy highs, like we saw at the dance last night, and lows...like this."

"Why didn't she tell anyone?"

"Afraid he'd get kicked off the baseball team. Which I don't doubt. Sad, sad situation."

"Amen." He brushed his fingers over the gauze dressing on my arm. "I'm glad you're all right."

"Me, too. Thanks for coming in. And for everything else."

"I'm always here," he said.

"That's good to know." I leaned the chair back and kissed him, then sent my story to Les and stood. "I think I've earned a day off."

"I'll drive you home."

* * *

Monday morning dawned bright and pollen-free. After a Sunday of sleeping in and letting Joey pamper me (his foot massages are as good as his kisses. Almost.), I felt nearly good as new.

And ready to have myself a little chat with my favorite copy editor.

I didn't find Shelby in her cube, or in Les's office. My head was on the verge of exploding when I walked past Bob's door and heard her shrill voice, patting herself on the back for doing such a stellar job filling in for Les while he was out. He chimed in to agree often.

I stopped outside the door and listened.

"And Nichelle wasn't even here most of the week, plus she leaked an important piece of information to the *Post*," Shelby said. "I think Les is right. She's overworked, Bob. Look how sick she got last week. It was a bad idea to give her the courthouse back last fall when we can afford another beat reporter's salary. Put me on the courthouse. You know I'm good enough to handle it, and we'll stand a better chance of staying on top of Charlie Lewis, too."

She had some nerve, that Shelby.

"Shelby, who takes care of your flying monkeys when you're here bothering me?" I asked, stepping through the door and smiling when she and Les both dropped their jaws on the tacky brown seventies carpet.

"I'd almost agree with you, myself," I continued, "except I had a very nice chat yesterday with Greg Lidner at the *Post*. Name ring a bell?"

Shelby's eyes widened for a split second before she arranged her face into a clueless expression. "Why would it?"

"Well, it seems he called here last week, looking for a comment about my story on TJ. Someone answered my phone. On Monday, at eleven. When I was on my way to TJ's funeral with Parker. A woman with a high-pitched voice who said she was me, and told him all about how I thought the sheriff was lying, reminding him three times to tell his editor where he got the information. Subtle, Shelby."

"I have no idea what you're talking about," she huffed, folding her arms across her chest.

"Sure you do. You hung around outside when Bob asked Parker and me to stay after the meeting." I didn't bother to inflect a question mark on the end of the sentence. "I'm just surprised you waited for him to call here instead of calling him. He got my cell number from Sheriff Waters and called me at home yesterday, quite surprised that I don't sound like a cartoon character on my cell phone. Nice guy."

"I would never—" Shelby turned an imploring look to Les, but the look on his face said he didn't believe her any more than Bob did.

"There's a line, Shelby," he said quietly, turning on his heel and walking out of the office. She tore after him and I dropped into a chair and grinned.

"I never believed it," Bob said. "But Andrews will be very interested to hear this."

"I'll let you tell him," I said. "He apologizes like a politician. It creeps me out."

"So, the *Post* called you?"

"For an interview. Not the job kind. Though the guy did say his editor was impressed."

"You can't leave. You love me."

"And I love Richmond. Right now, anyway." I smiled.

The rest of the section editors filed in and Spence stopped next to my chair, eyeballing the dressing on my bicep. "That looks nasty."

"I'm sure you could handle it, just like everything else about my job, right?" I said.

"I could have written the suicide coverage," he snapped.

"I think you ought to stick to your stat sheets and leave the criminals to the crime desk."

He opened his mouth to reply, but Bob's warning glare made him snap it shut.

He could stay mad 'til I left my house in garden clogs for all I cared. I sat back in my chair and pulled out a notebook as Bob started the rundown.

The meeting sped by in alternating throes of spirited discussion and laughter. Halfway through, my scanner squawked. I turned it down, pressing it to my ear. Hostage situation in a bank building.

"Holy Manolos." I jumped to my feet, waving the scanner when Bob gave me a raised eyebrow. "I have hostages today, chief. Save me some space."

"Have fun," he called as I ran for the elevator.

I got out of the garage and my phone binged a text. "Coming, Aaron," I said, stopping to glance at it.

Kyle: "Dinner tonight? I'm dying to know why the ABC's undercover guy says he met with a pretty brunette last week. Who looks just like you. And came and went with a Mafia big shot he met through a transport contact the moonshiners use."

Holy. Crap.

DEVIL IN THE DEADLINE:
Nichelle Clarke #4

A human sacrifice unlocks a chilling mystery, and leads Nichelle Clarke into a world of unimaginable danger.

When Richmond Police find a young woman's bloody remains spread across a candle-lit altar in an abandoned power plant on the banks of the James River, they give crime reporter Nichelle Clarke an all-access pass in exchange for her help.

But the information Nichelle gets from the victim's friends only draws her deeper into the mystery. Where did Jasmine come from? How did she end up on the streets of Shockoe Bottom? And why doesn't she have any dental records?

The answer trail stops at the front doors of a sprawling compound in the foothills of the Blue Ridge, where Nichelle finds a secretive cult leader and his devoted following. It is a world where lies become truth, and money is the true idol. Money some people would do anything to keep collecting...

Even if it means murdering a nosy reporter.

ACKNOWLEDGMENTS

So many people had a hand in putting this book in your hands, and each has my eternal gratitude. No matter how many times I do this, my biggest fear is always that I'll forget someone, so if it's you, please know it was unintentional and accept my thanks.

Jody Hynds Klann, my favorite scientist, thank you for spending a whole Saturday morning looking up medical and biological scenarios (in actual textbooks) and being my brainstorming buddy as I constructed this mystery.

Richard Helms, thank you for sharing your expertise in forensic and criminal psychology—and what's different about teenagers.

My resident expert on all things Mathews County and always-first reader, Julie Hallberg: thanks for...everything.

For sharing the unwritten history of Mathews, my thanks go to R.C. and Joyce Hernandez. Gwynn's Island is such a beautiful place, and I hope I've done it justice.

Thanks to Andrew Watts and the team at Severn River Publishing for being all-around fantastic to work with.

To the book bloggers and journalists who love Nichelle, and to my wonderful readers: thank you for following Nichelle's stories and helping spread the word about my books. There's no higher compliment for a writer than when you recommend their book to a friend.

This book deals with some serious issues that can affect people of any age, and I found some scary statistics in my research, but the one that sticks with me is this: the majority of people who survive suicide attempts tell stories of feeling the kind of hopeless that having one person to talk to can make a difference in. If you or someone you love struggles with suicidal thoughts, please, please pass on the phone number for the National Suicide Prevention Lifeline: (800) 273-8255.

I have a close friend who lost her son to suicide last year, but in true Sloane fashion, she flipped her tragedy into a miracle for other families by donating her son's organs. To learn more about donation, please visit www.-donatelife.net.

Thanks so much to all the readers who have connected with Nichelle, and especially those of you who have taken the time to let me know that. Those messages truly make my days brighter.

Last but never, ever least: eternal gratitude to Justin and my littles, who make time for me to spend with Nichelle and her friends. Our family is pretty amazing.

As always, any mistakes are mine alone.

ABOUT THE AUTHOR

LynDee Walker is the national bestselling author of two crime fiction series featuring strong heroines and "twisty, absorbing" mysteries. Her first Nichelle Clarke crime thriller, FRONT PAGE FATALITY, was nominated for the Agatha Award for best first novel and is an Amazon Charts Bestseller. In 2018, she introduced readers to Texas Ranger Faith McClellan in FEAR NO TRUTH. Reviews have praised her work as "well-crafted, compelling, and fast-paced," and "an edge-of-your-seat ride" with "a spider web of twists and turns that will keep you reading until the end."

Before she started writing fiction, LynDee was an award-winning journalist who covered everything from ribbon cuttings to high level police corruption, and worked closely with the various law enforcement agencies that she reported on. Her work has appeared in newspapers and magazines across the U.S.

Aside from books, LynDee loves her family, her readers, travel, and coffee. She lives in Richmond, Virginia, where she is working on her next novel when she's not juggling laundry and children's sports schedules.

Sign up for LynDee Walker's reader list at
severnriverbooks.com/authors/lyndee-walker
lyndee@severnriverbooks.com